SUDDENLY Rose heard voices. Her uncle and the guest were talking together in the library.

"You say she has a fortune in her own right?" asked the guest in a greedy, eager tone. "How much?"

"I'm not sure of the exact figures," her uncle replied. "Though I am sure it is a considerable sum."

"I see!" the guest answered. "I should want to be very sure, you understand. I am at my father's mercy, and I cannot be sure what he would do if the marriage did not please him—"

In a daze of horror, Rose turned and ran back to her room. She fastened the door, then leaned back against it. Her breath was coming fast, partly from the speed with which she had flown up those last few stairs, but mainly from the terror she felt at what she had overheard.

Her uncle was actually bargaining to sell her in marriage!

Tyndale House books by Grace Livingston Hill.
Check with your area bookstore for these best-sellers.

Grace Livingston Hill

ROSE GALBRAITH

LIVING BOOKS ®
Tyndale House Publishers, Inc.
Wheaton, Illinois

This Tyndale House book
by Grace Livingston Hill
contains the complete text
of the original hardcover edition.
NOT ONE WORD
HAS BEEN OMITTED.

Printing History
J. B. Lippincott edition published 1940
Tyndale House edition/1991

Living Books is a registered trademark of Tyndale
House Publishers, Inc.

Library of Congress Catalog Card Number 91-65339
ISBN 0-8423-5726-2

98 97 96 95 94 93 92 91
 8   7   6   5   4   3   2   1

I

ROSE Galbraith folded her work dress and apron neatly, and laid them in the top of the packing box; with a trembling and determined hand she drove in the nails that were already stabbed through the missing board; then she cast a quick desolate glance about the room. How empty it looked! How different from a few days before!

In imagination for an instant the dear old furnishings came back. The muslin curtains at the windows, terribly worn in places, but delicately darned so that their defects became adornments. The faded old rugs, one of them a hooked rug her mother had made when Rose was a little girl.

And over at the far side of the room the fine old bed and bureau and wardrobe that had been her mother's wedding present from her father's side of the house. And on that other side the corner cupboard with the frail lovely china that dated back a whole century. In the middle the leaved table which was alike their dining table by day, and their sitting room table around which she and her mother had gathered evenings. Oh, those days, and those precious evenings, gone now forever! But she would never forget them! Her whole life would center about them as long as she lived.

She turned away from gazing at those empty places. She could not bear it. A great tear slid out and rolled down her cheek, falling with a splash on the top of the box that now held so many of the things that had made up the background of her life. Curtains and pillows and blankets and quilts, several of which her grandmother, her father's mother in the "auld country," had pieced and quilted. Then tucked in between things there were pictures and dishes and a few cherished books and trinkets.

They had sold the little gas hot plate with its tiny oven that had served them so well during the lean years since her father died, sold it to a second hand man for a dollar and seventy-five cents!

"If I should ever be able to come back perhaps we could get a more modern one," her mother had said with a brave smile as they made the decision, for even a dollar and seventy-five cents meant a lot to them just now.

And that was only ten days ago!

Rose drew a deep quivering sigh and shut her lips with firm determination. She must not break down!

The cheap upright piano that her mother and she had prized so much had been sold to a little music pupil of hers. Her mother had always hoped that some day they would be able to get a better one. But now all those hopes were over. Her mother would never get any more meals in this scant little room that had been a home to them for four long beautiful years. She would never bring any more music from the dear old piano! She had gone to spend all her days in the bright eternal Home where she would go no more out forever! She would not even take this trip to

Scotland for which they had planned so long, to see the old home, and the old folk who were left back in the old country. The trip for which the tickets were all purchased and tucked away in the pretty little handbag that had been her mother's last gift, her birthday gift! And now Rose was going to have to take that trip alone! It seemed appalling to her!

It was too late to change her mind. The tickets might be returned perhaps, but where would she go? The tiny apartment had been definitely given up. The dear old furniture had gone to storage in the house of a friend. This box of left-overs was to follow in an hour. There would be only her own two suitcases left and they were now packed and ready to leave.

Her coat and hat were hanging in the closet, the pretty coat and hat that matched her suit. Such a pretty suit, and mother had loved it so, and insisted on buying it for her, because she said she wanted her family to see her girl looking the best she could. That blue suit was the kind she had always wanted to get for her child. But mother hadn't been willing to get anything much for herself. Somehow it seemed as if she must have known even when she had bought the gray tweed suit for herself, that she wasn't to stay here long, for when Rose begged her to get a few more things that she needed she shook her head determinedly.

"No, dear! No! Just the suit will do for me, and when we get over there I can buy some more. We'll get what we like cheaper. We'll maybe run over to London some day and shop!" And then she flashed a brilliant loving smile at Rose that almost made her feel that some of these day dreams might come true after all.

Rose had grown used to having to wear plain made-over garments. It had almost seemed wicked to her to have her mother buy this suit for her. But when she saw how much it meant to her mother to dress her child up for her relatives, she said no more.

Yes, surely mother must have realized that she couldn't stay long. It came to her with a quick sharp thrust how that last morning before she died she had called to her with sudden strength in her voice.

"Rose, dear, I want you to get that tweed suit and do it up to be returned. The ten days will be up tomorrow, and I've decided that I don't want to keep it."

"Oh, mother!" Rose had said in distress. "But I thought you liked it so much!"

"Yes, I liked it," she said with a faint smile, "but somehow I got to thinking about it in the night. I believe I'll find something I like better—"

Her breath was short and she closed her eyes wearily, as if the effort was more than she was equal to. But she roused herself a little later and begged Rose to tie up the package and ask the woman who lived next door and was a saleswoman in the store to return it for her. And because she had been so insistent Rose had done it.

It hurt her now, as it had hurt her while she was wrapping the package, that her mother never had that suit. Yes, surely she must have known she was going, even before the final symptoms came that made the doctor lose hope. And her mother had sent that suit back quickly to make sure Rose would have that little more money for her solitary trip to Scotland. Dear mother! It seemed to her that she would never be able to spend that money for anything for herself! It seemed sacred money. Yet her mother would never have wanted her to feel that way, she was sure.

She drew another deep quivering breath and tried to steady her lips, and her gaze. That mover would be back in a few minutes. She must not be weeping. He did not know that her mother had gone away from her and left her utterly alone. He was a man from down in the city that she had found from the telephone book.

She gathered the last few things together for him to take: the screen that had disguised the old gas hot plate, the decrepit waste basket, a few remaining chairs, and the little tool chest that had been her father's. She put the hammer and the screw driver carefully away in it and locked it, putting the key in her suitcase with other keys. Then she went to the closet and got her coat and hat, and the white blouse that was to be used on shipboard alternating with the blue one she was wearing now. She laid the crisp white one in smoothly, touching it tenderly. This was the last thing her dear mother had worked at, ironing that blouse, doing it late at night when she ought to have been in bed, handling it so lovingly, almost as if it were something holy. Could she ever bear to wear that blouse and take its crispness away? Oh, how was she going to bear the days of that journey without her mother? Why did she have to go now? Why couldn't she just stay here? Those people, her relatives in Scotland, didn't know her, and wouldn't care. How could she go and meet them all without her mother, who had counted so much upon it?

But there had been cables back and forth and they had been insistent. They had regretted that they could not come and bring her back with them. They were old, and not very well. And she knew it would be her mother's wish that she should go to them.

Besides, if she tried to stay, where would she live? Get a job? But it wasn't so easy to get jobs today. She might have to wait months, and she had but a very little money besides those tickets. Of course she could turn in mother's ticket. She meant to do that as soon as she reached New York. Perhaps she should have written to cancel it sooner. But there had been so many things to do and mother had only just gone! She couldn't think of everything at once.

Then she saw the moving truck stop in front of the house, and she hurriedly put on her hat. Her heart was beating wildly. This was the last minute that she had anticipated so many times during the days since they had decided on this trip. This was the moment when she had hoped to go forth so happily on a real adventure! And now her young soul shrank back. How she dreaded it. How she was going to suffer all through this thing that had been meant to be a pleasure.

Then she opened the door for the mover and he soon cleared the room of everything.

When he was gone she gave one last desperate look around the devastated room, and then with a quick motion took the key from the inside of the door, slipped it into the outer lock, stepped out and closed the door sharply, turning the key with finality.

She had already set her suitcases outside and now she took them and hastily marched down the path and out on the sidewalk, hurrying toward the corner where the trolley would be stopping soon. She was thankful that there was no one in sight. She could not bear the thought of prying curious eyes. She wanted this last act over quickly. She must not go away in a deluge of tears.

There was no one in the trolley whom she knew even by sight except an old woman who did some scrubbing at the high school, and she was sitting wearily looking out the window with a lack of interest in her face. She wasn't even looking toward Rose. Their ways had never crossed even casually. Rose had only seen her on her hands and knees scrubbing the cafeteria in the high school building. She drew a long breath. She didn't want anybody to be looking curiously at her now when she was leaving all the things that were known and dear to her. But she had no realization that scarcely anyone, even the neighbors, would have recognized her in her new blue suit and hat, with the handsome new coat over her arm, its lovely silver-flecked fur collar glorifying her whole outfit. She wasn't thinking about her new clothes now. All the joy of them was gone, now that the mother who had planned for them and selected them was not there to enjoy seeing her in them. She was only thinking of the great pain in her heart, and the heaviness of having to go out thus alone. Praying that she might go bravely, as befitted the daughter of the mother who had planned all this for her.

She left her suitcases at the station in care of the old station master whom she had known since she was a little girl. He had arranged about her ticket to New York, and told her about the trains.

She went across the street to the little real estate office where they paid their rent, to leave the key of their apartment, and then she came back to the station and sat down drearily on the bench that ran across the front of the station. There was no one about here with whom she could claim any degree of intimacy, although there were a number whose names she knew, and where they lived and what was their general station in life. But they had probably never heard of her, nor even seen her to notice her, except as she might have passed them on her way from school in a group of girls.

The conductor helped her lift her suitcases onto the train and she dropped into the seat nearest the door. It wasn't far to the city where she would get her New York train. She didn't care where she sat.

But then her eyes wandered out of the window, catching her last glimpses of the post office, the grocery stores, the drug store, the little shoe shop where she had had her shoes mended so often, the garage, the church spires in the distance among the trees, the college on the hill, and lastly as the train gathered full speed and swept around the curve out of town, the big stone high school where she had gone so regularly. She might never see it again. Would she miss it? Although it was nearly two years since she had graduated, it still seemed closely associated with her life, the background of all her contacts with young people her age.

There were the new tennis courts. There were people playing on them now. She couldn't tell who they were. Perhaps not anyone she knew, for this was vacation and there were likely to be strangers in town.

Then the train passed on and they were lost to view. She had a sudden quick yearning for one more glimpse of the old schoolhouse before it passed out of her life forever. She leaned forward and stretched her neck to look back, catching only a far flash of the old gray stone building; then the long low shed where they parked their bicycles hid it from view till the tall hedge wiped it out entirely. They went around another curve, and the old life was gone, gone!

She closed her eyes and the big sunny room of her school days flashed into her vision again. She saw the long aisles, the long pleasant stretch of blackboards, with windows at intervals, the neat separate desks. How interesting it had all seemed to her! How she used to love to describe it to her mother when she came home.

She saw again the rows of students, heads bent to books, others staring around and smiling. There was the first row; during her last year Annette Howells was in the front seat; because she always needed watching, Rose had thought. She never was still. She seldom studied. She was pretty and knew it, and was always trying to attract the attention of the boys across the aisle.

Behind her was Caroline Goodson, a stolid solemn girl, overgrown, and slow of mind. Annette would never bother to chatter to her. Then Shirley Pettigrew, so pretty, and so well dressed. Who sat next? Oh, Jennie Carew, and those girls from South Addison Street. Then up to the front row her mind jumped again. Mary Fithian, then Fannie Heatherow, and then herself.

She went down the line behind her, and wasn't sure of some names. She hadn't been one who turned around much.

The third aisle was all boys. Johnny Peters, Harry Fitch—how they used to carry on whenever the teacher's back was turned as she wrote on the blackboard! And next was Gordon McCarroll across the aisle from herself. Everybody liked him. Everybody had a smile, and a gay word for him.

Gordon belonged to a wealthy family. He might have gone to an expensive school, but it was whispered that his father preferred the public school. And certainly Gordon never acted as if he were trying to high hat anybody. He had a genial way with him that showed he counted himself one with them all. Rose was naturally shy, and she rarely went to the school parties, or she would have known him better, she supposed. But though she did not know him well she had great respect for his bright mind and his straightforward manly attitude. Of course he had always said "Hello!" to her when he came to his seat in the mornings, but that was about all the contact they had ever had. No—there was the day when she had been asked by the teacher to read her essay before the class, and they had clapped so enthusiastically; he had looked up as she came back to her seat and said in a low clear voice, "Swell!" There had been a look in his nice gray eyes that she had not forgotten. That had been the extent of their acquaintance.

Yet now as the memory of the last year of her school

life came so keenly to her heart, his was the only face that stood out vividly.

It was ridiculous of course, because she didn't really know him at all, and all the fancied virtues she had put upon him might be from herself, only figments of her imagination. Yet of them all he was the only one she felt she would truly miss. Of course she never would have had the opportunity to be real friends with him, even if she stayed in Shandon. Why should she? She had merely lived on the outskirts of Shandon, and he lived on the Heights in a big lovely stone house, so screened with evergreens that one could scarcely see it from the street. He lived in another world, and had only touched her world in those few school contacts. Some day he would be a great man perhaps—she felt sure from her estimate of him that he would—and she might hear his name, and be proud that she had sat across from him at school. Well, that was that!

There was poor Jane Shackelton. Jane was a good girl, dumb, but she always did her best. Rose had often helped her with her mathematics. She didn't even know where Jane was now. She had moved to another part of the state. She had promised to write to her, but Jane wasn't much of a scribe. She probably would put it off so long that she wouldn't think it worth while. And even if she did it might not get to her now, though Rose had filled out the card for the post master to forward her mail, in spite of the fact that she didn't really expect any mail. She hadn't had time to be intimate with anybody. There had always been somebody's babies to mind after school, to bring in a few extra dollars to piece out mother's small earnings. And since she left school she had been busy teaching her little music pupils. Well, it didn't matter any more. Everything was over, mother was gone, and somehow she didn't have much interest in the new people who would be waiting on the other side of the water.

She sighed and looked apathetically at the swift flying suburbs they were passing through. This was Comley where Cathy Brent lived. They hadn't any high school in Comley, and Cathy had always come up on the train. Another girl she didn't know very well, and didn't care whether she ever saw again or not. But still, she was a link between the old life in which mother had been the center, and the emptiness of today. Cathy Brent was likely married by now to Jack Holley. They hadn't done much else during the last year but saunter around the sidewalks surrounding the school building, or loiter in the halls on rainy days. How fast time went!

Or did it? It certainly wasn't going rapidly now. This journey to the city station seemed interminable, and interwoven everywhere with memories of things that were gone.

Then suddenly they slid into the big station and she gathered up her coat and her two suitcases and went on her way.

She shook her head at the red-capped porter who offered to take her baggage. No, the habit of her upbringing was upon her. She was able to save the few cents it would have cost, and there were things she might need more later. Of course if mother had been along they had planned to have a porter carry their luggage. But now it wasn't necessary.

She walked slowly, looking sadly among her fellow travelers. She didn't know one of them. She felt terribly desolate. Already she was in an unknown world of strangers.

Since she had her ticket to New York, she went straight over to the escalator, and reached the upper platform where the New York train would arrive.

She found an empty seat on the long line of benches, and put her suitcases at her feet. How happy she had expected to be when she reached this stage of their journey! And now it was all blank and sad! Mother wasn't along! Mother's dear precious body was lying in the quiet little corner of Shandon Cemetery, and mother's spirit was up in Heaven with the Lord. Somehow it seemed to put her mother so very far away to think of that, as if she had become a different order of being who would not understand her child's loneliness, till suddenly it came to her that mother couldn't be like that. Mother, if she was conscious—and she had always been taught to believe that the dead in Christ were conscious, and with the Lord—she would remember her child, and love her, and be thinking of her as she journeyed alone.

That thought was comforting, but it almost brought the tears, and she mustn't weep, here in the station. Mother wouldn't want her to go away weeping.

She sat up straight, and smiled a feeble little smile at a baby in a woman's arms, a stolid little baby who was interested only in her thumb which she was sucking violently. But she continued to smile at the baby until suddenly it lifted its head and reared away from its thumb for an instant, beaming forth with a toothless gurgling smile. Strange that an ugly whimpering little baby could suddenly smile like that! For no reason at all it seemed to cheer her. And then the light on the signal flashed brightly announcing the arrival of the train, and she arose and gathered her effects together.

The train swept up in a business-like manner, and the porters rushed hither and yon.

Following the direction of the voice that roared out from the signal box Rose found the right coach and hurried in, relieved to discover she could have a whole seat to herself.

She settled back and closed her eyes for a minute until the train was in motion, the people who had flocked in after her had settled down, and got their belongings established in the racks overhead. Then there was the bustle of the conductor coming for tickets, the intermittent stoppings at other stations farther out of the city.

For a little while she was intrigued with looking at the towns they passed. She had heard their names before, and often wondered what kind of places they were. Now she studied their roofs and towers and sordid tenements. After all you couldn't see much from a railroad train. People didn't live near a railroad if they could help it. The quiet lovely part of the towns was far away hidden under the trees. She dropped her head back and closed her eyes again. She was deadly weary. It was good just to close her eyes and rest. If she only could get away from her thoughts for a little while! But then there was the waking up! It was so terrible to wake to the thought that her mother was gone, for the rest of Rose's time on earth!

That was the last she remembered until she heard the conductor asking the woman with the baby if she wanted to get off at the Pennsylvania station, or to go to downtown New York. Then she came to herself in a panic and gathered her senses in a hurry. There was no one but herself to depend upon. She must not miss her boat!

She got out her directions and looked them over, though she had memorized them the night before. She wanted to be sure she hadn't forgotten anything. She was to take a taxi to the wharf. That would take care of her baggage too. She glanced over the directions the ticket agent had written out for her. He used to live in New

York and he knew just what she ought to do, even to the exact spot where she would find a cheap restaurant where she could get a bite to eat before she went on board, if there was much time before sailing.

Through the rush and noise of traffic in New York City she paid very little heed to the city itself, which had always heretofore held glamour for her. She had meant to look for the place where her mother had lived when she first came to this country, and the old location where her father had a clerking job for a time until he secured a better position in another city, but somehow the taxi didn't take the direction her mother had thought it would from the station, or else by the time she got accustomed to reading the street signs they were too far downtown for her to identify anything.

And then they were at the wharf! It was time to pay her fare and get out.

Arrived at last at the little cubicle that she and her mother had selected with such care from the ship's diagram, she sat down on the side of the bed with her baggage at her feet and stared blankly at the opposite wall. She was in a place at last where she had to stay, at least for a few days. She did not have to nerve herself up for the next act. She could sit right here all night if she wanted to and no one had the right to say her nay!

It was then she felt the tempest of tears coming, the first tear stinging its way out from under her closed lids, and rolling boldly down her white cheek, and there was an army of them coming with a rush. In an instant she would be down, conquered, giving way before her broken young heart, she who had meant to be so brave! But it was of no use to try further. She was done!

Then suddenly she was startled by a voice going by her stateroom door. "All ashore that's going ashore! All ashore that's going ashore!" Ringing footsteps hurried on, the clarion voice continuing the warning.

Within her heart came a sudden fierce yearning to see this parting from the shore of her native land, to take one more glimpse of the country that had been the scene of her life thus far, and she sprang up dashing away those few tears that had ventured out.

A more sophisticated girl would have gone at once to the tiny mirror and done things to her eyes which were no doubt red from even those few tears; she would have gotten out a powder puff to remove the suggestion of tears, a neat little lipstick to brazen out the lack of a smile on her trembling lips. But Rose Galbraith had never been very conscious of self or appearance. She had worn plain, sometimes faded, often made-over garments, and shoes that had had to be carefully polished not to show their shabbiness; she had carried it all off with a grace, even in the company of better dressed people, just because she wasn't expecting to make a good appearance, and wasn't thinking about it enough to worry.

And so she went along the devious way from her little cubicle to the deck, remembering well how she and her mother had traced the way again and again with a pencil along the diagram of the ship. She arrived just in time to get a place next to the rail where she could look down to the dock. A great throng were standing there, and many more were hurrying down the gangplank to mingle with them and turn to look back at their friends above on the boat.

Rose looked down on that gay throng and couldn't see a face she had ever seen before. Of course. She hadn't expected to. But it gave her a most desolate feeling. A quick fear came that she might be going to cry again. She shouldn't have come out here of course. She might have known it would only make her homesick to see all these happy people going off to have a good time, with so many to see them off. And she hadn't anybody in the world to say good-by to her!

Of course those relatives to whom she was going might be kind enough to welcome her when she got to Scotland, even sorry to see her go if she ever could come back again, but they didn't know her yet. She had never so much as seen them; it probably would not matter much to them if she never got there.

Well, she must stop such thoughts if she didn't want to be disgraced right here among a lot of strangers. She would try and find something amusing to look at down on the wharf. There was a man holding a little child in his arms, and the child was shouting funny little farewells to some playmate who was sailing. She looked at the gay face of the little playmate near the rail beside her and almost envied her her joy. A pleasant looking man and woman were with her. She wasn't going off on a journey alone.

She turned her attention to a group off at the right. They were saying good-by, happily.

"Now, Herbert, don't you and Gladys turn the house upside down while we're gone off pleasuring," admonished the pretty white-haired mother, obviously talking to a handsome son whose wife was bidding the father-in-law good-by.

She turned sharply to the left and there were more people saying last things to dear ones. On every hand everyone but herself had someone who had cared enough to come down and bid farewell. It brought a great lump into her throat, and she was having another struggle with her tears. How silly! Tears! Because there wasn't anybody, not *any*body to say good-by to her.

Of course there had been people in Shandon to whom she might have paid farewell visits, and they would have been kind, maybe would have given her little gifts or something to remember them by; but she just hadn't had the courage to go around and hear them tell how they had loved her mother and how sad it was that she was gone. It was her own fault that she had said good-by to so few. There was Harry Fitch. If she had given him half a chance he would have offered to bring her all the way up to New York in his car, and see her off. He would have brought his sister Mary along perhaps, or maybe John Peters, or that silly Fannie Heatherow, and they would have stood now down there on the dock and yelled things she couldn't hear, and laughed and carried on the way that crowd down there near the man with the child were doing, and she would have been mortified to death and been only too glad to sail away into oblivion out of their reach. Oh, she ought to be glad there were no people like that down on the wharf to see her off!

So she tried to smile, and most unexpectedly there came great fat hot tears plunging down her cheek and splashing on her hand on the railing. Someone who was passing, a young man in well-cut tweeds, paused and looked down at her.

She decided not to look up till he had gone on, because she was just sure another tear was on its way down and would be sure to fall right before him. She mustn't be seen crying, even by a stranger.

So with eyes downcast she stood there, and sighted the neat creases in the tweed trouser legs there just at one side.

But he wasn't moving on. Was he just going to stand there? She lifted an investigating glance, and met a puzzled gaze looking down at her. And then a friendly voice asked in an astonished tone:

"Why, isn't this Rose Galbraith? It surely is! What are you doing here? Not leaving the country, are you?"

Then she looked up with a radiant face. "Oh," she said with a great relief in her glance, "why, it's Gordon McCarroll! I'm so glad you spoke to me! I was just feeling awfully forlorn because everybody else seemed to have someone around, who knew them, and I didn't have *any*one to even say good-by to."

Rose looked up with her lashes all dewy and gave a shamed shy little smile, like a child that was embarrassed.

The young man looked down at her with a kindling smile.

"Say, now, that's hard lines. I certainly am glad I happened along! The company sent me here with some papers for an Englishman who is sailing on this boat, and I didn't dream I'd see anybody I knew. Say, are you going over for the summer? Just a trip? My! I wish I were going! I love the water, and maybe we could get really acquainted. But I've got a regular job now and haven't any time for playing around in Europe. I suppose you'll have a great time. Where did you say you were going?"

"I'm going to Scotland," said Rose soberly, almost sadly.

"But say! Aren't you thrilled? I've never been to Scotland, and I've always been crazy to go, ever since I read those books we had in lit class. I liked them so much I read a lot of others too. I want to see Loch Lomond and Loch Katrine, and all the others. But you don't seem very happy about it. Aren't you anticipating a good time?"

Rose dropped her gaze for an instant and drew a deep trembling sigh, with just a faint glimmer of a smile on her lips as she looked up.

"I'm not feeling very happy about it just now," she said, drawing a deep quick breath to keep the tears back, "because you see mother and I were going together. It is mother's native land, and she was so happy to be taking me back there to show me everything. But just last week she went home to Heaven to live."

"Oh!"said the young man with a great gentleness in his voice. "Oh, I'm sorry. I didn't know. And now it is going to be very hard for you."

Rose struggled to answer, but instead two great tears swelled out and rolled down her cheeks, and she could only lift her tear-drenched eyes to his face for an instant's apology and then look down again. Suddenly the young man reached out both his hands and took her small trembling hands in his.

"I am so very, very sorry," he said tenderly, and as she lifted her eyes again she met a deeply sympathetic glance. "I know how hard it must be for you," he said, "I have a very dear mother myself."

She flashed a look that was half a smile, yet full of sudden sorrow.

"I thought you would have a mother like that," she said shyly.

There was an answering glow in his eyes and his fingers pressed hers again as they still held them lightly.

"Thank you," he said appreciatively. Then after an instant's quiet he asked, "And now, who are you with?"

"Just myself," she said with a sad little smile.

"Oh, that's too bad," he said sympathetically. "I wish there were somebody on board I knew to whom I could introduce you. But you'll get acquainted."

"Perhaps," she said wistfully. "But I guess I don't get to know people easily. That was why I was so glad to have you speak to me. It seemed so strange and lonely here."

"I'm glad I was here!" he said with a sunny smile, and then his handclasp gave a quick close pressure, and it was not till then that either of them realized that he was still holding her hands. Their eyes suddenly met and they laughed, a happy little friendly laugh. What would people think about it? It didn't occur to them. Other people about them were doing the same thing. Husbands and wives, brothers and sisters, parents and children, lovers, who had a right to be holding hands. They were only schoolmates. Yet because of her need and his nearness it seemed quite right for her hands to be lying in his in this pleasant protected comforting way.

Then suddenly out of the melee of laughter and tears and farewells came the screeching of the siren, and the voice of the ship's official, calling: "All ashore that's going ashore! *Last call!*"

People all about gave a moan and started away from the rail making for the exit, leaving them in a little space by themselves. Farewell kisses and laughter and last words were in the air, and Rose realized that her friend was going! In a moment more she would be standing here alone again, but she would have his friendly words to remember, his smile, his kindliness, the warm clasp of his strong hands on hers.

Then came another warning whistle.

"I must go!" he said. "I'm sorry. But—we are friends, aren't we? And—you will be coming back, won't you? When?"

"Oh, I don't know," she said sadly.

"Oh, but where are you going? I must have your address!"

She murmured the name of the little Scottish town to which she was going. Her hands were still in his clasp.

"Have you friends there?"

"Yes, my uncle, John Galbraith. It's Kilcreggan."

"Write me please, as soon as you land, and again when

you reach your abiding place. I shall be anxious to know how the trip went. Will you?"

"Yes," she breathed shyly, "if you want me to."

"I certainly do!" he said fervently.

"Last call!" came the echo from below.

Suddenly he stooped and laid his lips on hers in a warm friendly kiss. "Good-by!" he said earnestly. With another lingering pressure of her hands he let them go and hurried away.

Then, just at the head of the steps he flung back and pressed a card into her hand.

"My present address," he said breathlessly. "Don't forget to write at once!"

And then he was gone, so swiftly and so fully that his presence seemed almost like something that had not been. Yet she still felt the warmth of his handclasp on her hands, the thrill of his good-by kiss on her lips, and her cheeks were glowing with the memory.

2

ROSE stood there for several minutes searching before she could find him in that crowd waiting down below. The gangplank had been hauled in and she leaned over the rail and watched breathlessly, searching the throng. Would he perhaps be carried along and have to go back on the pilot boat? It would be her fault if that should happen to him.

But then her gaze swept the whole side of the ship and she saw him hurrying off from the other plank where the baggage had been loaded aboard.

All about her were excited voices; confetti and paper ribbons flung over the rail, landing at the feet of friends, or about their necks; handkerchiefs waving; people crying; people laughing and contributing to the general symphony of sound. There were many smart sayings that were never heard above the noise of the boat as it thundered its final farewell to its native land.

But Gordon McCarroll was making his way through the crowd toward the end of the dock that was below the forward deck where he had left her. He looked up and signaled, and then smiled with intent gaze, for all the world as if she were an old friend, the kind of friend she had always in her heart wished she might be.

He was standing there and waiting, as if he had brought her down here and put her aboard. He was taking away that deathly loneliness and making her feel as if she belonged, as if he really cared for her loneliness and wanted to comfort her.

Suddenly she smiled, a radiant glow like sunshine illumining her face. As they stood there looking at one another during those last seconds, while the ship began to move, it was almost as if words, pleasant assurances, passed between them.

And when at last the ship passed on into the dimness of the blue mist that was the sea, Gordon McCarroll still stood there, looking out at the mere speck that the ship had become, thinking amazing thoughts about the little girl who was alone out there on a strange sea! The little girl whom he had known so slightly during the years of their school days together. How she had suddenly become of importance to him! Just the clasp of her hand, the touch of her lips, and something dear had crept into his heart that he could not understand nor fathom. Was that merely a thing of the flesh? No, he thought not. There seemed something almost holy about it.

She had always interested him. Her quaint answers in class had frequently drawn his attention, but he had looked upon her as someone out of an unknown world, for he had never met her elsewhere than in school, and his interest in her had always been but passing. Yet he remembered now that he had often marked the blueness of her eyes, the lights of gold in her hair that curled so naturally about her delicate refined face. And now he had seen in her today a beauty he had never noticed before. Perhaps it had always been there only he had not been looking for it, or perhaps the sorrow of her

mother's death had touched her with the beauty that
sorrow brings. But anyhow the memory of her face as
he had just been looking down into it, stayed with him
and intrigued him strongly.

The twilight was settling down over the pearly tints in
the sea, and the ship had become a part of the distance,
with possibly a mere speck of light stabbing it somewhere to show where it had gone, but he felt sure the
little girl was still there by the ship's rail looking back to
the land of her birth wistfully, and perhaps, as he was,
thinking of their brief farewell. Would he ever see her
again? His heart cried out to be assured. Would it be
possible for him to do anything about it sometime?
When? Would he still wish to do it when the time came?

He turned sadly away and walked the length of the
wharf, took a taxi to his hotel, and sat down to think
before he went down to get his dinner.

And later, after going out to call on some of his
mother's friends, the memory of Rose Galbraith was
with him again on his way back to the hotel. Her eyes
reflecting the blue of her garments, their beauty holding
his thoughts even against his will. He felt again her small
soft hands in his, the thrill of her shy lips so sweet against
his own. He wasn't a boy who made a practice of kissing
girls. Kissing had always seemed a very special sacred
thing to him, and now that he was looking at his own
action past, and the fact that it was he who had stooped
to lay his lips upon hers, he wondered why he had done
it. What impulse had stirred him to it? Was it pity for her
loneliness? No, not that. There was nothing forlorn
about her. Nothing in herself that had claimed such
intimacy. She had seemed almost surprised, yet she had
yielded her lips. No, it was not pity for her, nor was it
wantonness. It had seemed a fitting sacred thing. As if
somehow she suddenly belonged to him and he wanted

to kiss her. The farewell gave enough occasion for it, even though they had never been intimate. He was not ashamed of his action. He thought about whether he should tell his mother of it when he went home. He would not be ashamed to tell her. In a way she would understand. There had always been a sweet intimacy between himself and his mother. But yet he wondered if she would fully understand. He had to think it over carefully and be sure he understood himself before he would feel like bringing it out into the open that way. Maybe it was just something that should be kept in his own heart till time should pass over it and set some kind of a seal upon it. Perhaps it was only a pleasant salutation, a farewell, like a handshake, that would pass into history and be no more. It wasn't likely that he would see her again, ever. Yet that thought was not pleasant, for the memory of that kiss held a strange sweet thrill that was full of beauty, and seemed something akin to a heavenly friendship. It was as if suddenly he was aware of having known her a long time.

Always in his school days she had been somewhere about, though usually shy and quiet. Excepting of course when it came to recitations. She had always been smart as a whip in class. The teacher's attitude toward her had been one of utter confidence. She could always call upon Rose when there were visitors present and know that there would be a perfect recitation. Yet withal it had never given her that look of pride and self-importance that many bright ones wore like a garment. Much praise had never made her try for a position in the limelight. She had always been so sweet and unassuming no one had seemed even jealous of her.

Of course he had never known Rose Galbraith socially. She almost never attended the parties and picnics and gatherings of the class. Only when in the line of her studies her presence was required was she always present. She had never been out with the crowd skating, or attending any of their special outings, and it had never occurred to him to ask why. He hadn't even known except vaguely, in what part of the town was her home. But now he began to wonder why she had always been so apart from the rest. Could it be an invalid mother, or poverty and hard work that was the answer to that question? Yes, perhaps it was both, for she had told him that her mother had just died.

Poor little girl! There was such a stricken look in her face! It had seemed to call forth the finest feeling of his heart. He had felt a strange new desire to take her in his arms and comfort her. He couldn't quite understand himself. But somehow he felt glad that he had happened along before she left.

Happened? Was it chance? Could a thing that lingered with him so keenly be just a happening? Or was it somehow planned as a kind of climax to their school days? What, that quiet plain girl whose life had touched his so rarely? Why should she seem suddenly so fine and rare? Why should the thought of her linger so poignantly in his mind? She seemed so utterly alone to go across the great ocean, going to strangers!

"Oh, God, keep her safely," he prayed as he knelt before he slept.

Rose Galbraith, as she stood on the deck alone and watched the land recede, was conscious of a comforting gladness. The touch of his hands on her hands, the touch of his lips on hers, the look of his eyes into hers, for just that last minute before he went! It was wonderful! Breathtaking! As if God to comfort her had prepared a friend for those last few moments. She probably would never see him again, but for that moment she had had a perfect friend for her own, and it was something she could remember all her life.

His face upturned from the throng on the wharf, the radiance of his smile! How lovely it was that she had that to remember! A symbol of her happy school days! How glad her mother would have been to know that the nicest boy in her high school had given her as much honor for those last few minutes as if she had been a princess. Maybe it would be something like that when the end of her life came, and she was about to enter the heavenly Home. Only—would there be anybody to bid her good-by then? But she wouldn't need them, for she would be going Home.

Then at once she became aware that the deck was almost deserted. People had gone to their staterooms. There would be things to be done. Her mother had told her about it all. She must unpack some of her belongings, smooth her hair, and get ready for the evening meal. Also she must get acquainted with the small compartment that was to be her refuge during this voyage.

Slowly she found her way to the cabin, reluctant to leave the spot where that pleasant good-by had taken place. It would always be the bright memory of her voyage, for surely none of the rest could be especially pleasant, now that her mother was not along and she knew no one else on board!

It seemed almost sacrilege to her that she must now get out the pleasant garments her mother had insisted upon and apportioned each to a certain time. The pretty little frock of soft rose silk, simple in the extreme, but fair with loving stitches of the dear hand that was gone, was the order for tonight. The tiny string of pearls from the five-and-ten that made the neckline so becoming. How far her mother had made their few dollars go in getting ready for this homegoing which had meant so much to her, but now was not going to mean anything to the sorrowful girl who was taking it as a pilgrimage alone. How it hurt to have to go through each activity that they had talked over so carefully together! How well her mother had remembered what had happened each hour of the voyage when she came over on her wedding trip.

The tears were almost at the surface now as she stood before her own stateroom. How she hoped she was to have the whole room for herself! But she had canceled her mother's ticket, and perhaps they would have to put someone else in with her.

She opened the door and snapped on the light, for the twilight had preceded her here. It was bright enough now and she looked about her. There were her suitcases still locked. But no others! What a relief. She must hurry to get out her dress and hang it up in the breeze from the porthole to take the wrinkles out.

She hastened over to the suitcases, and then before she stooped to them she saw the big box on the dresser. An enormous box it was, a florist's box. What was it doing here? The boy must have made a mistake and brought somebody else's flowers to her cabin. Nobody would be sending her flowers of course. Or perhaps someone else was coming in with her after all! How unpleasant that would be!

She stooped to look at the name on the cover, and was amazed to find it was her own name! What did it mean? Surely the ship didn't provide flowers for the passengers! Her mother had told her how many pleasant things were provided, but not flowers!

She untied the cord that held the cover, and there on the top was a card with the penciled words "Bon voyage." Turning it over she found Gordon McCarroll's name engraved, and her heart gave a little leap of joy. How lovely! How wonderful! But when had he done it?

Ah, that must have been what he was doing after he left her before he appeared leaping over the baggage entrance plank! He must have passed the flower shop. She had seen it on board in her first wanderings. How thoughtful of him! To think he would go to that trouble for her! How kind he was!

Suddenly she felt again his lips upon hers, felt the sweet thrill that flooded her young being, the clasp of his hands on hers. Oh, that was a precious moment, that parting, that she had so dreaded! And now it was climaxed by these wonderful flowers!

She took them from their box almost reverently. Roses! They were great crisp buds folded each in its own rosy sheath of baby-like petals. Exquisite roses! She had never had a gift of roses in her life that she could remember. She had often looked wistfully at them in the shop windows. Her mother had meant to send up a bouquet of roses when she graduated but Rose had found that out in time to prevent her spending the money on flowers that would fade, when they needed it so much for necessities. How pleased her mother would have been to know that she had these gorgeous roses! Suddenly she sat down in the little chair in front of her dressing table and buried her face in the cool sweet flowers, her tears dropping upon them. It was like having a dear sweet face against her own comforting her. They almost seemed to have a human touch. They were not just inanimate things, they were *alive!*

Presently the sound of distant unfamiliar gongs startled her into getting up and putting her flowers in water. There were several vases about as if flowers were an expected part of the voyage.

Then as she took out the soft rose dress and got herself

ready for the evening, just as her mother had planned, her heart was made glad again, thinking how pleased her mother would have been about the roses. Of course if mother had been along she would have had mother, and that would have been gladness enough. But mother was not here, and would have been greatly pleased that someone else had comforted her girl.

She had dreaded inexpressibly having to go out into this new world of the ship and learn its ways, but when she was ready, and looked herself over carefully as she knew her mother would have done if she were here, she drew one or two of the smallest of the lovely rosebuds from the vase, and breaking off the crisp long stems, fastened them in the soft folds of her dress at her shoulder, where they lay like a lovely jewel and gave grace to her whole outfit, the loveliest adornment that she could have had.

She went shyly down to the dining room and in due time found herself seated at a table with several other people. There were two young men, an old lady, another one of indiscriminate age, and a young girl with a good deal of make-up and wearing a low-backed evening dress. Rose felt uncomfortable and out of place there. She wished she didn't have to stay. She tried to think how different it would have been if her mother had been along, and then put that out of her mind because it brought the tears too near the surface.

After all, she reasoned, this was no worse than a first day in a new school, and she had been through that experience twice in her short life. She must get over that ridiculous dread of meeting strangers, anyway. She had nothing to do but mind her own business, speak pleasantly when she was spoken to and eat her meals. It wasn't in the least likely that any of them would be at all interested in her. Her mother had told her so much about a ship and its ways that she felt she was fairly well informed, and if she just held her head up and went on her way why need she be disturbed?

So she lifted her head, and happened to meet the eyes of the alert looking old lady. She smiled brightly. That was better than just sitting silently.

The old lady gave her a faint glimmer of an indifferent smile, but turned away to speak to her companion, so she felt she hadn't got far.

She ordered a simple dinner and ate it mostly in silence, answering now and then a question put to her by those who were seated near her.

As they rose from the table and were making their way slowly out of the dining room one of the young men from the table came up beside her, looking down at her admiringly. He was noticeably good-looking, with strong white teeth that gleamed engagingly as he smiled, and very large black eyes with long curly lashes. His hair was crisply black and curly in long polished waves, and he looked as if he gave a great deal of attention to his appearance.

"Nice night!" he said familiarly. "How about a little walk on deck? Been around the ship yet?"

"Why, no, not very much," said Rose shyly. Somehow she didn't just take to this young man. He was too familiar on such slight acquaintance. Perhaps unconsciously she was comparing him to Gordon McCarroll. And then she laughed to herself. Why, Gordon had even gone so far as to kiss her! But that seemed different. Besides, she argued to herself, Gordon was not a new acquaintance. She had known him for years. The young man helped her up the companionway, she all the time wishing that he wouldn't. Still he was only being polite and friendly, and Gordon McCarroll had suggested that she would get to know people. He was a fellow traveler.

She mustn't be snobbish. He was probably just trying to be kind.

She would much have preferred walking on deck by herself, but unless she absolutely refused his company and fled to her cabin she didn't quite know how to get rid of him. She was not versed in the ways of the world, and she was innately courteous. It didn't seem the right thing just to go away by herself when he had asked her. There was no harm of course in walking about among others and looking at the sea, with its sunset lights, and its silvering approach of the moon which would rise presently.

So she drifted around with him, letting him do most of the talking, but thinking her own thoughts. He was talking about the list of entertainments on board. He told her in detail the story of a movie he had seen on his last trip, with a knowing flavor of worldliness that showed plainly what his character and tastes were.

"Do you play tennis?" he asked suddenly.

A wistful light came into her eyes.

"No," she said a bit sadly, "I wish I did."

"Well, here's your chance to learn," he said gaily. "I'm just nuts about tennis, and I'd be delighted to teach you."

"Oh!" she said with a startled look, torn between interest and a kind of reluctance. "You mean deck tennis. Why, that would be wonderful! But I couldn't let you do that. I would be an awful dub at it. I've never played on land, you know. I don't know the first thing about it."

"Oh, that's all right," said the young man easily, "I'll see to that. When can you play? Early in the morning?"

Now she was almost frightened. Did she want to play tennis with this man? Of course it was a perfectly proper thing to do, yet she wasn't altogether sure that she wanted to be under even that much obligation to this stranger. True, they had been introduced at the table, but she didn't like the young man. She had a feeling that he wasn't her kind. So she hesitated.

"That's kind of you," she said thoughtfully, "but I think I would like to watch a few games first before I made any attempt. Of course I have seen court tennis played, but I've never had much time to watch it. I think I would like to watch awhile first. You know I am entirely green at it."

"Oh, sure, we'll watch a game or two first," said the young man, "but you'll see. It's nothing. You look limber and agile. I'll warrant you'll make a good player. Of course it's all right to watch for half an hour, say, but there's nothing like getting into it yourself to make you lose your timidity."

He rattled on affably, and the more he talked the more Rose shrank from being at all friendly with him. She was relieved when at last they came back into the region of her own stateroom. She was meditating how she could excuse herself without being rude. She felt that she had already wasted enough time over this individual, and she didn't want to waste any more. There was so much that was new and wonderful about this trip which she wanted to be free to enjoy by herself. Of course if he had been one who would enjoy looking at the wonderful tints of sky and sea, one who understood her thoughts about them, that would have been different. But once when she tried calling his attention to the silver path coming toward them from the wide rising moon, he only stared at her and laughed.

"Sentimental, aren't you?" he said patronizingly. "Well, of course that's all very well for a first trip, I suppose, but personally I got used to the moon on water long ago, and I don't waste time getting an eye full of that any more. There goes the orchestra. How about going in and dancing? That suits me down to the ground, and I'll bet you're pretty good at it yourself. How about it?"

Rose looked up almost amused.

"Oh, I don't dance," she said pleasantly. "I think I'll go in and write some letters."

"To heck with your letters!" said the young man. "Waste this perfectly gorgeous evening on writing letters! How quaint of you! Come on in and we'll try each other out. That's another thing I'm pretty good at teaching, dancing!"

"Thank you," said Rose disinterestedly, "I wouldn't care to learn."

"Say, you aren't by chance going old-fashioned on me, are you?"

"Not going," smiled Rose. "I *am* old-fashioned."

"Well, you ought to snap out of it," advised her companion. "I can help you to get a different outlook on life and you'll be ready to thank me the rest of your life for bringing you up to date!"

"But I'm not a bit interested," she said quietly. "I think you'll have to excuse me now, I have other things I want to do."

"Aw, don't get that way, baby! I rather like you. Really I do! You certainly don't look old-fashioned, darling. You've got a swell outfit on and I picked you out as the most interesting girl in the dining room. Come on! Let's go the rounds and have a good time together. By the way, I've forgotten what your name is. It doesn't pay for us to run around nameless this way. My name's Harry Coster. Just Harry'll do. Everybody calls me that. What's yours?"

She smiled distantly.

"Why, my name's Galbraith," she said with a pleasant little dignity. "Miss Galbraith." She said it so gently that it lost in some degree the rebuff she felt like giving. But he stared at her and then burst into his gay laughter.

"Miss!" he said mockingly. "Well I like that! High hat, are ya? Well, you can't get very far with a handle like that, not these days. Haven't you got a first name? I think I'd rather use that."

She was greatly annoyed at the intimacy of his tone, and felt like shrinking into herself. He was laughing at her of course, but why not hide behind a certain quaintness if he wanted to call it that? She certainly did not wish to establish a close friendship with him. She felt herself falling into her childish habit of shyness, and knew that it would get her nowhere with him. He would just think he could say anything to her and she would be too shy to resent it. So she lifted her sweet eyes distantly and said with that cool little smile of hers:

"I think Galbraith will do, if you don't mind."

She could see that astonishment was strong in his eyes. He didn't know any girls like this, and was intrigued to pursue her and break down her defenses.

"Well, all right, baby," he said with a genial smile on his handsome lips, "have it your own way. If that's what you want. How about going down to the bar and having a little drink? I'm thirsty as a fish, aren't you?"

She looked at him really startled now, and then suddenly she shook her head.

"No," she said, "I don't drink either!" and she gave him a steady glance from her clear eyes.

There was a certain dignity about her that made him drop his bold glance before her level gaze. There was something about her that actually compelled his respect.

"Excuse me," he said embarrassedly, "I never met a girl like you and I didn't know. But—" he lifted his eyes and studied her—"just how do you get by when you're in a crowd? You don't find other girls or fellows who agree with you in that, do you? There are two vacant deck chairs over there. Let's sit down and talk this thing out. I'd like to get to the bottom of it. You can sit and look at your silver poem on the water while I ask you questions. Here! Have a cigarette and then we can talk better," and he handed out his cigarette case.

"Thank you, no," said Rose, a twinkle in her eyes now, "I don't smoke either!"

"You don't *smoke!*" said the young man pausing with his case extended, and staring at her in genuine astonishment. "Say, this is something really worth looking into. You haven't got some grim aunt or chaperon or poky old mother on board keeping guard over you, have you?"

Rose's face grew suddenly sober.

"No," she said, and a small sigh escaped her. "I only wish my mother were here. She was to have come, but—she went to Heaven instead."

"Oh, say, now that's hard lines! I didn't know, of course. But say, her being in the place you call Heaven isn't the reason for your being so different, is it? I honestly would like to understand you. Why don't you do these things that everybody else is doing? Why are you so different? I really don't see how you get by not harmonizing with all the people around you. You live in this world. I should think you'd have to do as the rest of the world do."

She gave him a bewildered look.

"But you see it isn't my world! I live in a different world. I always have. The world I know and love doesn't do these things."

"Do you mean you belong to some queer kind of religion that has certain rules? Aren't you allowed to have a good time?"

"No, I don't belong to any queer sect," said Rose.

"I'm just trying to live my life as I think my Heavenly Father would have me live. You see I don't belong down here. My Home is in Heaven and some day I'm going Home."

"Good *night!*" said the young man. "You talk about it as if it were a pleasant thing to consider dying. Not me! I try to forget there is such a thing as going out and leaving this jolly old world. I try to think I'm going to live always."

"You are, of course," said Rose thoughtfully, "but your attitude down here makes all the difference in *where* you go to live forever, you know. And if you are expecting Heaven forever the earthly things don't seem so interesting. Good night! I'm going to leave you here!" And Rose turned and dashed down the corridor to her cabin.

3

LOCKED securely in her cabin with her tall lovely roses like guardian angels silently watching over her, courage came back again to Rose. But there was no mistaking the fact that she was frightened. Partly by the things that Harry Coster had said to her, and the way he had looked at her, and partly by the way she had dared to talk to him.

Never before had she spoken like that to any living being, about Heaven, and dying. She had never supposed it was possible to talk that way, especially to a young person. At least no one but a clergyman would do it. Oh, she was a church member, had been since she entered high school, but even the ceremony of uniting with the church had been an ordeal to her. She had meant it with all her heart, but to stand up before a church full of people and say by the bowing of her head that she belonged to the Lord Jesus Christ, had required actual physical courage. She had never supposed that she of her own free will would start a line of conversation that could end in the way this one had ended. She hadn't thought it was in her to say such solemn personal things. She hadn't been trained to do it. Yes, she had been to young people's Sunday night meeting for several years, and once in a great while had taken the brief part of reciting a Bible verse, or a line or two of poetry appropriate to the topic, but it had been hard, much harder than reciting a difficult lesson in school.

And here she had taken the initiative and gone straight to the point with this gay young man. Or had she? Had she told him enough, at that? She hadn't even mentioned the Lord Jesus Christ. Perhaps she should have explained to him the way of salvation. But she couldn't preach a sermon to him, could she? Well, even what she did say astonished her. She felt as if she ought to thank God for it, for surely the words had been given her. She felt a joy, past understanding, that she had said them. She never could have thought them out for herself. And they had seemed to work. She was puzzled at the singing joy in her heart and puzzled that the young man had no gay repartee wherewith to mock her. She had managed to get away and was safe in her room with the door locked.

But in spite of her strange feeling of triumph she felt weak and very much alone. She dropped down in the chair beside her bed and stared ahead at her roses. They seemed a living testimony to the fact that God was watching over her, though she hadn't realized any such thing before. Then she bent her head, and her lips touched the rosebud nestled in her dress, reminding her of that farewell kiss. Gordon McCarroll's lips upon hers, his hands holding hers hadn't seemed rudely intimate like the look of this other young man as he stood fairly insulting her with his intimate amusement.

Well, perhaps she was silly and old-fashioned as he had said. She had been brought up to reverence tender words and intimate touches, and it did grate on her senses to see them lightly treated. Yet she hadn't felt there was anything wrong in that good-by kiss, nothing but utmost courtesy and kindly thoughtfulness for her. But then Gordon was a schoolmate of years. A stranger had no right to rush into intimacy as this other one had done. Of course a great many of her other schoolmates had these careless ways of acting and talking! She hadn't been so far out of the world but that she had overheard plenty of it. Yet never before had it been addressed to herself, and now she found her finer feelings affronted!

Perhaps she was judging this strange man too harshly. Perhaps according to his standards he was only offering her honest admiration, but she didn't like it, and some-how she must protect herself from such contacts. Strange! She had never had trouble of this sort before. It must be her new clothes! That was it! She had always had decent garments, though extremely simple, sometimes almost shabby, in school. The scholars had grown used to her in everyday clothes, and had taken her for granted as a shy little person who belonged in the background. Now here she was appearing in pretty new clothes, and it had somehow brought her into notice. She mustn't let her head get turned with it all. Gordon McCarroll had probably noticed her for the first time because of the new clothes, too. He had suddenly discovered her, forlorn and needing comfort, so out of the abundance of his own charmed life he had paused to give her thought enough to send her on her way comforted. That was all it was of course, but it was something dear that she would always treasure. It wasn't to be expected that there would be many such bright spots in the days that were ahead of her. Her life was set henceforth in drab loneliness, and very likely some kind of hard work, and she must not allow her longings to go ahead of all probability. She would probably never see Gordon Mc-Carroll again in this life, but she would always remember to ask God to bless him greatly because of what he had done for her this day.

As for the other young man, she must keep him in his place, and keep out of his way as much as possible. That was all.

And now it was her happy duty to write a note of thanks for the roses! Or would it be better to wait until morning? She was suddenly very tired, and the motion of the ship and the music of the waves lured her to rest. She must take time to think what she would say in that letter. It was her privilege at last to speak to the boy who had all her school days been her ideal of what a young fellow should be, and she wanted to consider each word she wrote, and have it such that she would not be ashamed to think it over afterward. All the years of their school life seemed to have culminated in this one happening today, as if it were a lesson long anticipated, and now she wanted to fulfill her part creditably.

She went to her porthole and looked out over the far stretch of silvery sea and sky, stabbed with stars and bright moonlit wave-crests. A strange wide sea. The moon was up there somewhere, but she could not see it from this point. God was up there somewhere, and God was watching over her and caring. It was hard to realize sometimes, but it had been the last thing her mother had said to her the night she went Home, that God would be caring for her, and He was always there. How she wished she knew someone who could talk to her about God as her mother used to do, or her wonderful father! She sometimes felt such a longing to know God better. Well perhaps He would send her some friends some day who knew Him. He surely must have sent Gordon McCarroll and his roses to cheer her lonely way.

She turned from surveying the wide strange night and

laid her face against the flowers, softly touching a rosebud with her lips.

"Good night!" she whispered softly.

Quickly she arrayed herself for the night and kneeling bent her head to pray. There were so many things for which she was thankful, and so many places where she needed God's keeping power. Then she snapped out the light and crept into her bed, thinking how strange and sorrowful it was that she was here in a great boat tossing on the wide sea, and her dear mother's body was lying in the cemetery back at Shandon Hills.

Perhaps there were nice people, of course there must be some here on this ship, but she hadn't seen any yet that she cared to cultivate, and she was lonely, so lonely.

Gordon McCarroll had helped her through those last few moments before she left her native land, and the memory of his lips on hers still thrilled her, but she was afraid she was in danger of making far too much of it. The thought of it grew more precious every time it recurred, and she was quite certain that he had not intended it to be anything but kindly friendship. He wasn't that kind of a boy, never had been. She had watched him with the girls. She knew his reputation. And he, if he knew anything about her at all, would be sure she wasn't that kind of a girl.

As she lay there in the darkness with the sound of the sea all about her, the motion of the ship and the throbbing of the engine all blending into a sweet quietness, with a distant strain from a fine orchestra in the far distance, her tense sorrowful heart relaxed, and all the weariness of the day, and of the last few days, began to drift out and make itself known. It seemed good to be resting.

Rose was up early in the morning. It came to her that she wanted to see the early sea while the day was young, and perhaps there would not be so many alien watchers about before breakfast.

That young man called Harry Coster, if he'd done all the things he asked her to join him in last night, would surely not be up very early. It would be nice to get her first morning visions without him as accompaniment. Perhaps he would not be so anxious any more to companion with her after the way she had answered him last night. He doubtless was through with her. She sincerely hoped so. But at least she was running no chances. She wanted the sea all to herself for just a little while, to get acquainted with it, and try to read in it the moods her mother had said were there.

So with her big blue coat about her and the soft wool cap on her head that matched the fur collar, she stole out to the deck and reveled in the early morning loveliness. Pearly tints of sky and sea, illimitable space, golden morning air. Was it like that where her mother was, she wondered? More beautiful of course, only it was impossible to conceive of anything more beautiful. "Eye hath not seen . . . neither hath it entered into the heart of man to conceive." The words so familiar, yet never tangible before seemed to speak themselves to her heart. It was infinitely comforting to think of her mother in a beautiful place at last. Mother who so loved lovely things, and who had had so few of them during the after part of her life! Mother who had been brought up to have plenty, and to expect beauty. Brought up to instant discernment of what was good and what was shoddy, and who couldn't help it that imitations and ugliness caused her actual physical discomfort. Mother who had sometimes sacrificed a trifling extra for the table that she might have a flower. And now she was where there was plenty of beauty, no stinting! How grand for her! Mother amid eternal joy and loveliness! And mother must be glad that she was here watching the morning rise out of the sea, and thinking of her at home with God!

Suddenly a voice interrupted her.

"Well, beautiful, how are you this morning? Why so pensive? What are you thinking about? A penny for your thoughts!"

She turned annoyed to find Harry Coster beside her, handsome and sporty-looking, taking things for granted just as he had the night before. Was she going to be pestered with him all through the voyage? Would she be driven to stay in her cabin?

"Oh, you wouldn't be interested in my thoughts," she said reticently. "They were just plain thoughts."

"What about?" he insisted. "Sure I'd be interested."

"Oh no," she said gravely now, her eyes very sweet and far away. "I was just thinking about my mother, and if she sees this lovely morning I'm in, and if it is so much more beautiful where she is now than any mornings we have down here. Or whether this is just a piece of it, only with some of the glory dimmed so we can bear it."

She was talking more to herself than to him, letting her thoughts go on into the infinite.

"There you go!" said the young man gaily. "How do you get that way? If you'd gone dancing with me last night and had a little drink or two you wouldn't be so morbid this morning. What you need is a good hard walk around the decks to get up an appetite, and then after breakfast we'll play tennis. The other girl and fellow at our table are going to join us, and we'll have a great time. Come on now and we'll have a constitutional."

He seized her arm and laughingly forced her into step with him, getting into double-quick time and starting off on a brisk walk about the deck. Other people were coming out now, and were walking, two by two, some of them singly. Rose wished she could get away by herself. She didn't really like this dominating young man who insisted on forcing her to do what he wanted to do. Yet perhaps it was easier just to fall into step and go on than create a scene here on the deck with all these staid older people taking businesslike walks with such careful purpose, obviously following a set plan.

But somehow the beauty of the morning had fled for Rose. She didn't want to fly along gaily with this young man who evidently had no purpose in life but to have a good time. She wondered what she ought to do about him. She couldn't very well do anything but be polite when he came around determined to be friendly. What did it matter? A sea voyage didn't last forever. Perhaps if she got friendly with some of the girls and women she could wish him off onto them. That girl at the table. She looked to be far more his kind than she was.

Just then Harry Coster spoke.

"I told Lily Blake and Vance Hoffman that we were going to play tennis with them this morning, and they're keen for it. We'll play together, you and I. Partners, you know, against them. Then I'll have a chance to give you pointers."

"But I couldn't possibly play," said Rose aghast. "I never played in my life."

"Oh, that's all right," said her would-be partner, "neither has Lily, but she's keen for it, and you'll both soon learn. Hoffman and I made it up we would both coach our partners, and you'll learn a lot that way in a short time."

He rattled on about how it was important to keep your eye on the ball. Then the breakfast call came, and they could go to the dining room.

Rose sat next to the old lady again, who put her through a catechism about where she lived, and what she had done in her life so far, and where she was going, and who were her relatives, until she was hard put to it not to have to tell her private affairs to the avid old gossip. She succeeded, however, by her quiet answers in getting away with New York State as her home, not far from New York City; and Scotland as her destination. Her relatives she avoided naming, and the old lady came off with the opinion that she must have something to hide or she wouldn't be so reticent about herself and her family, and she voiced this opinion freely on deck later that morning.

Rose played at tennis for a little while, and rather enjoyed the exercise, even though she didn't always succeed in doing what she was directed to do. But when the rest of the party decided to finish with a swim in the pool she pleaded something to do and got away. She found the deck chair that was assigned to her and enjoyed a little while with a book she had brought along to read.

All went well until she sighted Mrs. Adams, the old lady from her table, bearing down upon the empty deck chair beside her, and quietly, unostentatiously, she slid from her chair and made her way quickly out of sight before Mrs. Adams was near enough to realize she had been seen.

The swimming party arrived at the table noisily just as Rose was finishing her lunch, and she managed to slip away again without getting involved in any plans. If they only would let her alone and allow her to enjoy that deck chair and the wonderful breeze!

But at last she settled down to write that letter to Gordon McCarroll.

She had thought it out in the small hours of the night that if her mother were here and she asked her advice about that letter she would say, "Make it natural, and simple, and not too long."

So Rose set to work.

The roses were there beside her, his roses, and the memory of his kindly farewell was with her. So she wrote with a sudden sense of his having been near her for those few moments on the ship.

Dear Gordon:

It was so wonderful to me to have those few minutes with you before we sailed. To feel there was somebody I knew to say good-by to me. I shall never forget how it comforted me.

And then to find those gorgeous roses in my cabin when I went back! To know that you took the trouble to send me flowers, and give me a taste of what it was to be just like other people with friends to see them off, and flowers, and thoughtfulness! I can't thank you enough.

I feel as if I wanted to give you my mother's thanks too, for she would have been so grateful to you for being kind to her lonely daughter. Maybe up in Heaven now she knows about it and is glad.

The roses have made my little stateroom a palace and they have given me a great deal of pleasure. I do not know any words to make you understand how I prize them, and prize your friendly thoughtfulness. You don't know how much I needed a friend just when you came by!

I will write you again as you have asked when I reach my aunt's house.

Thank you again for all you have done for me.

Sincerely,
Rose Galbraith

She put the letter into its envelope, addressed it in her clear pretty hand and then slipped out to mail it. She wanted to feel that it had started on its way, though she knew it could not really start until they landed. After that she took her book and went to her deck chair again, thankful to find the adjoining chair vacant.

For a long time she lay there quietly watching the sea, because she felt too happy over the thought of her letter going to Gordon McCarroll to settle herself for reading. It seemed such an important thing, that letter.

How surprised she would have been in her school days if she had been told that she would ever write a letter to Gordon McCarroll!

4

SHE was lying back in her chair with a dreamy expression in her eyes, thinking with quickening heartbeats about that letter she had just written and mailed. Thinking of the way Gordon McCarroll had looked at her when he gave her that good-by kiss. "Like a real friend" she told herself, the rosy color stealing into her cheeks, her eyes bright with unexpected pleasure.

There was a pleasant little smile on her sweet lips and her eyes were off at sea, her book lying in her lap with her fingers between the leaves keeping her place, when Mrs. Adams bore down upon her again, and clumsily writhed herself into the vacant chair by her side. But Rose wasn't aware of what had happened until it was too late to escape, and her heart sank. Oh dear! Could it be that that was Mrs. Adams' own chair? And would she have to endure her presence perhaps every time she wanted to sit on deck? That would spoil a good many nice quiet hours upon which she had counted, for the woman talked incessantly. She just couldn't keep still. Rose had found that out already.

But perhaps she would go to sleep and then it

wouldn't be so bad. She turned her disappointed gaze and gave a wan little smile hoping to find Mrs. Adams looking sleepy.

But no, Mrs. Adams had no intention of going to sleep! She got out her knitting from the large substantial bag which she carried, and prepared to entertain her companion as she knit.

"Well, I'm glad I've found somebody to talk to at last!" she said ponderously, with great satisfaction. "It certainly does bore me the way some people sit selfishly and refuse to say a word. Over on the other side of the deck where my chair is located there are three women right along in a row with me and not one of the three has a civil tongue in her head. If you ask them a question they either don't answer at all or else they get off a lot of modern slang that doesn't mean a thing, and they are the most unfriendly lot I ever saw. And *sleep?* Why they pretend to be asleep every time I come in sight. I'm glad they're not at our table. I intend to see the purser and get my deck chair changed. Do you know if anyone has this chair? I like your looks and wouldn't mind having a young person to talk to. Do you knit? I could teach you some new stitches perhaps. I'm a real good knitter. And by the way, I don't remember your name. What is it? I like to put all the names down in my travelogue. Do you mind?"

"My name's Galbraith," said Rose quietly. "Isn't the sea lovely this afternoon, Mrs. Adams? And I really don't know who has that chair. I haven't had time to be out much yet. But I thought I saw someone sitting here a little while ago when I looked this way from a distance. No, I don't knit. I've never had time. I'm not long out of school."

"Oh," said Mrs. Adams looking at her narrowly. "Well, that explains why you look so sweet and wholesome, I suppose. No lipstick, and no rouge, you know. I can't abide make-up. Like that other girl who sits at our table. She doesn't look to me like a really respectable character, does she to you? Or perhaps she's an old friend of yours, is she? How long have you known her?"

"Oh, I don't know her at all," she said. "They asked me to play tennis with them this morning, and I did for a few minutes, but that isn't very conducive to getting acquainted with people, you know."

"Well, no, I suppose not," said Mrs. Adams dryly. "But I do think you ought to be a little careful till you really know people, don't you? There are so many adventuresses and divorcees going about these days you can't tell who is respectable and who isn't. It's my opinion this Blake person—Lily Blake she says she is—is di*vorced!* Don't you think she is? I was looking at her hands at the table today and she looks as if she had been wearing rings on the third finger of her left hand, wedding rings you know, and if that is so you can depend upon it she's divorced. My dear, I think you can't be too careful. You don't look like a girl that would run around with women like that, and I thought I'd warn you."

"Well, but I'm not running around with anybody," smiled Rose amusedly. "I don't see what harm it would be to play tennis with anybody for a few minutes, do you? We're all God's people in the world together, and we've no right to judge one another. Besides, playing tennis a few minutes isn't choosing them for intimate friends and going in their ways if they happen to be wrong."

"Yes, of course you'd excuse it! Young folks will, but it's a dangerous thing to be easy about such things. You can't tell—! By the way, are you and that Harry Coster old friends? I can't help feeling *he'll* bear watching. He's too good-looking to be all right, don't you think? Did he give you those roses you were wearing to dinner last night?"

"Oh, no," laughed Rose. "They were from a box of roses that a friend from home left in my cabin." Mrs. Adams favored her with a speculative stare.

"Oh!" she said thoughtfully. "From *home? Boy* friend?"

Rose laughed aloud, a merry little sound between a giggle and a joyous laugh.

"Would that make any difference?" she asked, looking Mrs. Adams over amusedly.

"Well, yes, I think it would!" said that good woman decidedly. "At least it might make a difference to the young men you went around with on board."

"Oh!" said Rose. "But, you see, I don't have any idea of going around with the young men on board."

"I saw you myself walking around with that young Coster last night, and again this morning. If that isn't going around then I'm blind. If you are engaged or anything I think the young men at your table should know it, and I should consider it my duty to inform them. There are too many girls going around these days flirting with this one and that one, and it isn't right. You don't look like that kind of a girl. And you're not wearing an engagement ring either. I think a girl that is engaged should wear an engagement ring."

She gave Rose a condemning glance, and clicked her needles menacingly.

"Well, but you'd have to be very sure it was true, wouldn't you, before you told the others a thing like that?" asked Rose demurely.

"Oh, I'd be good and sure," said the old lady confidently. "I don't go around telling lies about people, you know."

"Of course if the girl had told you herself and given you permission to announce it, that would be a different thing," said Rose sweetly.

Mrs. Adams lifted her chin contemptuously, and snorted.

"There are more ways of finding out the truth about such things than having people *tell* you," she said offendedly. "Give me a few brief glances, a chance to watch a girl a little while, and I can tell. And as for her permission, what's that? If a girl doesn't want things known she shouldn't do 'em, and I for one am not going to be a party to keeping things to myself that ought to be told for the sake of right and wrong."

"Well," said Rose quietly, "I wouldn't feel I had the right to jump to conclusions and then go and tell things that the people most concerned were not ready to have told yet!"

"Ready!" sniffed Mrs. Adams. "Ready! Humph! Well, it's easy to see where *you* stand, and it doesn't take long to size people up. If people are ashamed of what they're doing, naturally they wouldn't be ready to have it known! I didn't take you for that sort of a girl, and I certainly don't intend to let a little chit like you tell me whether I'm honest or not, and if I'm justified in what I think is my duty."

"I'm sorry," said Rose. "I didn't intend to criticize you. It just didn't seem fair to me that anyone should go around announcing other people's engagements even if they were true. But I probably didn't quite understand you. And now if you don't mind I think I'll just excuse myself and go to my cabin for a little while. I'm getting awfully sleepy, and I wouldn't like you to think I was like those other people you said were always going to sleep."

Rose got up with a sweet smile and slipped away,

wondering if it would be at all possible for her to secure another deck chair where there was no likelihood of having undesirable neighbors.

But that very afternoon, coming toward her deck chair cautiously, viewing it from afar lest Mrs. Adams would still be there, she sighted another woman as different from Mrs. Adams as one could well imagine. She was sure she had not seen her in the dining room yet. She was a fair sweet woman with white hair and a distinguished bearing. She looked as if she belonged among the wealthy "first class" travelers. If so what was she doing down on the tourist class deck?

Rose hesitated shyly, and deliberately walked on past her chair, before she could make up her mind to come back and sit down. She felt that perhaps the new lady would think she was intruding if she sat down there. But when she finally ventured the lady looked up with a lovely smile.

"Isn't this your chair?" she asked, laying her hand over on the arm of Rose's chair. "I wonder if you were expecting some friend to sit here with you this afternoon?" she asked apologetically. "I found this chair was vacant, and I asked to be allowed to take it, because, to tell the truth, I saw you yesterday when you came on board, and I want very much to get to know you if I may. You see you look so very much like a dear friend of my girlhood days that I was drawn to you. Do you mind? If you had other plans I'll gladly withdraw."

"Oh, how lovely!" said Rose, blooming into a smile. "I'll be delighted for you to have this chair!"

Rose sat down happily, studying the beautiful face of the woman.

"Let me introduce myself first," said the lady. "My name is Campbell and I live in Edinburgh. And now, may I tell you about my friend whom you resemble? She was a very lovely girl. When I first knew her we went to school together in a little town in Scotland, and we loved each other very dearly. Then changes came and we were separated. She was married a short time after I was married. I went to London to live, and I lost track of her. I tried to find out about her but the family had moved, I don't know where. There were two brothers. I understood the older one had gone to Edinburgh University, but before I could trace him there he was graduated, married and gone to America to live. No one seemed to know the address. But I have often wondered about her, I would so like to know if she is living. When I saw the startling resemblance you bore to her I determined to find out whether you might possibly be her child. I don't want to presume, but would you mind my knowing your name? I could have asked the captain of course, but I thought I would like to ask you yourself. And I don't even know my friend's married name, you see, because in those days people did not send out such careful invitations as they do now. But her maiden name was Rose Galbraith!"

"Oh!" said Rose, her eyes growing large and eager. "Why, that is my name, too. And my father had a little sister whose name was Rose. I never saw her because she went to Australia to live, but my father used to say I looked like her. Oh, how wonderful that I should meet somebody who used to know my lovely Aunt Rose!"

"My *dear!*" said her new friend, eagerly as a girl. "What was your father's name?"

"Gilbert Galbraith," said Rose almost reverently. "And he went to Edinburgh University. And then when he was married they went to America."

"Oh, and where are they now?" asked the lady.

"My father died seven years ago," said Rose, and then in a lower sad little voice added, "and my mother just last week! We were coming over together, but—she went Home to Heaven instead."

"Oh, my dear!" said the gentle voice, and the older woman's hand came out sympathetically and lay on the girl's hand.

Rose was all of a quiver.

"To think that I should meet someone who knew my own family!" she said with quick tears in her eyes. "Oh, I'm so glad you came to sit here! And to think you knew my sweet Aunt Rose. My father loved her so much, and used to tell me about her."

"Do you know about her? Is she living yet?"

"Yes," said Rose eagerly. "But away out in Australia. I have a picture of her that I've always loved. I'd like you to see it. Perhaps I could have it copied for you when I get back to my things in America, if I ever do."

"Oh, and you are not sure of going back?"

Rose caught her breath and answered with a trembling lip.

"Oh, I don't know what I am going to do. I haven't dared try to think. Mother and I were coming over to visit and going back to America of course. Mother felt she ought to come over and see her only sister. She wrote and asked her to come. And mother wanted, too, to go and see father's mother, my grandmother Galbraith who is pretty old and not very well. And his brother John and his family with whom grandmother is living. And then we were going back to America to stay."

"Oh!" said the lady. "Your mother preferred America?"

"Well," said Rose, lifting her eyes honestly to the lady's face, "you see, mother had been sort of alienated from her people because of her marrying father. They are all dead now but her sister and brother-in-law. But the sister was older, and sided with them all. They didn't want her to marry father because he wasn't rich. They had in mind a wealthy lord who owned a castle and was very influential. He wanted to marry my mother. But she didn't love him. She loved my father. So when he was graduated she went to commencement, and they were married and went right to America. Her family never forgave her. At least they were very angry. You see they had been wealthy people and highly connected, and they felt it was a disgrace to marry just a poor student who had no great prospect of rising in the world."

"Oh, yes, I remember hearing about that," said the lady. "Poor mistaken people! And your father was worth so much more than that worldly lord. Yes, I remember being indignant about it, for the Galbraith family were wonderful people, fine and cultured, and truly royal in their characters. Your father wrote some notable things before he died. I remember reading them. I have some of his writings now. I know they were very highly spoken of, and brought him honorable mention from his university more than once. But my dear, I'm so glad I have found you! And now, what are your plans? Are you going straight to your Uncle John's to see your grandmother? Or do you stop in Edinburgh to see your other relatives?"

"I must," said Rose with downcast glance. "Mother wished it. She wanted her only sister to see me. She said we owed that to father, too. And of course after years they sort of forgave her, and wrote to her occasionally. Sometimes they sent her useless presents, things that seemed to mock our comparative poverty. And yet her sister, after father died, sort of seemed to yearn for her, and at last mother gave in and wrote that we would come. But mother didn't live to get there. And sometimes when I think about it I wonder if it wasn't easier for her after all. Of course her own mother and father were dead, long ago. They had been very hard on mother. They were proud and domineering, and they died without ever coming over to see her, or saying they were sorry she had been so treated, though mother had often written loving letters and begged them to get over it and love my father. Their only answer was to write and offer to *adopt me!* But of course neither mother nor father would have that. And I think my aunt sided with them largely. Naturally I don't anticipate my visit there with joy, and I shall get it over with as briefly as possible, I think."

"Yes," said the sweet Scotch woman, "they were a hard people and very proud. I knew them but slightly myself, but they were so known in the city. They couldn't brook the thought that their daughter had married a poor man when she might have lived in a castle. It all comes back to me now. But my dear, it is right, I suppose, that you go to them for a visit at least."

"Yes, I shall have to go," sighed Rose. "I think I'll stop there first a few days and then go on to grand-mother."

They sat there talking a long time till the sun began to dip in the western water and the sea to put on its holy jeweled look. And then suddenly they remembered it was time to be getting ready for dinner. Rose went to her stateroom with the memory of a soft clinging hand when they parted, and a gentle tender word in her ears.

"I'm so glad we have found each other!"

"And oh, so am I!" responded Rose with a long drawn breath of relief.

"And I hope you will come and sit with me a little while this evening," said her new friend. "We have a great deal more to talk about."

So Rose went to her own table that night with a pleasant thought for the evening that was to follow the meal, and with a good excuse to offer if Harry Coster tried to monopolize her again.

But how they did stare, especially Mrs. Adams, when the gracious lady appeared behind Rose's chair before she had finished dinner and spoke a few low words in her ear, then with a smile went slowly on.

"Well," said Mrs. Adams in a tone that could be easily heard over the table, "you certainly are flying high! I didn't know you knew her."

"Yes," said Rose sweetly, "she's an old friend of my aunt's."

"Oh, *really?*" said Mrs. Adams. "On which side? Father or mother?"

"Oh, she's a friend of the whole family, you know."

"Well, I thought you were sort of high hat," said Lily Blake. "Now I see you had some reason."

"High hat?" said Rose, puzzled. "What reason could I have to be high hat?"

"Why, because it isn't everybody who knows Lady Campbell intimately, of course. I heard somebody say today that Lady Campbell was so high up in society she was almost royalty."

Rose tried not to show her surprise. So her friend was *Lady* Campbell! Not just plain "Mrs." "But why should *I* be high hat? That doesn't make *me* royalty, surely!" She laughed.

"Now," said Harry Coster with his scornful grin, "don't pretend you don't know why. You can't put that over on us. I say, how about giving us an introduction? I wouldn't mind knowing some near-royalties myself. It might come in handy sometime."

They did a good deal of kidding and laughing, but Rose could see that they looked at her with a trifle more respect than they had done, and when Harry Coster gave his evening invitation to her to go and dance awhile, he only bowed low when she said, "No thank you," and stared after her thoughtfully, instead of arguing with her about it.

So the days grew to be pleasant ones, with such a friend as Lady Campbell to sit beside her occasionally, and sometimes to invite her up to have dinner with her. She was a friend who could advise her and was wise about things of the journey that she needed to know.

It was pleasant, too, to have Lady Campbell invite her for a visit in her own home. She began to look forward to her stay in Scotland with a possibility of pleasure. For her mother's sake if not for her own she wanted to enjoy it, and see the beautiful things and places and people her mother had loved. So the approaching end of her voyage did not cause her as much anxiety as it had before she knew Lady Campbell.

One night when she crept into bed and lay there listening to the beating of the waves, and thinking about her pilgrimage, she reflected that Lady Campbell was another person like Gordon McCarroll, a person with a heart of gold and a life full of love and helpfulness. People were in sort of stripes in the world. Some were one kind and some another, and you had to meet all kinds and adjust yourself to each, but there was only one kind that you could take to your heart truly and admire and fellowship with. Was it perhaps because they loved the Lord? She would have to think about that. She would have to know people better before she found out how much a knowledge of God helped to make them of the right kind.

Then she fell asleep with a smile of peace on her lips.

5

BACK in New York Gordon McCarroll had not forgotten the girl whom he had helped to speed on her way, who was now out upon the wide ocean. He thought of her often, especially at night when he was alone in his room. He wondered a great deal about her. How was it that he had not known her well, at least as well as he knew the rest of his schoolmates? He had a strong feeling that she was more worthwhile than any of the others.

He had always known that scholastically she was above the rest. She was more of a scholar, or else she was a patient plodder. He had never troubled to find out which. But now, strangely enough, those few minutes he had spent with her on shipboard had made him feel that she not only had a superior intellect but that she had character, and that she was sweet and original.

Not that he deliberately set to work to analyze these thoughts at first. They came gradually to him like a pleasant revelation, and it was then he wondered at himself that he had not somehow discovered this before. Why had he never noticed her before?

What had there been about her on shipboard that was different?

For one thing she seemed prettier. He had never thought of her as being pretty or stylish. But now she seemed very lovely, garbed quite as other girls of her age.

Then suddenly he remembered that he had noticed once before how pretty she was. That had been at Commencement. She had been wearing white, like all the others, but something filmy and soft, and her young face had shone out from among the others like a star. He remembered looking at her several times that night and wondering about it. And then of course had come vacation days and he hadn't seen her any more till he found her on that boat, with blue eyes like the blue garments she was wearing.

He scoffed at himself for thinking such thoughts. When had he ever noticed clothes, or taken account of them as a measure by which to judge a girl? Probably, though, clothes did count for something in the general appearance of a person, and not everybody could afford lovely garments. As he remembered the Rose Galbraith of school days, she had always been extremely clean and neat, tidy and almost tailored if one could use that description for garments that sometimes were quite faded, worn almost shiny. Poor little girl! She had probably come from a plain home where money was scarce. And now her mother was gone, and her father too perhaps, because she had said she was alone.

And when he thought about it he was glad he had kissed her. The touch of her lips seemed still to be upon his own, and a strange thrilling wonder lingered, too, whenever he brought her flower-like face to mind.

He was glad he had happened to pass the flower shop on his way from the ship, glad that he could snatch time to give his order and scribble those few words on the card. It warmed his heart to think he could have that much touch with her. And now, he positively must put her out of his thoughts. He never had a girl entangle herself in his mind this way. And she had not tried to do it either. She was just a lonely child, genuinely glad to see a face she could recognize. No, she was never a girl who would set herself to attract a young man's attention. She had always kept so utterly in the background in school. Strange that he should be so interested in her now, after just those few minutes. That he should so long to do something more for her. He felt he would like to give her another word of cheer as she went on her way. That was impossible of course. Just because he had kissed a girl good-by didn't mean he must follow her all across the ocean and cheer her up. He couldn't yet understand why he had kissed her. It had been so sudden! But it had been wonderful, the sweetest thing he ever remembered. Well, he could write to her later, though he didn't feel that she had given him a full enough address. He could send her a book or two he thought she would enjoy. That would be perfectly legitimate, without seeming to be rushing her. He must keep steady.

Yet the wish to have another contact with her continued, and toward the end of the week it occurred to him that he could send her a radio message.

He called himself all sorts of names as he turned the idea over in his mind, but in the end the thought appealed to him more and more, until at last one night he resolved to do it. It certainly couldn't do any harm, and if he worded it casually it wouldn't seem ridiculous. She wasn't a girl with whom one would take liberties of attention. So he gave careful thought to the wording of his message and at last sent it off.

Dear Rose:

Hope you have a pleasant voyage. Best wishes for a happy arrival among your friends. Be sure to send me your full address as soon as you are located. I want to send you a book I think you will enjoy. Hope everything is fine.

Your friend,
Gordon.

That message was brought to Rose late Saturday night after she had been asleep for two hours. It filled her with a new contentment. It made her feel that she had one friend who meant to be not a mere casual acquaintance, but a good friend that might last through the years. Such a friendship could be as fresh and pleasant after time had rolled along as when they were just children in school, a friendship of two people who liked the same things, who would enjoy talking and reading about the same subjects. It made life an entirely different thing to Rose, as if she had happy wholesome contacts like other girls, and were not absolutely alone in the world. Well, anyway, however she reasoned it out, she felt happier, and didn't quite dread the new scenes and relatives as much as she had done. Someone away back across the water was thinking of her now and then and wishing her well, and some day if she ever met him again, she would remind him of how he had said she would make friends on the voyage; she would tell him about Lady Campbell and how lovely she was.

Lady Campbell was very kind and helpful at the end of the voyage. She saw to it that all the details of landing were made clear and comfortable for Rose, and that she was put on the train that would take her the short journey to where her mother's people had promised to meet her.

But before they parted Lady Campbell made definite plans for Rose to visit her, making sure of both the addresses where she expected to be. She kissed her good-by, calling her a dear little girl, and said she was so glad she had found her. She warmed Rose's heart and kept away the tremor of half fright at the thought of meeting the new relatives.

She wasn't anticipating any pleasure in this visit. It was going to be hard for her to like the people who had treated her mother so cruelly, on account of her wonderful father. Probably it was right that she should be willing to forgive them, but it seemed impossible. She couldn't help resenting them for her father's sake. And they didn't even know him! She meant to get through this visit as soon as possible and get on to her father's family who had been so lovely always to her mother that she felt as if they were more her relatives than the others.

The way along which the train sped was most interesting. New scenes, lovely lakes, verdure, flowers, and wide expanses of heather. How lovely it all was!

And then the enchanting little villages, Scotch and quaint; and there—she caught her breath—was a tall old craggy castle!

Just then the train stopped at the station where she was to get out and she arose in fear and trembling to gather up her belongings. There was the tall old castle on the hill not far away and she was glad for that. Perhaps it would be within walking distance and she could go near and study it. She had always wanted to see a real castle. There was a foreign looking car drawn up at the station and a man in livery standing by it.

"Are ye gaen tae Lady Warloch's?" he asked cautiously.

Rose hesitated, then realized that that would be her aunt of course. Mother had always spoken of her as Aunt Janet, but her name was Warloch. Janet Warloch. And mother, if she had stayed here, would have been called Lady Margaret. Well, her mother was a lady, that was right, but it would have to be proved to her that her sister Janet who had treated her own sister so contemptibly was a real lady also. But mother wouldn't like such thoughts and she must stop it.

She got into the car and the drive began, through the lovely town out into the countryside, where charming vine clad cottages nestled among the trees by the roadside. Then up, up, winding about a hill, with always that castle above and a little beyond. Perhaps they were going to pass it. Wouldn't that be wonderful!

At last she summoned courage to ask a question.

"Is the castle a private dwelling, or some public building?" she asked timidly.

The old Scot looked back at her and raised his bushy red eyebrows.

"Thot'll be Warloch cossel," he said cryptically. "We'll be soon thur the noo!"

"Oh!" said Rose awestruck, almost speechless. Of course! Mother had always addressed her letters to Warloch Castle. But would she be able to live up to life in a castle?

The car swept around the drive, and up, until they circled the castle itself, and came to a standstill before a great entrance. Another servant also in livery, opened the front door, and stood at the top of the stone steps. Back in the shadow of the doorway she could see a lady standing, tall and quite angular and haughty. Her hair was white, and although there was a slight family resemblance to her mother, it was not a pleasant one. She had a firm determined mouth, and a disagreeable determined tilt to her chin. But there was so much shadow up there inside the hall that Rose decided perhaps it was only her prejudice that made her think that. There was a tall elderly gentleman standing just back of her, with an arrogant lift to his head. Oh, she was quite sure she was not going to enjoy this part of her visit. She wondered how it would have been if her dear mother had been with her. Would she have enjoyed getting back to her people, such people as these were? Could one love even one's own when they had done a thing such as these had done?

These thoughts raced through Rose's mind as she went slowly up the steps, and stood finally in the dark hall, facing the cold-eyed woman in stately garments. Then her mind went harking back to the gentle words of her mother, how she had instructed her to be entirely natural with these people, to forget all she had heard about them, and to remember that Aunt Janet used to be very dear to her mother when she was a child. Determinedly she took a deep breath and summoned a smile, and a gay little cheery voice which was far from being her own natural one, and asked sweetly:

"Is this my Aunt Janet?" and then thought too late that perhaps her aunt wouldn't want to own her as a niece and added: "I mean is this my mother's sister Janet?"

"It is!" said the lady icily. "Will you come in?"

But suddenly, because there came a quick rush of memory that if her dear mother were here there would surely be a warmer greeting, impulsively she put her arms about the tall repellent woman and laid a soft little kiss on her cold lips.

The amazed woman returned the unexpected salute with a cold semblance of a peck on Rose's pretty cheek, stepped back with a motion of rebuff as if to forbid further demonstrations, and turned toward the gentleman.

"This is Lord Warloch," she said formally, "that is, my husband, your uncle, I suppose he must be, if you are my sister's child."

Lord Warloch put out a clammy bony hand on a long arm and grasped her hand ineffectually. Rose stood there wondering what to do next.

"You will come in and sit down for tea with us while the man takes your luggage to the room," said Lady Warloch. "Your name is—? Margaret—I suppose, like your mother's."

"Rose Margaret," said Rose trying to steady her voice and speak brightly because she was so very near to tears, and knew she must not cry.

"*Rose* Margaret!" said the severe cold voice, that was all the more severe because of the bit of a Scotch accent on her thin tongue. "And who is the Rose for? Surely not just a fancy name! I should have thought Margaret would have been enough since that was your mother's name!" She looked at Rose as if it were somehow her fault that she had too much name.

"Why, Rose was the name of my father's sister, a very dear sister, and mother was very fond of her too." And then she stopped aghast. She had meant to be so very discreet and not mention her father's family any more than she could help. Her mother had warned her of that, to be careful at least until they were well acquainted. And now, what had she done?

"Indeed!" said the cold aunt-voice. "I should have thought it was enough for my sister to have married your father without taking on his whole family." "My mother loved them all," said Rose simply, struggling to keep her voice steady and her lips from trembling.

"So it would seem!" said the cold voice, and subsided into a disapproving silence.

Then the uncle took up the conversation.

"You came over *alone?*" he asked with more disapproval in his tone. "Or did you have friends with you?"

"No, I had no one with me," said Rose quietly, "but I met some very pleasant people on the boat."

"It is never wise to pick up strangers indiscriminately," averred the aunt autocratically. "You never can tell about them. The very people you judge to be nice might turn out to be quite common, and become a nuisance afterward. If I had known you were coming alone I should have given you that advice beforehand. But of course we couldn't foresee that your mother was going to pass away before you came. It would have been so much better if she could have lived to come back to her own first, but of course it is too late to say that now. Hereafter, however, if you ever have occasion to travel alone make no friends whatever! That is the safest rule."

Rose was struggling to keep back the tears which her aunt's ruthless words brought to the overflowing point. She lifted a sad little smile.

"Well," she said, "I guess God must have taken care of me, for I met the dearest lady, and she was so sweet to me. She knew who you were, had met you once in London, I think she said."

"A great many people know who *we* are of course, whom *we* have never really met," said the aunt loftily. "What was her name?"

"She was Lady Campbell. She was charming. I am sure you would approve of her."

"Campbell?" said the aunt, "I know some Campbells of course but probably not the same. The Lady Campbell I refer to would never be around getting acquainted with stray girls traveling alone. Was she introduced to you by someone?"

"No," said Rose, "she came and sat down beside my deck chair and told me that I looked so much like an old school friend of hers that she wanted to get acquainted with me."

"Yes, that's an old trick. Quite unscrupulous women have sometimes used it, I suppose, to get young unsuspecting girls under their influence. It is never safe to trust unknown people. I suppose this person didn't tell you where she lived, did she?"

"Oh, yes," said Rose smiling at the remembrance. "She's invited me to visit her. I have her address right here in my purse."

"Well, don't go near her! That's all I have to say. You would find yourself caught in some terrible situation."

"Oh, you don't understand, Aunt Janet. Her husband is something in the Government. They are very noted people. I heard people on the ship telling about them. They were at the captain's table, and everyone thought a great deal of them. Here is the address!" and Rose handed over the dainty engraved card.

The aunt looked up after glancing at it.

"Why, I don't understand!" she exclaimed in astonishment. "Robert," she said looking sternly at her husband as if this were suddenly all his fault, "it seems to be *the* Lady Campbell. My dear, how did you say you happened to meet her?"

"She just came and sat down in the deck chair next to mine which did not seem to belong to anyone, and she told me she had asked permission to sit there because she wanted to get to know me. We had a very beautiful talk, and I found out that it was my father's youngest sister who was her friend. And she knew my father when he was in college; she had often visited at my grandmother's home when she was a girl. She knows and loves my grandmother though she has not seen her in a good many years, because after my Aunt Rose married and went to Australia she lost track of them, as they had moved away about the time she herself was married."

"We shall have to look into this," said the aunt, handing the card back to Rose. "we cannot of course have you intimate with any people who are not genuine."

Rose felt her anger rising, but she dropped her glance and reflected that no good could come from answering back. She was here only for a few days anyway, and why get up an argument? It was best to be peaceable whatever was said if she possibly could.

But just then a servant arrived to announce that the young lady's luggage was unpacked and she might go up to her room. Rose was relieved when she found that she was to go with the servant and that her aunt was not accompanying her to her room.

"You'd best lie down and rest awhile," Aunt Janet's cold voice followed her out of the room, "and then you can dress for dinner. Maggie will tell you what to put on if you have anything with you that's fit to appear in. We are expecting a guest to dinner. If you didn't bring along suitable evening garments we can send a tray up to you tonight."

Rose hesitated at the door and looked at her aunt.

"Would you rather I stayed upstairs?" she asked with quiet dignity.

"No, not if you have a dinner dress with you. If you haven't one I shall have to see about getting you something," went on the implacable voice.

"I have dinner dresses," said Rose quietly, and followed the maid out of the room, resolved that she would make her stay in this castle brief indeed.

But she was intrigued by the stateliness of the old building, as she followed the woman up the great stone staircase. The lofty gloom of the stone walls seemed so to fit her preconceived ideas of what an old-world castle should be. Her heart thrilled with the thought that it was some very old castle like this in which her mother used to live when she was a little girl. Tomorrow she would manage to ask a few questions and find out all the family history that she could get from the severe taciturn old aunt. Surely she would be willing to tell of old times. She must be patient and get as much as she could to carry away for the sake of her own knowledge of her mother's early home.

Up in the great room that had been assigned to her she found her meager wardrobe spread out, some of it upon the bed, some hung in the wide old wardrobe.

"I thot yo'd be wearin' this the nicht," said Maggie, pointing to a simple blue crepe with a froth of lace about the becoming square neck and the brief sleeves. The very dress that mother had wanted her first to appear in before her family! There were others as pretty perhaps, but this was the one upon which mother had spent the most of her delicate workmanship, and Rose loved it very much. She had safely guarded it and packed it most carefully, so that it was fresh as when it was first made.

"Yes," said Rose, "that is what I intended."

But when the woman left her Rose did not lie down immediately. Instead she went to the great wide windows and looked off across the hills of Scotland, and thought how when a girl like herself her mother might have stood and looked at almost this same view of the far beautiful stretches of country, not knowing then how it was to fare with her in life; how she was to love one of God's noblemen, go to a far land, and be separated entirely from her family, her proud worldly family!

There were so many things to look at. The furniture was quaint and old, and of rarely fine workmanship, but the needle point of the chairs was much of it faded and worn. There was nothing bright nor modern about the room. The carpets dim and thick and pretentious spoke of other days, and the pictures were oil paintings in great gold frames, ancestral pictures most of them, earls and dukes and lords and ladies, periwigs and farthingales, high ruffs and headdresses. She spent much time looking at them, studying their faces for some likeness to her beloved mother, wondering who they were.

She had not been told what time she would be expected downstairs, but at last her little watch which had been her mother's commencement gift to her, the result of savings from the years, told her it was time to be dressed and ready for whatever was suggested.

When she was ready she sat down with a quaint old book she had found in the bookcase, a book of Scotch traditions, wit and wisdom, tales of the old days.

And so she sat and read until the twilight came down, making it hard to see. Then she looked about for a way to turn on the light, but there seemed to be no lights save tall candles against the grim stone walls. Of course an old castle wouldn't have electric lights, though she wondered at it. Would it cost so much to have a castle wired?

She was sitting dreamily beside the window looking out across the moors, watching a lovely sunset in this strange new land, and thinking that God's sun was alike everywhere. She was wondering too if her mother could look down and see what her child was doing, thinking, here in this great lonely castle among almost hostile relatives.

It was perhaps these few minutes of communing with her dear mother's hopes and wishes for her, that gave her a gentleness during the trying places of the evening, and helped her to wear a high look of victory when at last there came the summons to go down into the candlelit castle.

She went down the stairs slowly, pondering on the words of the old servant who had called her.

She had paused in the doorway and looked her over with a satisfied glance.

"Ye favor some o' the gowans in the garden," she said happily. "Ye'd best be gaen doon the stair the noo. The yoong Lord MacCallummore will soon be arrivin'."

MacCallummore! Where had she heard that name? Ah! That was the name of the man they had wanted her mother to marry! Could it be that they had invited him for her to see what her mother had missed when she married her father?

She entered the great gloomy room where her aunt and uncle were sitting, and looked about uncertainly. They sat in stately manner as if they awaited royalty.

She saw at once that they had changed into evening dress. Her aunt was wearing black, gleaming and sinister with jet strewn about it, from which her skinny bare arms protruded gauntly, and her long bony neck like a yoke of tan leather.

Rose sat down on a low hassock not far from the open fire which burned inadequately in the great barracks of a room. She gave a little shiver as she drew the hassock nearer to the fire. For now that the dark had come the castle seemed wide and chilly. It was of course a wonderful place, and it was so different from any dwelling she had ever been in that it much intrigued her, but there was nothing cozy or homelike about it. Or, she reflected, perhaps it was the coldness in the faces and glances of the owners, rather than the atmosphere that made that involuntary shiver as she sat down. She wondered.

For almost a full minute after she entered the room,

neither the aunt nor the uncle spoke. Then a solemn old clock spoke, chiming out the time, and Lady Warloch, looking up at it as if it had been a servant who had announced a guest or a meal, said:

"Our guest will be soon arriving now."

She did not look at Rose, so she concluded the announcement was for the benefit of Lord Warloch.

At last he cleared his throat impressively, sepulchrally, and said "Yes!" And then as if suddenly he was in a hurry, he looked at Rose and said:

"There are questions I want to ask you."

His piercing eyes looked through her and made her feel as if she were all at once a prisoner at the bar. His voice had long ago been wrung dry.

"Yes?" she said politely.

"Several matters that I wanted to satisfy myself about before the arrival of our guest. It is well to know just where we stand, you know, in introducing relatives, especially to our friends; and of course, under the painful circumstances, we have not been in touch with you through the years, and have therefore not the knowledge that we should have had if we had been residing in close proximity."

He paused as if expecting an answer, and Rose smiled and said once more, "Yes?" There seemed nothing else appropriate to say.

"Very well, then, suppose we begin at the beginning. I would like to have you tell me fully and definitely what are your circumstances?"

"Circumstances?" repeated Rose in bewilderment. "Circumstances? I don't know that I understand just what it is you want to know, uncle. I am sure mother must have told you in her letters all that you would need to know."

"No," said the uncle severely, "I don't recall that she

said one word with regard to your circumstances. She merely said that now that her husband had passed away she was contemplating visiting her homeland and wanted to know if it would be acceptable to us for her to make us a short visit, as she longed to see her sister."

"Yes," said Rose. "She gave me the letters to read before she posted them. I knew what she said, but I don't know just what you mean about circumstances. What is it you want to know, uncle?"

"Why, naturally I am speaking of money," said the old man with great dignity. "In other words, to speak plainly, I am wanting to know about your financial circumstances. I have always understood that your father was not a financial success. In other words he did not exert himself to get into any sort of lucrative business. I am inquiring to know if your father was able to leave you and your mother in comfortable circumstances. In plain language, did your father leave you anything at all?"

Rose's cheeks were glowing by this time, as she gradually became aware of her uncle's meaning, and her loyal young heart sprang to quick defense of the father whom she had almost adored.

"Oh!" she said with quick lofty unconcern, and a sudden memory of the fund of five hundred dollars in the bank that her father had started for her the day she was born by depositing a few scanty painfully saved dollars. By the time he left this world it had grown to the sum of five hundred dollars, and was supposedly to be for his daughter's education, or her start in life. She recalled his sadness as he talked it over with her mother the night before he died, regretting that he had not been able to save more. She recalled the fact that her mother would never let it be touched for anything, not even when they were in their worst straits, saying: "No, child! Your father wanted that to be kept for you, at any cost.

He said there might come a time when you were in dire stress, and would need it. He wanted to leave you something material that would show he thought of your future. It isn't much of course, but we'll not touch it ever unless we have to for a matter of life or death."

And so she had remained firm about it, even when the cherished trip to Scotland was in question. She would not let even a hundred dollars be withdrawn from it to make the trip more luxurious.

So Rose lifted a proud young head, and looked at her uncle with eyes alight and said:

"Yes, my father left me money. Of course!"

The uncle bored her sensitive soul with eyes that were evidently weighing her words to be sure she was not lying.

"How much?" he said at length, looking straight through her again. His words were like pistol shots that sent rebellion quivering along her being.

Her eyes were flashing now, and her face had gone very white. But after an instant she controlled her feeling and tried to speak sweetly.

"I don't think my father would care to have me discuss that," she said, as gently as if he had asked for something pleasant.

The chilly old face of the uncle hardened.

"You certainly must understand that we couldn't do anything for you without knowing every detail of your financial standing," he said severely.

"Oh!" said Rose, suddenly appalled at the situation. "Why, I wasn't expecting you to do anything for me."

"You didn't expect us to do anything for you?" he said unpleasantly. "Then I confess I do not understand the object of your visit."

"Oh!" said Rose aghast, her face crimson with embarrassment. "I came because my mother was anxious for me to at least see some of her family. She said it was not right that we should bear grudges for things in the past, and she wanted me to know you both. Just a few days before she died she told me that if anything should happen to her, she wanted me to come on anyway. I think she knew she was going before it was time to sail. The passage was all arranged for and she made me promise I would do it."

There was a strange wetness stealing down the withered cheeks of the thin angular woman who sat across the hearth from Rose. She appeared unaware of it. She sat there steadily looking at the girl and let the tears flow down through the many fine wrinkles of her cheeks unmolested. Once or twice she opened her lips as if to speak and closed them uncertainly again. At last she murmured:

"You know it *may* be that my sister did not expect financial assistance." She raised mildly pleading eyes toward Lord Warloch. "My sister was never of a worldly turn of mind, and of course if they managed to get something together, it may be that she only wished us to use our influence to bring her daughter into the correct social circles. Having found out through experience what she had missed herself, she may have wished to atone somewhat for what she had done by saving her daughter from a like fate."

"I understand," said the cold voice of the uncle. "But even so we could never be of any use whatever to further a suitable marriage unless we knew exactly how she stands financially. If she were well off of course the whole matter would be comparatively easy. There are plenty of noble husbands to be had for the asking, provided the bride is a woman of means. It is for this reason that I am asking for full information."

But Rose was suddenly on her feet.

"Stop!" she cried. "Don't say such terrible things to me! I did not come over here for any help of any kind. I do not need your money, and I do not want a husband! I have no idea of getting married at present, and if I had I would prefer to do my own choosing and make my own arrangements. I will not listen to another word like this. My mother would not have wanted me to come if she had known you would think such insulting things about me!"

She had backed away from them in her excitement and as she reached the great arch that separated the room from the wide hall she came in sharp contact with someone who was just about to enter. Turning suddenly to apologize she saw staring down at her a tall lanky man in evening garb that didn't seem to fit him very well. She realized that she had met the evening's guest in no proper manner.

"I'm sorry!" she said. "I did not hear anyone come in," and she was about to offer further words when Lord Warloch arose and introduced her while she had still that royal light of battle in her usually sweet quiet eyes.

"This is young Lord MacCallummore," he said, addressing Rose. "And this," he turned to the stranger, "is our niece, Margaret Galbraith, of whom we have told you."

Then Rose stood back aghast. *They had been talking* to this stranger *about her!* Was this the son of the man her mother had refused to marry? She gave him a level quiet look, a slight inclination of her head, and stepped back to the low seat she had been occupying before he came, but she felt his speculative eyes upon her with a look that made her want to shudder. It was silly of course to feel so just because he was the son of the man her mother had not wanted to marry, but she could not seem to help it. She wished with all her heart that she could escape from this dreadful place and go up to her own room and cry her heart out.

Then suddenly there came the summons to dinner. Just a moment before she had been heathily hungry, but now it seemed to her that to swallow a single mouthful of food would be an impossibility, if it had to be eaten in the presence of this stranger. Nevertheless she rose and followed her aunt.

6

IN New York Gordon McCarroll was getting ready to go back to Shandon Heights to spend the week end with his mother and father. He hadn't intended going so soon, but that morning there had come a special delivery letter from his mother asking him to come that week end if he possibly could. She said the daughter of her old friend in California, Mary Repplier, was visiting in the east, and was arriving early Saturday for over Sunday. She wanted to give her a pleasant time and she didn't see how she was to accomplish that unless Gordon came home to help.

"You know her mother was my very special friend in school and I want her to have a good time while she is here," she wrote. "I don't know the girl at all, but if she's anything like her mother she is wonderful. At least, I understand she is very bright. I do hope you can arrange to come, dear, and I do hope it won't prove to be a bore. She ought to be interesting. She's traveled a great deal, and done a lot of the things you've always wanted to do."

Gordon had frowned when he read the letter. He would so much rather go home just to have a quiet time with his father and mother, and not have a fool strange girl wished on him. But of course, since his mother wished it, he would go.

So he packed his bag and started off.

It was almost dinner time when he arrived, and his first meeting with the girl was at the dinner table.

She was very attractive. He saw that at first glance. She had big black eyes and black hair, piled on the top of her head in carefully arranged carelessness. She had delicately tinted cheeks that looked merely like a rosy flush, and her lips were not too red, neither were her fingernails deeply tinted, but the nails were highly polished and everything about her was extremely well groomed. She was quite sure of herself, and her mind fairly scintillated with bright sayings.

Gordon could see that his mother admired her, and his father thought her unusually bright. He wondered what was the matter with himself that he wasn't especially charmed with her. She seemed to be the right kind of girl in every way. But he just wasn't interested. Well, he was here to save his mother and see that the girl had a good time, and he would do his best.

He was relieved that she wasn't the kind of girl who wanted night clubs and dances. At least she didn't ask for those things, so as she professed to be exceedingly fond of music, and it happened that there was some unusual music in town just then, he managed to secure tickets and took her to a concert. She proved to be a good listener, her comments were intelligent, and they spent a pleasant evening together, nothing thrilling about it of course. But when the next morning a telegram called her to an old schoolmate's home some ten miles away, Gordon drove her to the place and came back distinctly relieved that she was gone. He looked forward to a pleasant talk with his mother and father.

"You didn't like Sydney Repplier, did you, Gordon?" his mother asked thoughtfully when they were seated around a little late supper after his return.

"Why, yes!" said Gordon heartily. "She's a fine girl! Rather pretty, too, don't you think?"

"I think perhaps you'd call her handsome, wouldn't you, instead of pretty?" said the mother, still studying her son keenly.

"Yes, that's it, mother. Handsome. She has fine eyes, and she's keen too. She knows a lot about music."

"Yes. She's had a fine education. Her mother was a delightful musician. But you didn't quite like the girl, Gordon, did you? At least you weren't very enthusiastic about her, were you, son?"

"Oh, why, mother, did you want me to be?"

"Well, I don't know that a mother is ever very anxious for her son to be enthusiastic about a girl, but that is the way of the world of course, and it is a thing that is likely to come, I suppose, sometime. Of course when it comes for my boy I hope she will be a good girl. Our kind of girl. A Christian girl."

"Well, I should hope so, mother. But did you especially admire this girl? Did she fulfill all the requirements? Maybe she was, but to tell the truth I wasn't really taking much thought about it except to make her have as good a time as I could. Of course I haven't known her long, mother. I might think her great after I'd seen more of her. But—well, she seemed just a nice girl, that was all!"

The mother drew a relieved sigh, and then with still a troubled glance at her boy, wondered if he was seeing any girls at all in New York.

But the talk drifted to other matters, Gordon telling of his work in the office and how they had promised that the training he was receiving now would prepare him for a departmental head. He would eventually be located in the region of his home town, and that was great news to his parents.

At last he hurried up to his old room to get some sleep before the early train that he had to catch to New York in the morning. As he lay down to sleep it occurred to him that he hadn't said anything about Rose to his mother, and perhaps it was just as well. Since she had this girl matter on her mind it might only have given her something more to worry about. Why should he say anything? It was a matter that he had to work out for himself of course, and there might not be anything to it but a pleasant farewell to a lonely young school friend. He might never see her again and likely the memory of her would soon be dimmed.

But, he added, with his last waking thought, her memory would never be dimmed by the vision of a girl such as Sydney Repplier!

And day after day as he went about his work he found himself counting the time and wondering when a letter could come from Rose, thinking that when it came it would likely clear away his illusions and make it possible for him to stop thinking about this girl whom he had known so long, and yet whose vision of loveliness had only just come to his soul.

But the next evening his father and mother talked him over together.

"I can't quite make Gordon out," said his mother after her husband seemed to have finished the evening paper and was ready to be sociable. "I thought he would be interested in Sydney, and he didn't seem in the least so. He seemed much more interested in our old cat and whether she'd had as much meat as she wanted for dinner. I am just as worried as I can be about him."

"Why, mamma, you surely aren't troubled because he isn't interested in any special girl just now, are you? He's got plenty of time, you know. He's not very old, and he's just getting started in business. I think it's much better for him not to have other interests just now."

"Oh, but that's it, daddy. I'm afraid he may get interested in some little good-for-nothing, now that he's away from home and all the nice girls he knows. He looks lonesome to me, and there's no telling what he might take up with if he gets lonesome enough. You know New York must just be full of little adventuresses, watching out for a good-looking personable young man."

"Nonsense, mamma, don't you think our son has any sense at all? Did you ever see him in any stage of his career so far get into a fix like that? You know Gordon doesn't let anybody put anything over on him, much less a silly girl."

"Daddy, human nature is human nature, and some of these little fool adventuresses that are going around loose look like young angels and haven't any bringing up whatever. It would be so dreadful for him and for us too if he should suddenly get interested in one of those!"

"Well, Agnes, I never thought you were a woman who went around hunting for trouble. I thought you trusted your son with God when he went out away from our home. I thought you thought God was watching over him. I thought you believed in His keeping powers for yourself and all yours! And here you are going around setting up ideas to worry about! Why, you remind me of Sarai in the Bible! You actually do!"

"What do you mean, Malcolm?"

"I mean you're acting as if you had to play God for Gordon, the way Sarai did when she suggested to Abraham that he'd better marry her bondservant so that God could keep His promise about giving Abraham a son. Look here, mamma, it's all right for you to get Gordon home to help you entertain a girl you don't know what to do with, but when you try to sick him onto her and make him get interested in her, you'll defeat your own end. Didn't you see Gordon wasn't interested? If I were you I'd quit fretting. God has allowed him to grow up fairly decent so far, and you don't think He's going to fall down on the job now, do you? I've always admired the way you took everything that came so calmly. I thought that had a great deal to do with your training of our boy. You made him feel that everything was sent by God and we must accept it that way. You made him feel that it was important how he judged himself in every act and every thought. Now you don't think he's going to forget that right off because he's gone away from home, do you? He's got principles and beliefs, the kind he's been trained in, and he's going to stick to them. He may make mistakes sometimes, but you won't find him losing his head at the first silly girl he meets. And for the matter of that you can't find any sillier ones than some we've had in this very city through the years. Didn't you always find him judging them just as we had? He'll size 'em up. You know, mamma, it isn't as if Gordon wasn't a Christian himself. You don't think he wants to make a mess of his life, do you?"

"No. No, I don't think that, but Malcolm, I couldn't help feeling all the time he was here that he was sort of reticent and preoccupied. Why, sometimes when Sydney was talking brilliantly he didn't even seem to hear her."

"Yes?" said the father. "Do you know what he said to me? We were standing out by the car waiting for her to come downstairs the morning she left, and Gordon was looking a bit bored. I said, 'Nice girl?' and he nodded unenthusiastically.

"'Oh, yeah, nice all right. She's got a powerful lot of information stowed away in her sleek little brains and she's quite willing to impart it. Knows all the answers and likes to tell 'em. And advice! Good night! You can get enough of that on almost any topic you can name to carry you safe through life!'

"He just got that far and she came smiling out, and he put on his courtesy manners and shut up, but he had a queer twinkle in his eye. You know, mamma, Gordie knows his onions! He doesn't miss a thing! And you don't need to worry about him. When he gets a girl she'll be all right!"

"Well, I hope so," said the mother. "But somehow I thought it would be so nice if he took a girl we knew something about. A girl who had been brought up with nice ways. I didn't know she was like that. She seemed awfully pleasant and sweet, and her mother wasn't like that a bit. I knew her mother very well indeed."

"Well, mamma, you have to remember she had a father too. Maybe he's like that, always setting you right on every topic in the world. You didn't know her father, did you?"

"No," said the mother. "No, of course not. But children don't inherit everything from each side, you know. Well, I'm glad if it was that reason he didn't like her. I was just afraid he had got hold of some silly little nobody in New York and had his mind on her, and so couldn't see anybody else for the present. I worried a lot because he didn't tell me anything about what he was doing with his spare time. You know he always used to tell me about everything."

"Yes," said the father, "but you can't expect him to keep that up always. As he gets older he's bound to have a few reserves. We can't hope to have him running to us every time he meets a new girl. Besides, mamma, he did tell you what he was doing with his spare time. He said he was reading a lot."

"Yes, I know, but that wouldn't likely be all."

"Well, there mamma, you'd better learn your lesson too. You can't keep a fine young man like our son tied to your apron strings always. A girl's bound to come sometime, and when she does he'll tell you, all in good time. Perhaps he'll hold off a bit till he is sure of himself, but you'll know when it's right you should, and till then can't you trust him to the Lord? He's a good boy, you know, and he's the Lord's own."

"Yes, I know!" sighed the mother, and smiled a quivery little smile, till Papa McCarroll came over and kissed her the way he used to do when he was courting her, and her eyes met his with peace.

"Yes," she said sweetly, "I suppose you're right, and I know I oughtn't to fret. God has been good to us, giving us such a wonderful son. You know, I feel he's just like his father," and she gave her husband a worshipful look.

"Now why did you have to spoil it all by that last sentence, Agnes? You know the only wise thing I ever did was to marry you, and I've always been proud to think that my son was so much like his wonderful mother!"

And then the picture faded out in peace and quietness.

7

ROSE was very quiet at the table. She felt that the whole outlook on things had been utterly changed by the few words her uncle had spoken. And it was all the worse because in all probability the guest had overheard both her last words, and what her uncle had said to her. She felt she could not bear to look at the man, and it seemed as if the shame she felt must certainly show. Her cheeks were still burning with embarrassment. She did not know how becoming it was to her, nor how it brought out the blue of her eyes till they matched her frock.

But it presently became evident that it was not necessary for her to take part in the conversation. It was not expected of her. They were talking on without her, above her head, out of her knowledge. It was as if she were a naughty child being reproved by being ignored.

The dinner was very good, but Rose did not feel like eating. It seemed as if she had swallowed a stone. She minced away and tried to appear to be eating, but no one seemed to notice her in the least, and she felt so exceedingly uncomfortable that in spite of her a deep resolve was formed in her young soul to get out of this place at once. Tomorrow morning if she could.

Only tomorrow was Sunday, and there might not be service to help her on her way. Could she get through the Sunday? Her mother had told her that her family were ardent church people, going through all the forms and ceremonies, though without much knowledge of real spiritual values. A look at either aunt or uncle would make that plain almost at first glance, she thought.

And the guest? She didn't like his face at all. A narrow thin cadaverous countenance with high cheek bones and eyeballs that protruded somewhat. Yet those queer eyes could look right through one, and every time she looked up she saw him looking at her. It made cold chills go down her back, as if he might be a wizard who could cast a spell over her and waft her away to a grim castle where she would be a prisoner and no one would be able to find her. Able? The word startled her. Who would want to take the trouble to search for her? Not these indifferent relatives certainly, who were mostly concerned lest they might have to spend a little for her, or perjure themselves perhaps to get her suitably married so that she would do credit to the family.

Through her bitter thoughts she looked up once to find her aunt looking speculatively at her, and at last, in a pause, while they were waiting for the dessert to be brought in, she deliberately aimed a question at her.

"Would you like to see your mother's piano?" she asked, whether as a favor, or for ulterior reason Rose could not be sure.

She looked up with a great eagerness growing in her eyes.

"Oh!" she said, "is it here? I would so much like to see it. She has told me all about it of course. It almost seems as if I had seen it myself. The little line of inlaid wood along the edges. Even the lettering. Mother drew it for me, so I knew just how it was. I have the paper with me on which she drew it."

There was a kind of line of satisfaction on the grim old mouth of her aunt as she spoke. The guest sat back in his chair and watched her with indifferent attention, analyzing her, putting her in a category all by herself; and whether approving or disapproving was not apparent. Only the uncle took no part in the little byplay, seemed to have no interest whatever. He seemed almost distraught as if some other weighty matter were absorbing his mind.

The pause was long. Rose almost feared she had somehow offended again, but at last her aunt said, as if she were granting a very great favor:

"Very well, you shall see it. Of course we have kept it in perfect repair. That's one thing I've always insisted on."

She shut her grim lips firmly and Rose could not help noticing that she cast a baleful look at her thin-faced husband, as if she were recalling battles and victories won on that score.

Were they really poor, Rose wondered? Then why didn't they move to a cheaper house? Or, could it be that Uncle Robert was a little "close" with his money?

Then Aunt Janet spoke again, almost as if it were for the benefit of the guest.

"I wish you could have heard your mother play. She was a very wonderful player for a girl so young. I suppose you never heard her play?"

"Oh yes," said Rose eagerly, "I heard her all my life. It was she who taught me to play."

The aunt looked up astonished.

"You can play?"

"Oh yes, of course," said the girl. "It's the thing I love best to do, next to reading."

The uncle looked up with almost approbation in his eyes, but the aunt was still astonished.

"But I don't understand," she said haughtily. "I don't see how she could play without a piano. You had no piano, did you? Long ago she wrote me that she missed her piano."

"Oh, but we soon had one!" said Rose proudly. "My father went without many things to get her that piano. And we had that when I was a baby. We didn't live in a castle, but we had a piano!"

"Oh! I see!" said the aunt, almost as if she were offended; almost as if her ammunition had been stolen away from her.

Nevertheless when the dessert was brought in she gave the order to the butler:

"Thomas, light the candles in the east room, and open the piano."

The butler gave a quick, almost frightened glance toward Rose, and murmured stiffly: "Yes, my lady!"

After that she heard him go across the wide hall and into another part of the castle.

Rose was hoping that her uncle and the guest would not come with them when they went to see the piano. They left them at the table with their wine glasses. But when they reached the great room of the castle where the piano was enshrined there they were bringing up the rear, as if they were in a procession.

It was a huge room, stately and wide and high, and there were many ancestral paintings on the walls. The piano was at the far end. There was one enormous painting hanging over it, of a lovely young girl about Rose's age. Rose saw them both, the piano and the painting, at once, and her eyes lifted to the eyes of the girl in the painting, drawn as if by mutual recognition.

"Oh, that is my mother!" she breathed, and moved forward toward the picture, her eyes looking into the eyes of her girl-mother.

And so she arrived at the piano, and stood, but looking up at the picture for a long moment, as if the picture and she would read each other's thoughts. There was a radiance upon the daughter's face that drew the eyes of the others in the room, even the butler, pausing at the entrance to see if aught was required of him before he vanished. There was something almost spiritual in the room, they all felt, as if the spirit of the mother might be hovering near, or others perhaps, even angelic beings. It was a moment in which all held their breath and watched. Even the grim uncle seemed held in abeyance.

Then Rose dropped her eyes to the piano, let her hand rest softly on its satin surfaces, traced the inlaid line, the golden letters, and then laid her fingers gently on the old ivories, yellow with age.

It did not seem to occur to her to ask if she might play it. Suddenly she dropped down upon the stool that stood in position, laid her hands lightly on the keys, touched a chord or two softly, like one who had a right to play there, and then she was off, into a sweet surging lovely sonata, one that her mother had played long ago. The sweet melody tinkled out gaily, wild and lovely, and filled the grim old castle rooms, casting a kind of spell on all who heard. It stole out through the halls and reached the ears of the servants and when the first movement was finished the other servants had crept up in the dim shadows of the hall and were looking in, with tears in their eyes. Especially the old woman, Maggie, who had taken her to her room, was weeping and listening with her face aglow.

"That is the first piece your mother ever played," stated the aunt in a hard dry tone.

"Yes," smiled Rose with a sparkle in her eyes, and looking up she was surprised to find that tears were flowing down among the wrinkles on her aunt's face.

Rose could not see the face of the guest. She was glad he was behind her. She wanted to forget him. It had seemed to her during dinner that he was watching her as a purchaser might be watching a horse he was about to buy, and she couldn't forget that his father had wanted to marry her mother.

However the delight of the piano was above everything else. When she reached the end of the movement, she paused an instant and went on with another and then another. Then she rippled off to Chopin, then Schumann and Beethoven. The audience dropped down upon chairs and remained silently listening. Even out in the hall the servants were seated out of sight as if some holy service had come to their abode and summoned them from all thoughts of work or any other consideration of life. If she could have looked behind her and seen the faces, even the face of the cadaverous guest she might have realized that some power beyond her own was in the room, and that she had reached her audience and was leading them to think perhaps of higher things than would have been their natural bent.

Rose had given to her music much of the time that other young people gave to fun and frolic. It had grown to be her great delight to practice. And her mother who had been under rare teachers in her early youth and had not forgotten what she was taught, was a rare teacher herself. So Rose's touch was clear and brilliant, her notes like dew and honey and rose leaves. Sunrise and sunset and the sea scintillated through her playing, visions of sky and woodlands and flowers. One could almost smell the meadows and hear the note of a bird trill as her music swept on.

And then suddenly she realized that she was playing all her old favorites, high classical music, and perhaps it was above her little audience. She dropped down to a softer strain, and began to play old church hymns, melodies that spoke of love and salvation, and life and death, melodies that touched experiences that every life had felt, until all at once she came to a sweet old Scotch melody or two that had been set to sacred words. Remembering how her mother had loved them, she played with her whole heart in her finger tips, and her own tears came too. Then she stopped as suddenly as she had begun, and lifting her hands, her fingers as it were still dripping with music, she whirled about upon the piano stool and faced their wondering looks with embarrassment.

"I beg your pardon," she said shyly, with her sweet little smile. "I didn't intend to monopolize the evening. I just felt so wild to play on my dear mother's piano! And that picture up there made me feel as if she must be here listening, pleased that I was using what used to belong to her. This was one of the things my mother wanted me to come here for, to try her piano."

She looked at Aunt Janet with her apology, but Aunt Janet was engaged in erasing the traces of tears and did not answer. Even her uncle was blowing his nose furiously. Who would have thought that that hard old customer would have been stirred emotionally by mere music!

It was the guest after all who felt the burden of an answer upon him.

"I am sure you have attained a large degree of excellence in the art of music!" he said stiltedly. "I should think that even a professional musician might commend you. One wonders that a lady would care to take the trouble to reach that degree of perfection, but I suppose some do, and of course it would be pleasant for her family to hear her play upon occasion." His voice was cold and hard and one could see that he was struggling with his ordinary vocabulary to find suitable words, but he was really doing his best.

Rose swept him an indifferent flicker of a smile and said a cool "Thank you" and then turned away. Lord Warloch cleared his throat and said "Quite so!" and Lady Warloch turned to Rose and said:

"It is getting late, Margaret. You must be tired after your journey. Perhaps we had better retire and leave the gentlemen to have their conversation uninterrupted. We will bid you good night, Lord MacCallummore." She swept from the room signing to Rose to follow her.

At the door Rose turned back to flash a good night glance toward her mother's picture on the wall, and then gladly followed her aunt up the great stone staircase.

"You really play verra weel, you know," said her aunt, lapsing somewhat into dialect as she stopped at the door of Rose's room. "I had no idea you could play. It seemed—weel—quite like the days whin we baith were yoong."

Aunt Janet was not quite over her emotion that the music had so unexpectedly brought upon her, and she was almost embarrassed before Rose. But she paused a moment at the door.

"I hope you are quite comfortable," she added, getting back into more sophisticated words, "and should you be wanting anything just ring the bell and Maggie will come! Good night!" She stalked down the hall to her own door, and Rose was dismissed.

Left alone Rose closed her door and went and knelt down beside the bed, burying her flushed face in the cool pillow. She was fairly trembling with the excitement of the last hour. Oh, if only she could talk to her mother about it! She could almost see the shining of her mother's eyes if she could have heard about how she had played on her own dear piano!

But the next best thing would be to talk to God about it. Mother was with God, and perhaps He would tell her about it. Or perhaps mother herself had been able to look down and see the whole thing.

So she knelt and poured out her young heart in a sweet trusting prayer.

"Dear God, if You can let mother know about it, please do! Oh, it would help me so much to know she is looking down and seeing what I do. But anyway I know You are and that You care, and I'm glad You are, and that You can be with me all through everything. And so, now, please I thank You for such a mother as You gave me, and I thank You for letting me see that lovely picture of her as a girl, and for letting me play on her dear old piano. I thank You too for making Aunt Janet keep it in tune all through the years. She must have loved mother some to do that of course! I'm glad she told me about it."

The prayer rambled on sweetly. Rose just talking softly to her Lord, as she might have talked to her mother if she had been alive. Alone in trying circumstances, she was realizing the presence of her Heavenly Father as she had never realized Him before. Ah! It was good to talk to God that way!

When she arose from her knees she felt refreshed.

She was just about to unfasten her garments and make quick work of getting into bed when she remembered her little silk handbag, such a pretty little bag, that her mother had made out of rosebud ribbon. It was exquisitely made and she loved it, counted it among her precious treasures. She looked about on the bureau and floor for it, but it wasn't there! She must have left it downstairs. Ah! Now she remembered! She had laid it on the piano when she sat down to play, and probably had left it there.

There was a dainty little handkerchief in it that her mother had given her on a birthday not long ago, and a tiny pink satin purse with a trifle of money in it. Not much of course, but she couldn't afford to lose any of it, and she would hate to lose the bag. It would be best to slip right down now and get it before the servants picked it up and perhaps thought it was of no account. She fastened her belt again primly and went swiftly over to the door, opening it cautiously.

The hallway seemed just as when she had come in, though she wasn't sure just how long she had knelt to pray. She left her door slightly ajar and slipped out into the hall. The dim stairway wound broadly down against the castle walls, gray and forbidding in the dim flicker of half-burnt candles.

Guardedly she stepped forth, daring a step at a time. Suppose her aunt should open her door and demand to know where she was going! She had been ordered to bed. What would Aunt Janet think of her daring to go downstairs alone again, with the two men still down there? Would she call her bold?

But surely she could tell her what she was going for!

She dreaded terribly to come under the further condemnation of her aunt, or her chilly old uncle. If she had only been sure about the servants whether they would touch her bag, her bit of money, she would have let it go till morning. Yet perhaps even that might call condemnation down upon her for being so careless as to forget her bag.

Softly, slowly she made her way down, anxious eyes

to the right where in a minute now she would be able to see the great archway leading into the ball room where the piano resided. Would the candles be extinguished yet? If not there would be no trouble surely. It would be but the work of a second to tiptoe lightly over the great Aubusson carpet whose softness would drown her footsteps. But, could she find her way if the candles were put out? Could she find the piano in the dark, and the exact place on the piano where she had left the bag? Perhaps she should go back and get her little flash light that mother had made her pack in her bag. But no, she would go on and do her best. If the candles were put out the piano would likely have been closed and it would be already too late to do anything more about it tonight.

There were voices plainly to be heard now. They were coming from the library behind the big room where she had been taken first. Her uncle and the guest were talking together and she could almost hear the words they were saying. She *could* hear!

"You say she has a fortune in her own right?" the guest was saying, and his voice had a greedy eager sound. "How much?"

She was startled that the words came to her so distinctly. They must be very near or else it was some trick of the walls, and an echo. Oh, she must not be discovered by them. She shrank from them both inexpressibly. She went more cautiously, casting anxious furtive glances to the left side of the hall to be sure they were not standing there just below the great staircase, but she could see no one, though the shadows were deep on that side of the hall. But the voices were sounding very close; a hollow sound though, as if the walls were tricky with echoes.

And who were they talking about?

Just then her uncle answered.

"I'm not sure of the exact figures, though I'm quite sure it is a considerable sum. She is very young of course, and the estate may not all be settled upon her as yet. You know her mother has just passed away."

"I see! I should want to be very sure, you understand! You know during the life of my father I am at his mercy. I cannot be sure what he would do for me in case the marriage did not please him. And of course since she is the daughter of the girl who jilted him—" his voice was suddenly hushed and she could not hear the next words.

Suddenly she knew that they were speaking of her. They were daring to discuss a marriage between herself and this obnoxious guest!

Her knees grew weak beneath her, and yet she dared not stop there on the stairway. She was almost down the stairs now, and she could see a flickering light from the great room on her right. Oh, the candles must still be lighted. Perhaps she could get her bag and get back quickly while they were still absorbed in their conversation!

She fairly flew down the remaining steps, silently on her soft little slippers, and dashing into the great dim room flew across to the piano. Yes, there was her little pink bag like a rose full blown lying on the piano just where she had laid it.

Then suddenly she was aware of the presence of her dear girl-mother up there in the picture, and she lifted frighted eyes and smiled toward her, her glance pleading that she would understand. And it almost seemed her mother smiled there in the dimness, in that one second of time that she dared to look, before she turned and fled back to the hallway and stealthily began to mount the stairs, very slowly now because she must not let a sound of her footsteps reach down there where the two were talking with long pauses between their words. Then she suddenly stood frozen with horror.

"No," her uncle was saying deliberately in his toneless voice, "I wouldn't be able to find out the exact amount at once. She seemed to think her father would not want the matter discussed. I shall have to go very slowly. You know these Americans have queer ideas."

"But I thought you said she was not an American. I thought she was pure Scotch on both sides. Galbraith, surely, is Scotch."

"Yes, her father was Scotch, of course, as well as her mother, but she was born in America, and doubtless is tainted with American ideas. But I think there is no doubt but we shall be able to win her confidence soon. You know she has but just arrived this afternoon. She really does not know us yet."

"Nonsense!" said the man. "*I* shall ask her. She certainly cannot expect me to marry her without knowing all there is to know. I shall arrange to take her for a ride, perhaps tomorrow. If necessary I shall take her over and show her our castle, and then I shall ask her frankly. It seems to me we cannot get anywhere till that is settled. It is you who are so anxious to find a way for me to pay what you loaned to me, to settle quietly that unfortunate affair. I still feel your rate of interest is exorbitant. But if you are sure this girl's fortune would cover the whole thing, I am prepared to go through with it. The girl herself is quite satisfactory, pretty and all that. But, understand, sir, it's to your own interest to carry the matter through quickly."

In a daze of horror Rose arrived at the top of the stairs, and the slow deliberate sentences were suddenly cut off by the thick walls of stone, and the formation of the hall.

She slid into her room and fastened the door behind her. Then she leaned back against it, her hand on her heart, and breathed hard, partly from the speed with which she had flown up those last few stairs, but mainly from the horror she felt at the conversation she had overheard.

Then her uncle was actually bargaining to sell her in marriage!

Had this uncle had anything to do with that other proposed marriage of her dear mother, from which the bride had flown so suddenly? She tried to think, to remember what her mother had said. Yes, her mother's sister had been married then, and it must have been this uncle who was at the bottom of all that trouble. What an old miser he must be! Or else he was now learning from that past idea to try the experiment again and feather his own nest in the same way that probably had been planned by the grandfather years ago.

Well, inadvertently perhaps, she had helped to further his plans by saying her father had left her money, without telling how very little it was beside the fortune they were figuring on. But of course her uncle had no right to ask such questions, and she simply could not discuss with him what her father had done. She had not intended to give him ground for supposing she had a large fortune; whatever conclusions he had drawn were of his own creation. And now short of telling him just what her father had left her the only thing that seemed left to do was to clear out of the neighborhood as soon as possible, which very well accorded with her own desires. The only things she would be sorry to leave would be that wonderful picture of her mother and that darling piano. Was it conceivable that sometime they would let her buy those? Why, she would feel justified in taking that money her father had saved for her in order to get possession of those. But of course that wasn't the thing to think about now. She must somehow get away from here just as soon as possible. And how could that be managed?

Just staying around and saying no to this possible would-be suitor wouldn't be enough. Her mother's experience had shown that. If this young man were anything like his determined father it wouldn't be worth the breath she used to say no. Her mother just escaped imprisonment in her own home, with an alternative of kidnaping or something like that if home imprisonment failed. But she had acted quickly, and gone away with her lover far out of their reach. And she must be watchful now. Of course as yet her uncle and aunt did not know that she was aware of any of their plans in the matter. She should be out and away before they had time to say anything about it to her.

Tomorrow was Sunday. Would they go to church? Could she get away while they were gone? No, she couldn't carry both her suitcases down the mountain alone. There would be no taxis, no way to get hold of them. Should she risk losing her clothes that her dear mother had prepared so carefully for her? No, she mustn't do that. The whole family had been so ugly to her mother when she spoiled their plans, they would in all probability keep her suitcases just to annoy her. No, she must plan a better way. It wasn't likely that the uncle and his guest could do anything much immediately. It would be better to wait till Monday, and perhaps a way would open for her to get away without exciting more antagonism. She mustn't lose her head. Just because she had overheard plans that made her very angry and just a little frightened, she mustn't go and make a mess in her affairs that she would have to live down afterward. She came over here at her mother's bidding, to try and make peace where disagreement had reigned. Aunt Janet was her mother's sister, and they used to be dear to one another. She remembered the tears which had flowed down Aunt Janet's cheeks while she was playing. Perhaps Aunt Janet had wanted to be friends with mother long ago and somebody wouldn't let her, perhaps the hard cold old uncle!

She crept shivering into the big bed, put out the candle and lay there feeling very small and alone in the great castle. Castles were interesting and beautiful, but when one was all alone in an alien and unloving group of relatives castles were dreary places to be.

She lay there trying to think how she could get ready to go at a moment's notice. It wouldn't do to pack up everything, because that woman Maggie would come up and look around, maybe think she had to make the bed and redd up the room for her. Well, she could do that herself before she went down to breakfast. But she must leave a few things hanging in the closet so it would not be noticed that she had packed, not until just as she was ready to leave. She must be very wary. If she only could get word to her grandmother and her Uncle John Galbraith to summon her at once so she would have an excuse to clear out Monday morning in a perfectly natural way. She did not wish to continue the ill feeling that had embittered her dear mother's life. Still, she knew her mother would never want her to compromise the matter so that she would be in danger of being married to the son of the man she herself had spurned.

"Oh, Lord, please fix it for me in the right way!" she murmured as she drifted wearily off to sleep. It had been a long exciting day and she was so tired!

8

THE Galbraith cottage was low and thatched and smothered in vines that dripped from the gables and encroached upon the small-paned windows. It was hidden behind a tall hedge where gowans nestled and brackens grew sturdily. At the back the ground sloped away to meadows and wilder rolling land where heather bloomed in abundance, and a little brook twinkled with a bright sparkle on sunny days, and even sang when it rained.

There were many rooms inside the cottage, wide and low, and broad low winding stairs in the wall. In the main room—it was built before the days of "living rooms," though they were all lived in a-plenty—there was a deep stone fireplace reaching up to the ceiling, large enough to step inside and sit if one desired. There were lovely old rag rugs strewn about on the firm old floor where they seemed fitted to their places in the wide warped planks pegged in place many many years before. It might have been the original setting for The Cottar's Saturday Night. Even the big "ha Bible" was there on a low shelf where Grandmother Galbraith could reach it from her big old rocker near one side of the hearth.

Always there was a fire of logs laid on that hearth, and a kettle hung ready for any time it might be required. It was one of grandmother's kettles reminiscent of her wedding day and now it was honored with a place above the hearth; for John's wife was a Scotch lassie herself and liked it. She loved grandmother and liked to keep her setting as perfect as it had always been. It was the kettle that old Grandfather John Galbraith had hung for his bride the night of their wedding day so long ago. The old John Galbraith's body had been lying in its grave many years now, but his spirit seemed ever near to grandmother.

Though there was a "but" and a "ben" to the cottage, with a regular kitchen, wide and convenient for "Johnnie's wife," still grandmother liked her kettle near to brew a cup of tea for her friends when they came in, just as she used to do it in her own home when she was first a bride.

There were bedrooms at either end of the big downstairs room, big airy affairs, with ruffled muslin curtains at the windows, and old furniture much of which had been made in grandmother's young days, made by men she knew. A four-poster with a real feather bed—that was grandmother's bed; and a dresser and washstand to match. Chairs of the same old mellow wood, and a tiny rocking chair that had belonged to her little girl Rose. Rose who had married long ago, married a good man, thank God, but they had gone far away to another country. Grandmother cherished the little chair. And sometimes she sat by the fire in her big old winged chair and stared into the brightness of the burning logs. Then she could see quite clearly her little girl who used to rock in that little chair: looking up from some small task of sewing queer stitches into a block of patchwork, she would smile at her mother and say "You and me!" And now she was so far away! Would she ever come back? It seemed so many years!

Her little Rose's children had been boys, sturdy little boys who wouldn't want a rocking chair, so she had kept the little chair in her own room because it somehow seemed to bring her little girl nearer to her, her little Rose.

But there was another little Rose, now, a granddaughter, the child of her son Gilbert. Gilbert had been very dear, and grandmother had loved his wife Margaret, too, perhaps the more because her own people had turned against her for marrying Gilbert. Just because he was poor and had no lordly title! Her mother must have been very proud and haughty. But Margaret and Gilbert had gone away to America and their little Rose, named after her own lost Rose, had been born in America. She had never seen the second Rose, but a letter had come saying Margaret and Rose were coming to see her. But then Margaret had died. Gone Home where Gilbert had gone several years before. And now grandmother thought about that dear young Rose who was alone and was coming to see her some day. She thought more and more about her as the days went by and the time was drawing near for her to arrive. Sometimes she sighed when she thought about it. She wanted to see the second Rose so much.

It occurred to her that perhaps she might not see her after all. She was getting old, and perhaps her call would come before Rose got here. Sometimes at the thought a tear would steal out down her withered cheek and drop softly on her folded hands. Then she would rouse, and take her knitting from the little stand drawer by her side and begin to knit quickly. She mustn't give way to tears.

She had never done so. She mustn't get childish and do it now.

Grandmother came slowly out of her own bedroom where she had been taking an afternoon nap and went and sat down in her big chair by the fire. It was a spring day, but there was a little fire for the air was brisk. She liked a fire.

But a nap was something grandmother didn't approve of. Why should one waste time like that? She had all John's stockings to knit for next winter, and stockings for the boys! They all seemed to think that nobody could knit such good socks as grandmother. Why, even those expensive ones that came from the London shops weren't nearly as soft as grandmother's, and didn't wear half as well.

Grandmother was knitting hard when John came in from his day's work at the office. Her needles were flashing in and out with quick bright clicks. Jessie, John's wife, had just come in from the kitchen, "coom ben the hoose" grandmother called it, and stirred up the fire. The dancing flicker of the flames glanced over grandmother's needles with a pretty bright rhythm, like soft music.

John hung up his cap in the little entry way by the front door, and came over to his mother, stooping to put a gentle kiss on her soft cheek.

"Weel, mither," he said in his kindly tone, "hoo air ye feelin'?" The family usually talked to grandmother in the old Scotch dialect. She liked it. She said it made her feel "mair't'hame."

Kirsty came in, John's child. She had dark clinging curls about her roseleaf face, and deep natural roses in her cheeks. Her eyes were bright like stars and she brought the breath of the flowers in with her when she came. She too kissed her grandmother. She was a dear child, but she did not look like the little Rose, nor remind her grandmother of the little rocking chair. She had been allowed to sit in the chair as a small child, but it had never been given to her, and she quickly grew out of it anyway. Kirsty looked more like her mother, Jessie, John's wife, who was a strong wholesome woman, though gentle in spite of her energy.

Kirsty hurried down presently with a pink cotton dress on and a little white ruffled apron. She pulled out the big table at the far end of the big room, opened up the leaves, and spread a clean linen tablecloth on it. She got fine old sprigged china dishes out of the corner cupboard and began to set the table. Then with brisk steps she went out into the kitchen and brought in a plate of bread, the butter, the pitcher of water fresh from the deep well, a pitcher of milk from a neighbor's cow. Then Jessie came in with a covered dish of some hot vegetable, and then a great platter of Scotch stew. Its odor filled the big room with cheer, and John put down his paper and went over to his mother.

"Mither, will ye set by the noo?" he asked, and reached down to help her rise, guiding her to the table.

Then the door opened and John's two big boys, Donald and David, hurried in, tossing their caps to their respective hooks and calling greetings to grandmother as they passed, dropping quick brusque kisses on her cheek. They hurried up to their room above and could be heard splashing in the wash bowl hastily. They soon appeared with fresh faces and wet hair scantily brushed, and took their seats just as their father bowed his head for the blessing.

It was a cheery happy table, full of love and good fellowship, the grandmother being a part of it all, not just tolerated.

The tasty stew was all demolished, every crumb of the

scones gone, even the second lot hot from the oven, and they were lingering over the "sweetie" as Jessie called her delicate pudding dessert.

"Well, say, when's that American cousin of ours coming, I'd like to know?" questioned Donald as he held out his dish for a second helping of pudding.

"Oh, no telling!" said David bluntly. "She stopped off at the high and mighty relations first, and if they find out she's coming here they'll put an end to that! They'll never hear to having her come to us."

Kirsty flashed him a warning look.

"That's silly!" she said sharply. "You know she said she'd stop off in Edinburgh first and get that off her conscience and then she could have a really nice visit with us! You know she'll be here as soon as possible!" She gave a glance at grandmother and saw a faint shadow of quick understanding dawning in her eyes.

"Well," said Donald with his eyes on his dessert, "she hadn't been there yet. She didn't know what she was up against. Those Warlochs are a determined lot, and they still hate the Galbraiths, or I'm missing my guess! You can't tell if she'll even get here at all!" Donald hadn't seen Kirsty's warning look toward grandmother. The only word that could bring a bitter look to the face of a Galbraith was "Warloch," because the Warlochs had let their beloved Gilbert go down to his death without reconciliation.

"Don!" came the reprimand from the gentle Jessie as sharply as Jessie's sweet voice could ever speak.

Donald looked up and saw his mother's warning glance toward grandmother.

"A' was no meanin' that, mither," he said. And then with a loving smile toward his grandmother he added, "She'll soon be comin' the noo, won't she, grandmither?"

The old lady looked at him lovingly, but her eyes bore the troubled hurt, and her smile was very faint. She didn't finish her pudding, and sat back with her hands in her lap and the shadow growing about her eyes. Before she knew it she had heaved a very heavy sigh, right out there before them all! She was usually very careful about not sighing when they were all there. They were a family who watched carefully, each not to trouble the rest more than was necessary.

"Now, grandmither, none of that!" broke out Donald. "It was naethin' but a bit jooke I was makin'. She'll be coomin' the noo, verra soon, I'm thinkin'. Dinna ye fret."

"I'm no frettin', Donnie," said the old lady in a small tired voice. "I was only thinkin', gin it micht be a'm nae tae see her on this side. Gin it's tae be lang a' micht be called awa' afore she cooms. But it's a' richt, laddie. Ye'll juist tell her a've slippit awa', an' a'll be watchin' for her on the Heavenly shore along wi' her grandfeyther, an' her feyther. An' that a' luve her!"

The boy Donald brushed a tear from his clear young eye and made out to smile.

"Oh, grandmither, ye maunna talk that wy. She wants to see ye the noo. She's lost her feyther an' her mither, an' she's come awa' acrost the sea tae see her grandmither, an' yir no tae gang awa' till she sees ye. Mind that, grandmither! Yir no tae *think* o' it even. It's agin the Lord's wy. He'll na be callin' ye yet, not afore she cooms."

"Of course!" said Kirsty briskly. "It wudna be richt!"

"Dinna ye feel well, mither?" asked Jessie anxiously.

"Wud ye like me tae ca' the doctor, mither?" asked John with concern.

"Na, na," said the old lady with sudden brisk determination. "A'll be a' richt! Nae fear aboot me! Kirsty, bring me the silver tae dry. A' like tae hev some pairt in the worruk of the day. A' get sair weary of juist sittin' tae knit."

Kirsty hastened with the silver and brought it in a

towel-lined platter to the table with a big clean towel, and the old lady dried each piece slowly, happily, while Kirsty and Jessie cleared off the rest of the table.

John went back to his evening paper, sitting at one side of the fire; David went out to get more logs, for the evening was cool and grandmother must not feel chilly; but Donald went over to the old desk between two windows and wrote a letter to Rose.

> Dear Cousin Rose:
>
> I don't want to spoil your plans if you are having a good time, but if you could see your way clear to come to us right away it would be a good thing for grandmother.
>
> You see she feels she has been watching and waiting for you a long time, and as the days go by she gets more and more excited about your coming, wondering if you'll come today, or how long it will be.
>
> She isn't exactly sick, she's up and around. But you know grandmother is very frail and she's getting old.
>
> If you can't get away from Edinburgh soon, perhaps you'll write her a bit of a letter, and say when you are coming.
>
> But it you can come soon let me know and I'll meet your train and we'll spring a surprise on her.
>
> Your loving cousin,
> Donald Galbraith

"Come on, Davie," he said as he sealed his letter, "walk doon tae the village wi' me."

"Oh, are you going out?" asked John looking up from his paper. "Suppose you stop till we have family worship. You might be late coming in and grandmother will want to be going to bed."

"No, father, we'll be right back," said Donald. "I'm just going down to mail a letter—some little business I wanted to have go off in the early post."

By the time grandmother had finished drying the silver, Kirsty had the dishes washed and put in the cupboard, the table let down and shoved back in its place against the wall, and Jessie had finished setting the bread and left it tucked up under its linen and bit of blanket in its warm corner against the chimney. They came in and sat down just as the boys returned. David handed his father the big Bible from grandmother's shelf, and they all settled for the bit of the holy Word, and the tender trustful prayer that followed. Especially did their hearts swell as the father prayed for his mother so tenderly, asking that the Lord would give her strength to go through her days to the end, and not be discouraged by the way, praying for the as yet unknown grandchild who was supposedly on her way to see them soon. Everyone kneeling there in that circle near the beloved grandmother was echoing that prayer in his heart, that nothing should happen to her before the expected Rose should come.

They arose from their knees, strengthened in might and gentled in spirit, and went at the various pleasant tasks that were reserved for this evening hour together.

But none of them thought to ask Donald what his business letter had been about, and it had gone on its way to Edinburgh.

9

SUNDAY morning dawned bright and clear and for a moment Rose could not remember where she was. Not at home in Shandon! Not on the ship!

And then she caught a glimpse of the grim stone of the castle and she knew. Her heart went down, down! Somehow she must get away from here as soon as she decently could. That was her first conscious conviction.

And yet as she went back over that conversation she had overheard so involuntarily, it did not seem so very dreadful as it had the night before. Not dreadful enough for her to throw her baggage out the castle window and risk losing it. Not dreadful enough to do something desperate and lose the little friendliness she had already gained.

Oh, of course, she would need to be exceedingly cautious. She would need to beware of the young Lord MacCallummore and her mercenary uncle. She must absolutely refuse to have anything to do with the young man beyond being merely courteous, but surely that would not be hard to do, not in broad daylight, in the presence of her aunt and uncle.

She lay still a few minutes trying to think her way ahead. She must have a talk with her aunt as soon as possible, and tell her that she could not stay, that she had promised to go to her grandmother. And yet, perhaps her going there was going to be made very hard for her. If they still carried on the feud in their hearts—and it had looked yesterday as if they did from what they had said about the name Rose—they might even go so far as to try forcibly to prevent her from going.

But a glance at her little watch sent her quickly into action. It was almost time for breakfast, and she was not up yet. She arose hastily and made a quick toilet, putting on a sober little dark blue silk, with white collars and cuffs. There was a little jacket made of the same, and a small stitched hat that her mother had cleverly fashioned from the pieces of silk left over from the dress. Her mother had said it would be suitable for church in the city, she thought. Not a word had been said about church as yet, but she assumed that there would be. Her mother had thought that her sister kept up the ancient family custom of attendance upon divine service, at least in the morning. So Rose went downstairs properly clad for whatever the day might bring forth.

The aunt and uncle met her rather formally, but with far more apparent interest and kindliness than the day before. Rose could but feel that the fact that she could play the piano, and the possibility that she might be possessed of some unexpected money had made the difference.

While they were still at the breakfast table the old clock in the hall chimed out the hour, and Rose looked up and asked pleasantly, "What is the hour of your church service, Aunt Janet?"

The aunt was evidently taken by surprise at the question.

"Oh, would you care to go to church?" she asked, as if the idea hadn't occurred to her before.

"Why, yes," said Rose brightly, "that is, if you were going anyway. I don't want to make you any trouble to take me there."

"Oh, of course, if you want to go," she said quickly.

"Lord MacCallummore would have been very glad to escort her to church, I am sure," put in the uncle. "I could send the butler over to inform him that our niece would like to attend divine service and that you are not feeling well this morning, Janet. There is plenty of time for him to come for her. He asked me last night if there was anything he could do to help us entertain our guest."

"Oh, no, please don't trouble him, Uncle Robert!" put in Rose quickly. "If Aunt Janet does not feel like going this morning I would far rather stay here with her."

"I assure you it will be no trouble whatever for Lord MacCallummore to take you. He is anxious to serve in some way and I am sure nothing could please him more."

Rose felt her heart beat suddenly with a frightened rapidity, and her voice pulsed in her throat so that she was almost short of breath, but she managed a firm tone.

"No, Uncle Robert! I would not care to go with Lord MacCallummore. I have no interest in him whatever, and I have so little time to be here that I would far rather stay in the castle than to go to church with a stranger. Please excuse me."

Suddenly her aunt spoke.

"I think I shall go, Robert. You had better come too. Our niece will like to sit in the old pew where her mother used to sit as a child. There will be a number of people there who will remember her mother of course. Then we can bring Lord MacCallummore home with us to dinner, and he can carry out his suggestion of taking her to ride. He would take you to his father's castle, I suppose, where your mother often went when she was a child. You would like that, wouldn't you?"

Rose's heart sank. Her eyes grew troubled.

"No, Aunt Janet, I don't think I would care to go there. My mother has told me about it, but I do not think she would care to have me go there. Thank you, no, I would rather stay with you!"

"But that is nonsense!" said her uncle with irritation. "The MacCallummores are our friends, and if you stay here with us they will expect you to be friendly also. We cannot permit you to be rude to our intimate friends."

"Besides," said her aunt decidedly, "it is wicked to carry on old feuds. I am surprised that your mother was so unchristian as to give you such an impression of a family that has been friendly with her family through the years. You will, while you are here, put all such ideas out of your mind. Your mother is dead now, and is not the one to decide any more what you shall do. We are your natural guardians and I intend to see that you meet the right people and do the things that carry out your family traditions. Now, if we are going to church it is time for us to go upstairs and get ready. I shall expect you to be down here, Margaret, in just an hour, and Robert, you can give orders for the car to be at the door then."

Primly she stood aside at the foot of the stair and motioned Rose to go on up to her room. Rose, as she climbed up the grim castle stair again, had a feeling that behind her back her aunt and uncle were exchanging confidences about her. So she went slowly up, with trouble in her eyes, and when she reached her room she went to her knees again.

"Dear Father," she prayed, "please take care of this for

me. Don't let me have to go anywhere or do anything
with that MacCallummore man, please, dear Lord."

When she arose she looked about her with eyes that
were touched with peace again. Now she mustn't just sit
here and brood over this thing. She had given it into
God's hands and that was all there was to do at present.
Should she find a book to read? Or should she write a
letter?

Then suddenly the memory of Gordon McCarroll
came to her mind. He had asked her to write at once, as
soon as she reached her first stopping place. This was the
first opportunity she had had, except those very first few
minutes and then she hadn't got her bearings yet to
know what to tell him.

But now it came to her as a pleasant task. She could
write and have the letter ready to mail tomorrow if there
came opportunity. So she got out her paper and pen and
sat down at the quaint old desk.

    Dear friend,

she wrote, and smiled to think she had a right to call him
her friend. She paused to look thoughtfully down at the
paper with a little frown, and then wrote rapidly:

    I reached here late yesterday after a comfortable
voyage. I find things strange and not altogether as
I had hoped.
    I am in a great old castle, like those we used to
read about in the old Scotch novels in lit class. It is
very grim and awesome, and I feel as if I were
somebody else every time I look around on the old
stone walls and see the old-time furniture. I can't
help being interested in it all, but somehow I don't

feel at home, and I don't think I shall stay here very long.

My mother's sister and her husband never knew my father, and they did not want my mother to marry him, so they have no sympathy with things that are dear to me. I would not have come here only that my mother wanted me to meet them. But they are very formal, rather worldly people, so I think I shall try to get away soon and go to my father's family.

My voyage over was very pleasant, and I did get acquainted with a few people. One woman, Lady Campbell, was very kind and has invited me to visit her in London. Her husband has something to do with the English government. She came and sat by me one day on the deck and said that I looked like an old school friend of hers. It turned out that her old friend was my own Aunt Rose Galbraith who is married and lives in Australia. I thought that was rather a wonderful thing to happen, and we got to be very dear friends indeed before we landed.

It seems as if God has just been taking care of me on this trip and making things nice for me. At least until I came here to the castle. And yet even here there is one nice thing, my dear mother's girlhood picture, painted by a famous artist! I would have been willing to suffer a great many hardships just for the privilege of seeing that. And standing just below that lovely picture is my mother's piano. They have kept it tuned all these years and they let me play on it for a long time.

It was very nice of you to ask me to write when I got here. It makes me feel as if I had a native country, and a home, and someone who is friendly over there. Thank you too for the delightful message you sent to the ship.

I hope everything is going well with you and that nice things will come to you every day.

With all best wishes,

Your friend,
Rose Galbraith

She had become so absorbed in her letter that she had forgotten about watching the hour. She had just sealed and addressed her letter when Maggie tapped at her door and told her the car was waiting below and her aunt wished her to come at once.

With a startled look at the clock she rushed for her hat and jacket and gloves, and putting her letter away in her suitcase hurried down the stairs to find her aunt and uncle grimly waiting for her in the hall.

The drive to church was most intriguing, down the winding way to the valley, and over a charming road through the village.

They stopped before an old stone church, fascinating inside and out, a quaint gem of the old world.

"Was this the church my mother used to attend?" she asked her aunt as they got out of the car and went up the path to the door. And her aunt answered grimly, "Yes, it was!" as if somehow the fact were condemnatory; as if a person who had been privileged to attend that old historic church, were a criminal indeed to have alienated her family, and married an unknown man; and as if this Rose were, at least in part, responsible for it all.

But the service was quite formal, and not at all the sweet informal gathering of the little chapel where she and her mother had worshiped in Shandon, and she was homesick indeed for the worship to which she was accustomed. Oh, was it just because she felt strange that it did not seem as if God were there? Or, if He was there He seemed so far away? Not the dear Heavenly Father she knew so well?

She had not been seated long before she discovered Lord MacCallummore among the worshipers, sitting along pompously in a pew a little to one side and in front of them. In that quick glance before she recognized him, it struck her that he had eyes and a mouth like a fish. Then as he turned his cold fishy eyes in that direction she suddenly knew him and quickly looked away to the other side of the church. But she could not get away from the fact of his presence there, and more and more her thoughts were turned from worship and filled with anxiety. Now he would be coming home with them to dinner, perhaps, and she would have to talk with him. At least answer his questions if he spoke to her. And how could she do that with the memory of his cold unfeeling words that she had heard the night before? Oh, it was all terrible, and how was she going to get through that dinner, and those trying hours that would follow? And how could she plan to get quickly away from this troublesome place? She simply couldn't stay here and let her uncle carry on negotiations for her that she would never be willing to carry out. She must get away as soon as possible, and yet do it in a way that would not look as if she understood what they were trying to do.

So she began to pray. When the heads were all bowed she bent hers and closed her eyes and prayed in her heart that she might be able to trust all this to her Lord and that she might be guided in what she should do and say. When they were singing and listening to the sermon, still she prayed in her heart.

And now and then her thoughts turned to Gordon McCarroll. He was her friend, and it would be so nice to be able to tell him everything about her life and ask his advice about some things, but of course this was something she could never write about, and it wasn't in the least likely she would ever be able to tell her troubles to him, or anybody like him. She would just have to realize that the Lord was her only confidant. He was her stay, as the lesson read from the pulpit was saying: "The Lord is thy keeper. The Lord is thy shade upon thy right hand. The Lord shall preserve thee from all evil: he shall preserve thy soul. The Lord shall preserve thy going out and thy coming in from this time forth, and even forevermore."

So, between prayer and the sweet repetition of God's word in her heart Rose was comforted and put at her ease, so that she was able to smile sweetly on the way home and respond pleasantly, whenever she was addressed.

Not that she was addressed frequently. Her aunt had paused for an instant as they came out of the pew and indicated to Rose where her mother used to sit when she was a little girl, right beside their mother, who was very particular about her behavior in church and would never allow so much as a paper and pencil to help her while away the long sermon time. Aunt Janet seemed to consider that a great virtue, but to Rose it seemed the very essence of the hardness of that grandmother's nature as manifested afterward in the way she treated her child when she was grown. Not that Rose's mother had ever said anything of this to Rose, but when she had mentioned her mother she had often sighed and said: "My mother was a very serious woman! She felt that a child should always obey her parents, no matter how old she grew." That was as near to criticizing her mother as Margaret Galbraith had ever come.

On the way back to the castle after church was over

Lord MacCallummore turned to her several times politely and pointed out places of interest.

"Over that way are lakes. The scenery is generally supposed to be among the most beautiful in the world. I'll be pleased to take you for a drive and show it to you while you are here."

Rose's heart leaped up into her throat almost with fright at the idea. She didn't understand why it was that this man frightened her so foolishly. He was just a man of course, and seemed rather courteous at that. But the story of the way his father had fairly pursued her mother to make her marry him hovered in the background for her, and spoiled all possibility of her seeing anything sincerely friendly in his attitude. Also she could hear his cold voice asking about her supposed fortune, the night before.

"My father and mother are planning to ask you all to dine with us some day this week," he was saying when Rose suddenly came back from her thoughts and gave attention. "I suggested Tuesday night," he went on, "if that would be convenient to you?" He turned to Lady Warloch, as if it were only a form, his asking her. Exactly as if he knew perfectly well that Lord Warloch would settle the matter himself.

"Of course they could make it Wednesday if that suited you better, Lady Warloch?"

Aunt Janet nodded her head noncommittally, but Lord Warloch said in his cold voice:

"Better make it Wednesday, Janet. I have an appointment on Tuesday that may keep me rather late for a dinner engagement."

Rose drew a deep breath of relief. Two days more of grace before that would have to come, and almost anything could happen in two days when her Lord was in command.

She got out of the car at the castle and sped up to her room as fast as she could. Dinner would be announced presently, and she did not want to leave time for talk with the young lord. Something would have to be done, too, about that promise he had made to take her riding some time. She couldn't go driving with him! She couldn't! She *wouldn't!* She knew now just how her mother had felt when she ran away with her father. Only there was no lover for her to run away with now, no one to defend her and protect her. She had to be on her own!

But no, that was not so! The Lord was her defense and her protector, and what could the Lord not do?

After she had smoothed her hair, and taken as much time as she dared in her room, she dropped down beside her bed again for just an instant.

"Oh Lord, You won't forget that I've nobody else to help me, will You? You will take care of me and help me in all the trying places! Please! I'm depending on You!"

Then she went down to whatever the rest of the day had in store for her.

It was after the lengthy dinner had drawn to an end, and they were rising from the table that Lord MacCallummore turned to her.

"And now, Miss Margaret," he said, "would you like to drive with me? I think I can show you some scenery whose equal you do not have in America."

She looked at him with a smile of kindly distance.

"I thank you," she said. "It is very kind of you to think of me. But if you don't mind I think I'll just stay here with my aunt and uncle. I've only just come, you know, and this castle is a delight to me. Besides, I found a book in my room I would dearly love to read, and I had counted on playing a little while on my mother's piano, some of the dear old hymns she used to love and sing to me when I was little—that is, if it won't annoy my aunt."

Unexpectedly Aunt Janet's eyes kindled.

"Why, yes, I should like that!" she said with sudden unusual enthusiasm. "Yes, I found a pile of her old hymn books that she used to play from when I was going through the closet by the chimney last night. I should like to hear you play them. Do you sing?"

"Why, yes, a little," said Rose shyly.

"Then we will have an afternoon of music," said Lady Warloch looking at Lord MacCallummore with decision in her face. "Perhaps you will stay and enjoy it with us?"

Lord MacCallummore was not accustomed to having his plans switched around in this way, and he looked at Lady Warloch with a deepening frown on his brow, and then speculatively at Rose, his eyes narrowing. Just who did this little American upstart think she was to decline his offer of a drive and make her own plans for the household? He was not used to having the girls of that region say no to his invitations. He was considered a great catch. A lord, living in one of the finest old castles in the neighborhood. Not rich yet of course, but he would be when his father died. Immensely rich. Or so it was supposed. What was this girl's game anyway? Didn't she know that he would not brook refusal?

But they went into the great ballroom and Rose sat down at the piano again. All the afternoon she played to them, and sang.

First she played the old tunes her mother used to play. She did not need the worn old books to play them for she knew them all by heart. Her mother had played and sung them to her many a time. And as the afternoon waned and the twilight brought deep shadows in the great room, her uncle, who had found the most comfortable chair the room contained and arranged himself

restfully, was deep in slumber. Audible slumber sometimes, but the piano covered all that nicely, and it was a
comfort to know that he would not rouse and begin to
criticize.

And Lord MacCallummore, with a hard calculating
look in his eyes, sat stiffly in a high straight backed chair
and thought his mercenary thoughts. More and more
the sweet girl with the big blue eyes, the lashes long and
lovely, and the little frills of golden brown hair about her
face figured in his plans. He was not a musician. He did
not enjoy music. But he sat and listened. There was
nothing else he could do at that particular minute, for he
had words to say to Lord Warloch, and he could not very
well say them to a man who was snoring in a deep bass
rumble. He could not touch him lightly on the shoulder
and suggest that they withdraw for a little, for he must
not offend Lady Warloch who had so suddenly developed a will of her own and an interest in music; she
might be needed as an ally later. He gave her a casual
glance and saw that her eyes were wet with tears again
the way they had been last night. She had always seemed
to side with her parents in this matter of her sister's
marriage but women changed sometimes, and sentiment
had a great power over them, it was said. This girl was
very attractive indeed, and there was no telling how
much influence she might not exercise over her aunt if
she stayed long enough. No, he could not afford to
displease Lady Warloch. So he decided to brave it out
and stay.

He stayed until tea was brought in. The butler lighted
the logs in the great fireplace that graced the big ballroom, and the soft flames played over the sweet face of
the girl-mother in the gold frame above the piano.

Now Rose was seated so that he could get a full view
of her lovely face, and see the lights and shadows that

played over it and brought out her sweet expression. It would be nice to have a pretty woman like that around belonging to him. She wasn't exactly a conventional Lady MacCallummore but perhaps his mother could teach her to be. His mother was high-born, of course.

So he stayed till Lord Warloch had finished his tea and invited him into the library for a smoke, and then Rose escaped to her own room, and the book she longed to read.

But first she got out her little Bible and looked up those verses that had given her such comfort in the morning service.

10

ROSE awoke very early the next morning. It came to her that she had a great deal to do before breakfast. She didn't know how she was going to manage things today, but she felt that she should be ready to leave at a moment's notice. Yet she had made no plans for getting away beyond her frantic young prayers. She was merely fearful of developments.

For there was no telling what her uncle and that other lord had talked about last night, nor what they had decided to do with her. She felt that at any minute now information concerning her financial state would be demanded of her, and she didn't intend to give it. It was not her uncle's affair, and she did not like the idea of their plotting to marry her off. She must get out and away from here. And yet she must do it discreetly.

She dressed quickly, in such a way that she could go as she was if opportunity offered, or at least have only to slip into another dress and fold the one she had been wearing and put it into the suitcase in a trice. It had occurred to her that there must be delivery men coming to the house in the mornings, and surely she could pay one of them to take her away if necessity made it expedient. She might even have to take the journey on foot down to the town, but she wasn't sure she could manage the two suitcases, even if she wore her coat and didn't have to carry it, and she was not minded to leave any of her few possessions behind her.

Besides she didn't want to go in any such stealthy way. She didn't want to leave a bitterness behind her. For by this time she was beginning to suspect that Aunt Janet had a heart hidden away somewhere behind that stiff exterior of hers, and that it had suffered more or less as it rattled around through the years in the midst of family traditions and formalism. Just for her mother's sake, if not for her aunt's, she didn't want to cause any more unpleasantness. She was convinced that unless she was driven by some dire necessity, as her mother had been, she must leave in a quiet rational way, with no dramatic scenes, and no discussion about it. Perhaps she might write her grandmother to send for her, but somehow that didn't seem the natural thing to do. She had prayed to be guided. She had handed this thing over to the Lord to manage for her, and it didn't seem right that she should try to manage it herself, especially as no way seemed open at the moment. She would wait for the Lord to show her. But she would be ready to go when the time came, and not have to delay about silly things like packing. She was safe to put her things in the suitcase now, she felt, for she had convinced Maggie that she could look after herself, and didn't need the services of a maid.

So she began swiftly to fold her garments and lay them neatly in the suitcases, so that at a moment's notice she could sweep the rest into place and get away if need be.

When she went down to breakfast in a neat morning dress she had made herself, a white ground with little blue flowers scattered over it, and a piping of blue edging the bands that finished the neck and sleeves and pockets, she looked very sweet and serviceable for the day. There was no hint about her costume that she contemplated a hasty departure. Indeed she really didn't, for she could not see her way ahead.

She was trying not to think about any plans yet, for she knew she was quite transparent and she didn't want her aunt and uncle to notice any excitement about her manner. But in the background of her mind there was that continual consciousness that Lord MacCallummore firmly intended to come over and take her to drive somewhere that day, and she as firmly did not intend to go. It probably would make a rumpus in the house if she refused, but she would try to do it sweetly, somehow. Meantime she kept reminding herself that she was under the immediate care of the Almighty. She must not fret her soul, she must trust.

At the breakfast table it developed that the invitation to dinner at the MacCallummore Castle had been made a definite date for Wednesday.

Rose drew a soft little breath of relief. She had been so afraid that somehow the young lord would manage it that they should come today, or tomorrow. Wednesday left a lot of leeway. Perhaps by that time she could manage to get away and the dinner which seemed to have been planned in her honor would not have to be discussed. It seemed that the dinner was actually for the purpose of having the older MacCallummores look her over and see if she were eligible for their son. At least she could not get away from the thought that this was why they were being invited. She shrank from the idea inexpressibly. Yet she knew it would surely make trouble for her to decline.

It appeared during the breakfast talk that there was a

funeral that morning which the Warlochs felt obliged to attend, and Lady Warloch looking at Rose with a worried expression said:

"We shall be gone some time, Margaret. The funeral is at a distance and as the family have been intimate acquaintances it may be late afternoon before we can return. Can you interest yourself in reading, or playing on the piano while we are gone? Or would you like me to send word over to young Lord MacCallummore to come over and take you driving? I am sure he would be glad to do that if he has leisure this morning?"

"No. He has not!" said Lord Warloch abruptly. "He told me last night he has very important business in Edinburgh which will take him practically all day."

"Oh!" said the aunt.

"But I would much rather play and read anyway, if you don't mind, Aunt Janet!" said Rose with almost a lilt in her voice. She felt as if she had an unexpected reprieve. "I shall be quite all right, and enjoy myself very much."

"Very well," said Lady Warloch as she arose from the table. "Then I think we shall start at once."

Rose watched them depart with a light in her eyes. She felt as if she had a very precious pleasure ahead of her. She could be alone with the wonderful painting of her dear mother. No curious eyes to watch her when she looked at it, and smiled at it. It was like having mother alone with her. Mother, just another girl like herself.

The morning began very joyously, alone in the big old ballroom with the piano and her mother's picture, with quiet all about her, and her happy eyes lifted now and then to the picture. Her own voice asked a question now and again as she finished playing something. "How do you like that, mother dear? Did I play it the way you used to play it?"

It was a beautiful two hours she spent, the first real comfort that she had felt since she came to the castle, because she had no present dread of any disapproving relatives in the background, and did not need to fear the sudden arrival of Lord MacCallummore.

Then suddenly the scene changed. Maggie appeared at her side with a letter.

"Special deleevery," she said excitedly. "It's for yirsel'. The b'y coom awl the wy oop the hill wi' it from the post, juist for ane letter!"

"Oh, thank you," said Rose, looking curiously at the letter. Now what was this? She did not know the handwriting. Could it be from Gordon McCarroll? The roses flew into her cheeks, and then she knew she was foolish. No letter could have come so soon from America, and besides, this letter had the Kilcreggan postmark!

Her trembling fingers tore the letter open and she read.

When she had finished she looked up to her mother's picture, and it was almost as if a look of assurance passed between the painted eyes and her own.

"God answered my prayer!" she breathed softly to the picture. "Here is a way out."

She hurried out to find the region of the kitchen and discovered Maggie polishing the silver in the butler's pantry.

"Maggie, do you know anything about the trains?" she asked eagerly. "Would you know what time there is a train for Glasgow? I've just got word that my grandmother is ill and is anxious to see me. They want me to come as soon as possible. Would there be a way for me to get to the station, or would I have to walk down the mountain?"

"Ah! The puir auld buddy!" said Maggie sympathetically. "Is she that bahd? A'm not sae shure aboot the trains, but the butler kens thae fine. Tammas, coom ye here a meenit. The yoong leddy wants tae ken aboot the trains. Cud ye tell her?"

The butler appeared, with interest. Not many things like this happened at the castle to break the monotony of the day.

"There's a train tae Glasgow aroond the noon oor," he said thoughtfully, "but ye scurce cud be ready by then, cud ye?"

"Oh, yes," said Rose eagerly. "I could be ready in almost no time, but how would I get down the mountain? Is there a taxi I could send for?"

"The baker's lad will be by ony meenit noo!" said Maggie helpfully. "But ye winna gang till my lady returns, wull ye?"

Rose caught her breath.

"Oh," she said, her brows puckered softly. "Yes, I think I must. They said I should come at once. I can leave a note for my aunt explaining about it."

"But was there no to be a pairty oop at the Mac-Callummore Castle coom Wednesday nicht? Ye'll be no missin' the dinner, wull ye?"

Rose flashed a quick look at her that had relief hidden behind it.

"I must!" she said. "They said my grandmother was 'wearying' for me, and she's very old, you know, and feeble. She hasn't been well for some time. Besides, my cousin is meeting the trains for me, hoping I'll get there soon. I really must go. You wouldn't stop for a party if it was your grandmother, would you, Maggie?"

"Deed 'n I wudna," said Maggie with quick tears springing to her kindly eyes. "Gin the dear auld soul were in Scotland I'd roon a' the wy tae Glasgow."

"Of course!" said Rose with a tender smile. "So now, Maggie, I'll run and get ready and write my note to Aunt

Janet, and you let me know when the baker's boy comes, will you please?"

"That I wull," said Maggie. "An' a'll be oop tae he'p ye."

"Oh, no need of that. I'll soon hustle my things in. I'm used to hurrying, and I know just where they go."

She fairly flew up the stairs to her room, and by the time Maggie had finished what she was doing, and got around to tell the butler to watch for the baker's boy, Rose had her suitcases well in hand. All she could give Maggie to do was to put in the little blue flowered dress she had been wearing, while she slipped into her traveling frock.

"The baker's lad has gane on oop the road a coopla miles tae take an order," she announced as she came in, "an' he'll be back an' get ye, he says, in a few meenits."

"Oh, that's nice," said Rose, "then I'll have plenty of time to write my note."

"Aye, mind ye write that. My lady wull be turrible upset. I fear me sair she'll gie me thae blame, lettin' ye gang wi' oot her."

"Oh, she can't blame you, Maggie. You couldn't have kept me. Why, I *have* to go! She'll understand surely! And I'll write her again when I get there. She won't be angry."

"Well, ye better coom doon an' have a bit loonch. Ye'll be hungry on the wy. It's a lang ride tae Glasgow. I cud get the baker's lad tae wait a wee whilie for ye."

"Oh, no, Maggie. I wouldn't want to run the risk of missing that train. Just give me a bit of that lovely cold bannock in a paper and I'll put it in my handbag."

So Maggie hurried down to get a nice little lunch for her, while she wrote her note. She dreaded writing that note, and yet it was far better than to have to explain face to face and hear the scathing tones of Aunt Janet's voice when she took in that it was the hated relatives who wanted her, and to whom she was rushing away, leaving that dinner party entirely out of consideration. So she sat down quickly and wrote:

Dear Aunt Janet:

I am so sorry to have to run away this way while you are gone, but I just had a special delivery letter saying that my grandmother needs me. She is very old and feeble and has been ill. She is fretting for my coming. She is afraid she may not live to see me. They have asked me to come at once and are meeting me at the train. I know you will understand and forgive me for going without saying good-by. If I had waited till you returned I would have had to wait a whole day for a train, you know.

Please make my apologies to Lord MacCallummore for not being able to attend the dinner. Thank you and Uncle Robert for all you have done for me.

Hastily, Love,
Rose Margaret

She hesitated over the ending. Was it strictly true? What had they done for her? And then that impersonal "love" at the end! Was that a lie too? A courteous little lie? No, but she *ought* to love them, oughtn't she? Or could she, when they had been so hard on her mother, and so ugly about her father? Well, she hadn't time to study over it.

So she folded the note and addressed it to her aunt, and hurried downstairs, for she heard a truck driving in and hoped that was the baker's boy.

The butler met her three steps down and took her suitcases.

"Sorry ye hed tae hoorry this wy," he deplored as they went down. "My lady will be sair tribbled that ye hed tae gang awa this wy."

"Oh, it's all right, Thomas," said Rose smiling and handing him a bit of money. "I'm just grateful to you that you found this way for me to go. I would have been very much worried if I'd had to miss my train."

Maggie was there at the foot of the stairs, with a "bit boondle" as she called the lunch which she had neatly wrapped in paper, and she got her bit of money too, for indeed Rose was grateful for this getaway which couldn't have been carried out without their help. She also was a little fearful lest they might have to endure some unpleasantness on her behalf, when the lord and lady of the castle returned.

But at last with her suitcases stowed away in the back of the baker's truck, she said good-by to the servants who had helped her so graciously, and climbed in beside the baker's boy.

"Tell Aunt Janet I was very sorry I had to leave in this hasty way," was her parting word to Maggie, and then they drove off down the mountain, Rose keeping a constant lookout to be sure that her aunt and uncle didn't appear unexpectedly on the scene and block her way even yet, though it was scarcely conceivable that a funeral at a distance could be over so soon.

But there were no such interruptions, and the baker's boy, eager and interested in the pretty young lady who wanted to catch a train, conversed with her pleasantly, telling a lot of bright little incidents out of his carefree young life, and unknowingly adding to her knowledge of her family's standing in the neighborhood.

She looked back at the grim old castle as they neared

the valley and wondered if she would ever come there again, looked back a little sadly and wondered if her mother would have been satisfied to have her go away in such haste, and yet sure she would not have wanted her to stay and go to the MacCallummore dinner. For she was really afraid of young Lord MacCallummore. Was it because her mother had once been afraid of his father? Fearful lest in some way he would wield a power he seemed to have to compel her to marry him even against her will. It didn't seem possible that this young lord could do that with her, but there was something about his eyes that made her feel he usually got what he wanted, and she was quite sure her uncle and aunt would not lift a finger to protect her. Yet it seemed incredible that such a thing could be possible in this day and age. Surely, even in this land which was to her a foreign land, she couldn't be forced to marry against her will!

And yet her instinct warned her that she would have a very unhappy time before she got free from them all in case the young lord should attempt any such thing. She felt they all had ways of working with which she would not be able to cope, so as the distance increased from the castle her relief increased.

As they turned into the city street and swept on toward the station, Rose looked back up at the faraway castle and smiled a little good-by toward the place where she was leaving that wonderful painting of her mother, and the dear piano. Maybe she would never see them again, but she was glad that she had them in her memory and nothing could take that away from her.

And so they arrived at the station, the baker's boy helped her down from the high seat, swung her suitcases down, and with a gay lift of his cap plunged up to his driver's seat again, and roared away.

Rose, feeling as if the last connection with the old

castle had left her, picked up her baggage and hurried into the station, glad to find that she was in plenty of time. She bought her ticket and then sat down to await the train. Not until she was aboard would she feel safe even yet, and it was with great relief that she presently sighted the train coming on to the station. She was aboard at last, and in a few moments more she could look out of her window and see the castle, high and faraway.

Now, what did the future have in store for her?

MRS. McCARROLL was quite troubled. She had just received a letter from Sydney Repplier saying she wanted very much to go over to New York and run around a few days, and she wondered if her mother's old friend wouldn't like to go over with her. She was thinking of staying there for perhaps two or three months to take a few lessons of a famous pianist whom she heard had been engaged to conduct private lessons and classes for a summer school there, and she hated to go and make arrangements for such a thing without someone along who knew the ropes, who could help her secure a place to stay in the right neighborhood, and make the right plans for her. Would dear Mrs. McCarroll be so heavenly good as to take the time and trouble to go, even if only for a day or so?

But Mrs. McCarroll, after she had read the letter over twice, began to feel that she could read between the lines. What the girl really wanted was for Mrs. McCarroll to intercede with her son Gordon and get him to escort Miss Sydney around to the various places and get her nicely and decently settled where he couldn't help but come and see her occasionally and take her out. And somehow Gordon's mother was very sure that such an arrangement would not please her son. Not after the conversation they had had the last time he was at home.

"What's the matter, Agnes?" asked Mr. McCarroll that night when he came home. "You've got your anxious pucker between your eyes, and you might as well confess what you're worried about."

Agnes McCarroll laughed.

"Why, daddy, I'm not sure that I'm worried," she said letting her smile grow thoughtful, almost puzzled.

"Well, I'm sure! I never yet saw that pucker between your eyes but something developed sooner or later. Let's make it sooner. What's to pay?"

"Oh, nothing much," said Gordon's mother trying her best to make light of the matter in her heart. "It's just that Repplier girl again."

"What? Is she coming here again? Well, Gordon isn't here. You don't mind, do you? You can refuse to send for him, you know, say he is too busy."

"Oh, but that's it. She wants me to take her up to New York."

"For what reason?" asked the father with a quick keen look.

"Why she says she wants to study music a few months there with a certain artist who is very famous, and she wants me to take her up there and show her the ropes." The anxious pucker came again, now that she had stated the case in bald language.

"H'mm! Is that the way the young things go fishing these days? Well, you were worried about Gordon, perhaps that would be a good solution of your perplexities. You thought that she was wonderful. You thought she would protect Gordon against all those other nameless impossible girls that you seemed to think inhabited.

New York, just lying in wait for him. Now you've got your wish, and the girl is pursuing Gordon, and he's much too courteous, you know, to run away from her. Why worry?"

"Malcolm!" said Agnes McCarroll with a grieved quiver in her voice. "Is that you talking that way to me?"

"Well, now, Agnes, didn't I understand you the other day to be terribly worried about Gordon up there in New York without any decent girls around to keep him company and keep his mind from straying toward the unworthy ones?"

"No!" said Gordon's mother, the tears in her voice now. "No! I didn't distrust Gordon. You know I didn't."

"Well, but you liked the girl tremendously, didn't you, Agnes? Then I don't see what you are worrying about now."

"I didn't say I was worrying," said the mother bracing up and smiling through her tears.

"Then what *are* you worrying about, little mother?"

"Well, I just don't know what to do. I don't know how to break it to Gordon that she's coming. He'll hate it, you know. This will be just the last straw, because she's coming up, and asking me to bring her, which practically puts her on his mercy."

"Well, mamma, I hope you see she isn't quite the girl for our son. A girl that foists herself on the family in such a direct appeal as this. If she had to go to New York of all cities to study music, why didn't she go quietly and not let anybody know she was there? Then she wouldn't have made a nuisance of herself with the young man whom she evidently hopes to attract and use as an escort while she's there."

"I see. Yes, I see," said Gordon's mother. "I'm awfully disappointed in her. I thought she would have had more delicacy and fineness than to put herself in such a position. But what I'm really troubled about is, what I'm to do? If I go up to New York with her I've practically got to drag Gordon into it, and oh, how he will hate it! What shall I do, Malcolm?"

"Why don't you put it up to Gordon, mamma? Ask him what he would like to have you do?"

Her face lighted up with relief.

"I will!" she said happily, and went over to the telephone and called for Long Distance.

Papa McCarroll retired behind his evening paper and kept an alert ear toward the telephone, but didn't interrupt nor offer any suggestions. But he could hear his son's clear voice. It was as if those two he loved above all others were sitting right there beside him and he was listening to their talk, as it had often been at home; for they had few reserves, these three.

"Gordon, I've got a problem I want you to solve for me. I want you to tell me honestly what you would like to have me do about it, because I just don't know what I should do."

"Yes?" said Gordon all warmth and sympathy. "Let's hear!"

"Well, Gordon, it's something you won't like, I'm sure, and I thought perhaps you could suggest some courteous way out of it."

"Oh, sure!" said Gordon. "Say, it's not another girl, is it, mother? Because I just can't possibly come home this week end, any way you fix it."

"No, Gordon, it isn't another girl. It's the same one. And she doesn't want you to come home to entertain her this time, she wants to come up to New York. She wants me to bring her up and show her the ropes of our great eastern metropolis."

"Oh yeah? When does she want to come, mater?"

"Well, I think she's set the first of next week as her goal."

"Okay, mother, bring her on. The sooner the quicker! I have to leave for Chicago on Monday at noon, or maybe sooner, for two or three days. Can you sight-see her in that time or will it take longer?"

"Well, she's made up her mind to study music in New York, and she wants me to get her settled, and show her the ropes, she says."

"Okay, mother, but don't you dare give her my address. You can tell her I'm about to change my address, and you aren't sure where it will be when I get back. That will tide us over the worst. After that I may be sent to Canada to investigate some business, and then possibly south. I wasn't relishing the idea of travel, but since things are so perhaps I'll encourage my superiors to go on with their scheme. Don't worry any more, mother. Just bring on your girl next week, and get her happily settled, and maybe when I return I may leave my card at her door some night, or even call briefly. I can let her know how busy I am, how I am leaving for Kamchatka the next morning, but I wish her well and so on. But seriously, mums, whyn't you wish her on Palmer Atkinson? She'd adore him, and he is just waiting around for some nice wise little girl like that to mould him!"

"H'm!" chuckled Malcolm McCarroll, grinning at his wife.

"There, now, mamma, what did I tell you? Our son has a wise head, and I knew you could safely leave it to him."

"Yes," sighed the smiling mother, "it's pretty safe to leave things to Gordon."

"And when is it you start up to New York?"

"Well, I was thinking of Monday or Tuesday, but really, Malcolm, I don't know why I have to go at all. If

Gordon is going to be away she'll miss her goal entirely. Why should I bother?"

"Yes? Well, I'm glad you don't feel it essential. Still if I were you I'd just run up a day or two and see her started, if you really think she means it. Anyway it would be a pleasant gesture to your old friend's daughter, and you can introduce her to two or three harmless people. Among them the gentleman Gordon mentioned, and then I think you've done your duty. Leave the rest of the responsibility on your son. If he wants to take her out somewhere, let him. But don't give her his address. He evidently doesn't want to be chased, and you must admit the girls of today do a good deal of chasing."

"Yes, I'm afraid they do," sighed the mother. "But surely, Malcolm, there must be some nice girls."

"Such as you were, Agnes? Yes, I suppose there are still a few real Christian girls left," said the father.

"But Gordon doesn't seem to have identified himself with any church in New York, and where will he meet Christian girls?"

"I wouldn't worry about that if I were you. He isn't going to be there so very long perhaps, and as for Christian girls, if God has one for him He will manage to get them together. Just don't worry. By the way, are you so sure your Sydney Repplier is one?"

"Well, no," said the mother. "She said she sometimes went and taught her mother's Sunday School class, but when she told me what she taught I wasn't so sure. She seems to have made a great point of taking all the courses she can in any line, but I'm afraid she has only a great deal of knowledge without understanding. She said she could learn something good from everyone."

Father McCarroll grinned.

"Yes? Well, in a way that is true, but probably not in the way she meant it. Even the devil might teach you a good deal of what not to do, I suppose. But mother, if I were you I'd just pray that our boy may walk very near to the Lord so that he won't be seeking his own worldly good as much as getting ready to live eternally. If our boy can be kept from the evil that is in the world I guess we don't need to fret about picking out a wife for him. Personally, I'm not so keen on that Sydney girl myself, but then of course I don't have to marry her."

So Agnes McCarroll took Sydney Repplier to New York and showed her the sights, and looked at apartments with her, and went to see the great pianist with her, and tried to show her a general good time as much as one older woman can do for one younger woman. But when the third day Gordon had not yet returned from Chicago, and a telegram informed his mother that he had been ordered farther west the young girl decided she was not interested in studying music in hot weather, and that the pianist wasn't her type anyway. When an invitation came from another friend bidding her to the mountains for a month she abandoned her musical plans and departed mountainward. Then Agnes McCarroll came home greatly relieved in mind. Three days in the exclusive company of Sydney Repplier had not increased her desire to have her for a daughter-in-law.

When she reached home she found a letter from Gordon.

Dearest mother:

Because of your recent interest in girls I am writing, partly to put myself on the level with you and dad, and partly to reassure you as to my immunity just at present from the disease known as "falling in love."

I am hoping that your recent experience with a

certain girl in New York will not have increased your desire to have me her constant attendant, because I am quite sure that you have discernment enough to see many little things in her when you have her at close range, which would not make her fit into our scheme of life.

In the first place, her beliefs are quite different from those in which you and father trained me. Not that I've flown very high in those lines, but somehow you don't like a woman to fling all faith to the winds. It's all a part and parcel of her knowing-it-all, and telling-about-everything, as I said. But isn't that enough for you, without all the other objections I could name?

But mother, just because you've been so nice about my running away when you brought this girl around again, I'm going to tell you something.

When I get a girl I'm going to be mighty particular about her. And there's just one girl I've ever seen who has come up to my ideal.

Don't get worried, for it's not any girl I've just met up here in New York. I've known her all my life. Her name wouldn't mean a thing to you. She's just a quiet part of my school life, though I never took much note of her till lately. I don't know why. It probably was my fault. I always admired her in the distance. It never occurred to me to try to get any nearer. I was too busy. But now I know she was all right.

She's lovely, mother! I know you would like her.

But again, don't you worry. She's over in Europe. I'm over here. I don't know that she means to come back, ever. But I thought you would like to know there *is* a girl who has given me a higher standard, and no girl can take my fancy now, unless I feel she would come up to it.

So there you are! If we ever have a chance again for a good old talk, I may tell you more about her, and about how I came to be interested in her. But it's not a thing to write about. Not yet.

So please don't worry any more. I'm not going to fall in love with every girl I see in New York. And you can tell dad I'm aiming, if I ever get a girl, to get one as good as the one he got, or I'll go alone.

Your loving son,
Gordon

With tears of happiness on her face Agnes took her letter to her boy's father, and he with his arms about her read it, and then kissed her tenderly.

"He couldn't get a better girl," he said fervently.

"Dear!" she said softly. And then added with a small pucker in her brow—"Only—I wish he had told us her name. I would like so much to know more about her."

"You must be patient, little mother," said Gordon's father. "When your son gets ready to have a name for her he'll tell you. If there's anything to tell, and she's not just an ideal who may vanish into somebody else, he'll tell you when the time is ripe. You can't hurry a bud in opening, you can't force a love tale until it comes true. If you try you may be sorry!"

Agnes McCarroll smiled understandingly, and later that evening she wrote to Gordon. "All right, dear son. And when you ever bring her here I shall be ready to receive her with open arms."

And that very night Gordon began to dream how it would be if he ever brought her. And just before he slept it seemed his lips were upon hers again, and her face close to his.

The next day he received, with great relief and joy, the letter from Edinburgh, together with the letter she had written from the ship. For the vision of her had begun to be so beautifully far away that he had feared it might vanish some day and turn out only a dream. Maybe there hadn't been any girl at all who was different from other girls. Maybe it had all been fancy. Only that the touch of her lips still stayed upon his.

So he sat down at once with a great light of joy in his eyes and wrote her a letter.

> Dear Rose:
>
> I was so glad to get your ship letter today, and to know that you are safely across and landed among relatives. I do not have to think of you as all alone on a ship full of strangers. Somehow I felt as if I ought to have done something about that for you before I left you. I hoped the flowers would tell you how I felt about it. So I am very glad you found a real friend in your Lady Campbell. I could not bear to have you lonely all the way across.

Gordon stopped at that and read over what he had written. Was he getting too intimate all of a sudden? Perhaps she wouldn't understand why he should care. Perhaps she would think he was getting silly. He might frighten her, acting as if he had a right to look out for her that way. Maybe he ought to tear it up and begin again. But after he had read it the third time he decided to let it stand. There was nothing in being solicitous for a friend's comfort on a voyage, and they had both agreed that they were friends. She would understand. So he dashed on with his letter.

> I have been very busy since you sailed. My job has been growing quite interesting. I have just returned from Chicago and "points west." I have also found out that I am in training for the possibility of going back to Shandon vicinity sometime to have charge of a branch. While I like New York, Shandon is home, and it will be good to get back.
>
> Of course I have a few friends in New York, but most of them are away on vacation just now, and I don't find many congenial ones to talk with, so I am rather shut up to reading, though of course I never get tired of that.
>
> I am sending you the book about which we talked on shipboard. I have just been reading it over again with you in mind and I think you will like it. Don't forget to write me your impressions as soon as you have finished it.
>
> Please tell me as soon as you know just when you are leaving Edinburgh. I want to keep in touch with you if you don't mind, because you know we are real friends now.
>
> Hoping you will have a very happy summer,
>
> > Sincerely,
> > Gordon McCarroll

Fortunately Gordon did not mail that letter that night, for the next morning there came the next letter from Rose intimating that she might not stay long at the castle, so he decided to send his mail to Kilcreggan.

"Kilcreggan!" he said with a pleased look in his eyes. "That sounds charming. I'd like to go there some day!"

And that morning on his way to the office he stopped and got a good clear map of Scotland and looked it up. "The Trossachs!" he said wistfully. "Well, sometime perhaps. If I could just get that chance that Haskell has this year, of being sent over to England, I sure would run up there and see things. I'd take a day off and do it. But of course there's no chance for that this year."

Then as he studied the map his eyes got dreamy and he gazed off into the shadows of the room.

"Well, maybe!" he promised softly. "We'll see!"

12

LORD and Lady Warloch reached home toward evening, just as the soft shadows of dusk were dropping down on the valley, and creeping up the winding drive. There above them towered the castle, sharp and dark against the sky, with the sunset pointing each pinnacle and tower, and turning into molten fire the windows that looked westward.

They had had a long day and were tired. They rode silently side by side.

The funeral had been long and notable. Many acquaintances had come from a distance, and divines that had much to say of the virtues of the dead. It had been enough to make one think of one's own possible end that might not be far away. Enough to start one planning to get a little richer before the call should come to leave it all.

Not much was said about the Hereafter, except by one unconventional old elder, who because of relationship and a flair he had for saying the wrong thing before the right people had claimed a portion of the program. He brought dismal thoughts of possible judgments and a needed preparation for a thing that didn't seem at all real to them. Lady Warloch knew in her heart that she was not ready for any such time, if there was really to be one, and she was cross and shaken.

Then, too, they had stopped at the country place of an old cousin and his wife who hadn't been very prosperous. They had owed these people money for a number of years and hadn't paid it because it cost so much to live up there in the castle. There had been pieces of jewelry belonging to her mother that Lady Warloch had been told to give to this cousin, but she had never given them. She consoled herself by reiterating often to her own thoughts that Cousin Mary Howe would have no use whatever for that jewelry because she never went to any affair where it would be suitable to wear it. But she made up for this lack in herself by paying a good long call every time she went by their humble home, and partaking of their best in the way of refreshment, though she well knew they could ill afford to serve it. So they had lingered and enjoyed a pleasant repast, and now as they drove toward their high castle the vision of the humble thatched cottage with its ill-cared-for outlying borders and desolate empty fields, stood out in contrast with their own apparent prosperity.

It was not unnatural that my lady should go on to think of others whom by rights she might have benefited, if she had not had to take such good care of herself. And then there was that enmity toward her dead sister that she had harbored in her heart all these years. Somehow, sometime she would have to make up for that. And the time had come now in the person of her sister's child who, after all that had been said about resembling an unknown aunt, did look like her mother.

"I think," said she, out of the silence that had enveloped them ever since they had left the cousin's place, "that I shall leave my sister's picture in my will to her daughter Margaret, and I feel that she should have her mother's piano!"

The stiff gray lips of Lord Warloch opened sharply.

"Don't think of it!" he said. "That picture was painted by a noted artist. It should sell for a good price! I have several times wondered if we should not send for some collector and have it appraised."

"It belongs to the family," said Lady Warloch. "It was my own sister's portrait. It is not decent to let it go out of the family!"

"Nonsense!" said my lord. "Nobody will know whose picture it is if you don't tell them. Besides we might be able to sell it to some great collection where it would be on exhibition and that would be to our credit, you know."

"It is mine!" said Lady Warloch coldly.

"Yes, but I am your husband," said my lord sternly, "and I say it should be sold. And as for the piano, if that baggage of a niece of yours wants her mother's piano she can pay for it. Since she says her father left her money there is no reason why we should give her anything valuable. That too might bring in a fair price. I will make inquiry about it."

"I will think it over," said my lady still coldly. And then they drew up in front of the castle and got out.

Maggie was watching from a narrow window, dreading what was to come when my lord and my lady found out what had happened in their absence. Would they be relieved, or would they be very angry? Maggie had no precedent by which to judge and she stood there quaking in her worn old shoes, trying to study their faces and see if they were in a pleasant mood or otherwise. But they were wearing their after-funeral faces and it was impossible to tell. So Maggie turned reluctantly from her post of observation and hurried about the dinner. They would likely be wanting it at once.

So she did not go to Lady Warloch to tell the news. Instead she saw to it that the dinner was a good one and was on the table promptly at the usual hour, and the summons given in good order.

It was not until Lord and Lady Warloch came downstairs and took their places behind their chairs and looked about them for Rose to appear, that they missed her.

"Did you call Miss Margaret?" asked Lord Warloch of Thomas as he entered from the butler's pantry.

Thomas gave a frightened glance behind him at Maggie who was following with a carving knife which probably belonged with the first course.

"She's gane, my lord," gasped Thomas out of a very firm determination not to seem flustered.

"Gone?" echoed the master of the house. "Where has she gone, Thomas?"

"Why, sir, she's gane tae her gran'mither's. There come a letter for her this morn aboot an oor aifter ye left, sayin' her gran'mither was took worse, an' was aboot tae dee, an' askin' wud she come queek!"

"And you let her go, like that!" exclaimed Lady Warloch in horror. "You let her go all alone? Where is Maggie? Oh, Maggie! Why did you let Miss Margaret go off that way? You should have kept her until we returned. It was not respectable for one of our family to go traveling off alone. A young girl? What will people think of us? And how did she go? Surely you didn't let her walk! Thomas, how did she get away?"

"There wes nae haudin' her, my lady! She wud awa'! She said she maun see her granny afore she deed, and sae the baker's lad wes passin' an' I speired him tae tak her. She set aff quite comfortable, my lady!"

"The baker's boy!"

Lord and Lady Warloch looked at each other aghast, as if all their respectability of all the years that were past was now shattered by this act of these feckless servants.

"But I don't understand it!" said my lady. "You certainly knew that was not the thing to do. Surely both of you knew that we would want her kept here until we arrived, and then we would have decided what was the best thing for her to do."

"My lady," said Thomas with Scotch dignity which he assumed on occasions of great stress, "ye said naethin' at a' aboot lookin' aifter the yoong lady. She seemed tae hev her mind med oop, an' there was nae disputin' her. She said she maun gang, an' gang she wud. There wes nae haudin' her!"

"Yes," sighed Lady Warloch, "she's her mother over again, I suppose."

"Yes," echoed Lord Warloch, "I told you how it would be when you wanted her to come. I told you it would be the old story of her mother over again if she came. And now you see! We just get nothing for our trouble."

"Trouble?" said Lady Warloch irately. "What trouble have you had, I should like to know?"

"We've got trouble now, haven't we? With the Mac-Callummore's dinner, and all this affair with the young lord pretty well fixed up, then she runs away. That's just what her mother did, isn't it? And now we'll have to traipse all over the country to hunt her, I suppose. Probably take all day tomorrow and I had a man coming to see me."

Lady Warloch flashed a look at Thomas whose curiosity was fairly popping out of his eyes; a glimmer of Maggie's eye glued to a crack showed through the pantry door that wasn't shut tight; and Lady Warloch withered her husband with a glance.

"I think we will discuss that later, Robert!" she said with finality.

Lord Warloch cast an eye at Thomas as if he had no right to be there and closed his lips in a hard thin line, and the meal proceeded silently thereafter.

But Lady Warloch was not done with the subject. As soon as the meal was over she summoned Maggie to an interview.

Maggie came in fear and trembling but she bore Rose's note which in her first flurry of their arrival she had forgotten.

"My lady, the young lady left this letter for ye," she said shakily. The servants had briefly and breathlessly discussed the situation in the kitchen, and the chauffeur had contributed some bits of conversation he had been able to overhear on the journey. Maggie was inclined to hold up her head a little over her rebuke. After all, she knew the family history, and she knew the high handed way they had carried on when this girl's mother went away to marry the man of her choice. Her sympathies were with the Galbraith side, though she never had seen any of them but this sweet child whom they called Margaret, after her mother. Rose Margaret, she had gathered was the name, with much indignation and resentment over the Rose part.

So Maggie handed over the letter.

"Oh! She left a letter, did she?" said Lady Warloch. "Well, you should have given me that at once when I returned."

"Well, a' was that flustered wi' yir sharp words that I compleetly forgot it."

"That's enough," said Lady Warloch. "You may go. I'll call you later when I have read the letter."

So Maggie scuttled away sniffing with relief. She could dimly remember the fracas there had been when Lady

Warloch's sister had departed. She herself had been a young girl at that time, just a scullery maid in the kitchen, but she had greatly admired the young lady, and rejoiced in her courage to run away with the man of her choice.

Lord Warloch came in just as his wife finished reading the letter. He glanced at it with a frown, and silently she handed it over to him.

He read it hurriedly, and continued frowning.

"Where did you find this?" he asked sharply.

"Maggie brought it to me just now."

"Why didn't she produce it sooner? Seems to me we have very negligent servants. I think we have sufficient ground for taking something off their wages for this. Such gross neglect of duty, letting a guest go off that way with a baker's boy! Now, where in the world has she gone? Do you know? Did she leave you an address? Do you know where those common people who are related to her live?"

"Why no," said Lady Warloch. "I never asked her. But surely Thomas will know what train she took."

Thomas and Maggie were summoned again, though they had scarcely tasted their own dinner as yet; and they were put through a questionnaire that seemed to them like an inquisition.

Yet when it was all over and they had administered all the rebukes they could think of, they had gained little. The girl had taken a train for Glasgow, but that was all they could find out. Maggie was under the impression that her relatives lived in a suburb of Glasgow, but when the matter was sifted down she wasn't sure whether they were to meet the girl in Glasgow or at the suburban station. So they finally decided that they would have to wait about that matter until the next day, hoping that Rose would have the courtesy to write them. Meantime, of course, they could get in touch with the baker's boy and see if he knew any more about where she was going.

"We must find her before Wednesday and compel her to return at least until after that dinner. I am sure you ought to be able to make her understand how exceedingly rude she would be to run away from an invitation like that. She certainly can't expect that we can do anything for her socially if she behaves in such an unseemly way!" said her uncle. "You wouldn't understand, but it may make a great difference to us financially. It is necessary that you find out just how much money that child has, and we must get it into our control as soon as possible. She is too young to handle a fortune herself, and I'm surprised that your sister didn't intimate in some of her letters that she would like me to take over the handling of the fortune her husband left to them!"

"Well," said Lady Warloch, "you can't tell what queer ideas American women have. I understand they are used to doing all sorts of things themselves in business. Besides, you have no assurance that there was any great fortune."

"Yes," said the uncle convincingly, "I feel sure there is. If there had not been why would she be unwilling to tell me the amount?"

"Well, I know nothing whatever about her financial affairs," said Lady Warloch coldly. "My sister never told me. In all the years she never told me anything about her husband's people. She was very reticent. She felt she had a great grievance, and I think her husband was proud."

"Proud! What did he have to be proud of? Had he a castle, or a royal name or fame? Of course, I've heard that there are people in America who have amassed great fortunes by chance out of oil, or coal, or even gold. It may have been something like that, you know. But she distinctly told me her father had left her money, and when I asked her how much she answered very impertinently that she didn't think her father would care to have her discuss it. So, you see. If she hadn't a pretty large fortune she wouldn't have been taught to be so canny about it. And we must be very cautious or we shall lose all advantage. The first thing in the morning we must try to find that foolish girl. Grandmother or no grandmother she must go to that dinner!"

"I don't see how you're going to find her until we know where she's gone. For my part I think it would be better to get in touch with Lord MacCallummore at once and tell him that she had word that her grandmother was dying, and she didn't know any better than to go traipsing off alone, thought she had to dance attendance on her relatives, just because they sent for her."

"Well, that might not be a bad idea. We'll see when the chauffeur gets back from town whether he has been able to locate the man who sold that ticket to her. And the baker's boy, too. That's important."

But though they made cautious inquiry far and wide they got no further information the next day.

And when the second night settled down they were no nearer to a solution of the affair than when they first discovered Rose was gone.

13

ROSE going on her way was seeing the wonders of a new world. For a time indeed she was tormented lest she had left something undone or unsaid about her going away. Had she done this thing in a way that would have pleased her mother and father? But as the train went on by new ways across an enchanting country, she forgot her unpleasant experiences of Warloch Castle, and only the pleasant things came to the surface of her memory. The dear piano, and her mother's precious picture. The lovely old books in the bookcase in her room that she had so hoped to read sometime. Would she ever go back and read them? Some of their names she could remember, and she took out a pencil and paper and wrote them down lest they might slip from her memory. Perhaps some day she would be able to buy some of them.

Ah, there was one thing she would like to buy and that was that dear piano. Her aunt did not play. It could not be so very dear to her. Would it offend them sometime if she suggested it? Of course not now. She had no money, except the tiny fortune her father had left. Would her mother have thought it right to spend that for the piano, when she would not let her use it for the journey, or for anything else she wanted to get?

Still, the piano would be a help to her. Her music was now her only fortune. She could earn her way so much better if she had a good piano. Yet this was a very fine piano, even though it was so old, a great deal finer than she would need to have for just teaching little children.

Of course if she were going to be a concert performer it would be well worth her while to have a fine piano. But that being the case, would her poor precious little five hundred dollars be enough to purchase it? Certainly not if Uncle Robert, Lord Warloch, had the say of it. Aunt Janet might perhaps be a little more lenient.

Of course she couldn't broach the subject now without letting them know that the five hundred dollars was her entire fortune, and that would be to put herself entirely under the power of her uncle, and she did not want to be sold in marriage to any lord no matter how honorable he was, and certainly not to one who was the son of a man her own mother ran away from.

She shivered a little and settled herself in her seat so that she could the better see the landscape they were passing.

There were other castles in the distance, high and clear against the sky. She wondered if these others held such hardhearted unhappy people as the ones in Warloch Castle. She wondered about the different places they were passing, and the people she saw at the railway stations where they stopped. How she wished she had an automobile of her own and could go exploring through the land until she knew all the places her mother had told about.

Now and again they passed wonderful scenery. Great towering rocks shrouded in masses of trees and vines, great stretches of forest, and moor and meadows covered with heather. Then lovely lakes, connected by silver ribbons of rivers. As they came into Glasgow her excitement grew. Try as she would she could not keep herself from thinking how she would tell her mother about it all when she got home.

But there was no home any more, and mother was not there. There was nobody to whom she could tell of this exciting journey. Only Gordon McCarroll. Would Gordon care to hear it? Perhaps if he wrote again, and seemed to expect an answer she would venture to describe how lovely it all was to her to see the sights about which she had read in the stories of George Macdonald, Ian Maclaren, James M. Barrie, and others. They had all come to life on this trip. She saw the beloved characters, beheld the mountains where they ranged, the cabins where they dwelt, the pastures where they led their sheep, the places where they folded them. In imagination she rode with old Doctor McClure over the hills to his beloved patients; she even found a real "bonnie briar bush" beside which she fancied Geordie Hoo might have lain in those last beautiful days of his lovely consecrated life. She wondered if there were now any such churches as they had in those days, where people knew the grand old doctrines that her father and mother had taught her from babyhood, and where there was a vital Christianity, a spirit of love withal, like the little chapel at home which she and her dear mother had attended. Would she find a place to worship where God seemed close at hand? Not far away as in the great cold sanctuary where Aunt Janet and Uncle Robert went. It seemed as if God had never been there, unless it was hundreds of years ago when it was first built, before all those unholy notables had been laid to rest beneath the paving stones. It seemed in that church as if only dead members were there, and the God they worshiped was dead also. She gave a little shiver of remembrance. Oh, she did hope so much that some of her Galbraith relatives went to a real church, where God was beloved, and Jesus Christ was a real vital Person who dwelt with men.

At Glasgow Rose followed Donald's directions and telephoned she was on her way. Donald told her carefully where to get a bus and just where he would meet her.

She had a few minutes there to get a bite to eat, for the bit of bannock Maggie had given her had long ago faded from her memory. Then she took the bus, and began the lovely ride among the Trossachs.

Now she felt she was journeying through old poems and began to fancy every bit of water was Loch Lomond, or Loch Katrine. Her face was bright with eagerness as she gazed upon the beauty of which she had heard so much.

At last she reached Kilcreggan, more beautiful than them all, it seemed, with a castle there on a mountain, and wonderful verdure all about. And there was her new cousin waiting for her!

She had had letters and Christmas cards from him and the other cousins now and again during the years, and there had been some snapshots, but she had little idea how any of them would look. It was good indeed to see this hearty, robust lad, red-cheeked and bright-eyed, waiting for her with all the welcome she could have wished.

It was a great contrast to her reception at the castle in Edinburgh. David came hurrying up just as the bus drove away. It was evident that they were genuinely glad to see her. David was as eager over her as his brother.

"And how is grandmother?" she asked presently, after they had put her in the ancient car, and were preparing to go rattling down the pleasant village street.

"She's not well at all," said Donald with a shade of anxiety in his eyes. "It's good you have come. She's been in her bed all the day. It seems that she got the idea a few days back that she was not to see you this side of the Promised Land, and she's well nigh given up. She stayed in bed Sunday, and she's still there. We haven't dared tell her you were coming lest she might be over excited. Mother is going to tell her when she sees the car from the window. I'm to wave a signal to her when I turn the corner of the street. Oh, but I'm glad you've come."

"And I'm glad I came at once!" said Rose. "You see, my aunt and uncle were away at a funeral when your letter arrived, and there were only a few minutes to make the only train on which I could have reached here tonight. So I had to leave in a great hurry, and the servants were terribly upset by it. They thought they would be blamed for letting me go that way. There was an invitation to dinner that my uncle had made a great deal of, and I know he would have insisted that I stay for it. So I was glad they were not at home. It may make some trouble later, but I'm glad I'm away, even if it weren't for grandmother. Oh, I'm glad you sent me word!"

Donald looked at his new cousin with approval, and lapsed into Scotch.

"Weel, and glad I am ye're takin' it that wy," he said. "Thae lord and lady uncle and aunt are what you call in America 'not so hot' are they no? Is that right? A've been wantin' to use that phrase on somebody, sae I'm glad ye've come!"

The three of them laughed and joked happily on the way home, till Rose suddenly sobered.

"Is grandmother really very sick?" she asked with a catch in her breath. "Oh, she isn't going to be taken away too, just when I've got here, is she?"

"I trust not," said Donald gravely. "I think she's got her nerves all worked up. Though that's not like gran'mither, either. She's always been so calm and matter-of-fact about things all our lives, that we couldna think what had come to her. And when she got to talking in that mournful way about not being able to see you before she was 'awa' I just made up my mind I'd let you know. It made us all heartsick to hear her grieve."

"Oh, I'm glad, so glad you wrote to me, and glad I could get away in time to make the train!"

They talked on, getting really well acquainted, and Rose had a quick thought once about how nice it was going to be to have some real relatives to tell Gordon McCarroll about when she wrote again. And then the thought struck her weary young heart that perhaps he wouldn't write again and so she would have no occasion to write further either.

But there was no time to think such thoughts now, for they were passing through lovely mountainous scenery, with charming old houses nestled here and there among the trees, perched up on young mountains, or beside a lovely glimmer of lake.

"That's where we go to church," pointed David suddenly, looking up toward a huge stone house that was almost big enough to be a castle, nestled among tall trees and looking down toward the highway.

"Go to church?" exclaimed Rose in wonder looking toward the building. "What do you mean? Is it a church?"

"Oh no," said Donald. "That is, it wasna till oor meenister took it ower. It's no kirk noo, though it's got a pulpit, an' a great congregation, an' the best preacher a've ever heerd. But it's no called a kirk. It's a conference place. Fouk come there from all over the country an' foreign lands, too, an' stay. But they let the villagers in tae their meetin's. Believe me they air blessed meetin's. Yoong people, a many of them, an' testimonies. It's a couthy place. We'll tak ye an' let ye see!"

"Oh, I'm so glad!" said Rose. "I was wondering where you'd be going to church. I went with my aunt and uncle last Sunday and it was so desolate and empty. No helpful words, except from the scripture. You had to preach your own sermon to yourself if you wanted one. I thought maybe that was why my uncle and aunt looked so sad and kind of grim and hopeless."

"Puir souls!" said Donald pityingly. "From a' we hear they've enough tae be dour aboot. They've na been kind e'en tae their own kin. But you probably know the tale weel."

"Oh yes," sighed Rose. "I know the story all the way through, though of late I've tried to forget it for mother's sake. She wanted me to think as well as I could of her own sister, you know. And I did try to see good in her, but it's terribly hidden under formality and subserviency to riches and what people will think, and all that."

"Weel," said Donald thoughtfully, "it may be maistly the auld lord's fault. Gran'mither seemed tae think that Lady Warloch micht ha' been something hersel' but she was merried yoong, an' the auld lord laid doon the law. It minds me my mither heard something o' the like frae yir ain mither. Maybe I'm wrang!"

"No, I think you're right," said Rose sorrowfully.

"That auld lord ne'er kent his Lord Christ Jesus, I guess. He cudna raelly ken Him and be sae dour."

"No, I don't think he could," said Rose. And then suddenly she turned a blazing smile of joy on her cousin. "Oh, I'm so glad you know the Lord," she said. "I've been feeling so alone ever since mother died. Hardly anyone I've met seems to know the Lord. I was almost afraid to come here lest it would be the same."

"Say, now, that's blessed!" said Donald with a shy beautiful light in his eyes. "We wondered what like ye'd be! Ye'll be havin' some guid sorta kirk ower there in America, I'll be thinkin'."

"Oh, yes," said Rose. "It was only a small chapel, and they were plain people who attended it, but it's where my father used to go, and mother and I loved it, and so did he."

"That'll be the uncle whom Davie and I remember sae weel," said Donald quietly. "I wes only a wee b'y, but I mind his prayers sae weel. It seemed like Heaven was juist coom doon in oor ain hoose, an' God was standin' close beside him. When my Uncle Gilbert prayed a' cudna forget the sins a'd committed when a' thought naebuddy wes thinkin' o' me!"

"Yes," said Rose softly. "He was like that. I remember his prayers, too."

"Ye wud!" said Donald.

They swept into a long lovely quiet street, with thatched houses and trees lining the way, and high deep hedges.

"Oh, how lovely! What a sweet quiet place!" said Rose.

"This is home!" said David with a boyish ring of pride in his voice, and then they drove into the yard and helped their cousin out, and she felt as if she had reached a dear resting place.

They took her into the house, and they all gathered around her. Her new uncle and aunt were there, and Kirsty, just scurrying in from putting a clean white cap on grandmother who had roused and was eager to see her grandchild.

Rose was taken to kiss the soft lips and cheeks of the old lady whose skin was like warm velvet, and whose soft tiny hands still had vigor to grasp the young hands of the girl. Such soft vital little hands. And such kindly keen old eyes with the light of love in them! Rose felt that they were all just as her mother had described them. And they were taking her into their heart of hearts every one of them just as her mother had said they took her in when she first came among them, a stray and an outcast from her father's city mansion. And how they had loved her mother. Rose could see they were going to love her just the same way.

The grandmother wasn't satisfied now to stay in bed. She wanted to get up and be one among them. But they persuaded her at last to let them draw the bed to the open door where she could watch them all as they ate supper. David sat beside her and fed her some supper too, only she was too excited to eat, and at last it was Rose who had to come and coax her to take spoonfuls of the smooth delicious porridge they had fixed for her.

Then supper over, Rose watched them from her quiet seat by grandmother's bed, as they cleared away the dishes, each one helping, and finally gathered around the fire.

Rose with her chair just inside the other door, her hand fast clasping the frail warm hand of grandmother, watched the lovely service of family worship with joy in her heart. Her mother had told her of this, and she felt now as if her mother were kneeling there beside her, as she knelt by her grandmother; as if mother, too, felt the other frail old hand upon her head in blessing.

Then the boys came and wheeled their grandmother back, tucked her up with a firm hand and bade her kiss Rose goodnight. They shut the door and left her to Kirsty's ministrations. Rose was taken to her own room and made at home, and then they all came back into the big room and got acquainted thoroughly.

Such an unusual family her father had had! Her dear

precious father! No wonder he was so wonderful when he came from a home like this!

As she crept into her bed at last she felt, for the first time since her mother had left her, a real joy. This was home. As near to home as she could get until she could see her mother again, and tell her all about it.

In the morning when she woke, there was the sun shining broadly through her window, and the song of a bird in a tree near by. There was the tinkling of the brook down in the garden, and the clucking of the hens, the mooing of the cow over in the meadow near by. It was all so homely and lovely. Her heart almost seemed bursting with the joy of it. Just to get home where people loved each other and were not dourly fenced inside great castle walls. Just to be where there was life and warm hearts, and loving glances, and where she was welcome. Ah, that meant so much!

The work went slack that day, because they had so much to say to one another, until Rose began to notice and begged to be put to work also, and then it went better.

Every once in a while Rose would go in and talk to grandmother, who was being forced to stay in bed at least till the doctor came, much against her fretting and fuming.

And then Rose was taken out in the garden, and down by the brook, and over the meadow. She had never had time to have a girl friend before, and now here was Kirsty ready and eager to be a friend as well as cousin, shy with her at first, but with loving eyes, and it was easy to see that they would be warm companions.

When Rose came in she brought a lovely sweetbriar rose to grandmother.

"Mother told me this was the first flower my father

ever gave to her," she said tenderly as she held it close for her grandmother to smell.

"Oh, I mind it weel," said the old lady with a glint of passing glory in her eyes. "My b'y luved thae roses weel. He used tae say they were God's fairest gowans. An' yir mither lookit a gowan hersel' wi' a bunch o' thae in her hair. She was a sweet thing, that Margaret wi' her blue eyes like twa stars; my Gilbert luved her like his ain soul. An' yir a bit like her, though yir mair like my ain little Rose that's gane the noo, sae lang, sae lang!"

So the day flashed on with a beauty days had not had for Rose since her dear mother had first been ailing. The evening and the morning were marked by worship, prayer, and scripture, and sometimes songs from glad hearts. Rose felt as if the home was blest from morning till night. And once she thought about the castle she almost longed to go and tell those poor souls she had left behind what a difference it would make if they only knew the Lord well enough to talk to Him all through the day and at night. Could they ever be made to understand? Would they ever be willing to yield their proud selves to humility? Would there ever come a time when she would feel she could go to them and tell them, once at least, what they were missing? Would God let her do that some day? It seemed so pitiful for them to live on in the darkness and gloom of a castle that was only a tomb, when they could come out into the light.

But such a thought was too startling to stay with her long and now that she had found her place in the home and could bring help to them all, and comfort to grandmother, the terrible ache that had come to her heart when her mother left her, grew more bearable.

And then one day came Gordon's first letter!

14

THAT letter from Gordon McCarroll, together with the book that arrived by the same mail, filled Rose's heart with a great deep joy. It brought back all the memory of her parting when she sailed. She felt again the touch of his lips on hers, the look of deep friendliness in his pleasant eyes, the warmth of his voice as he spoke those last words, and somehow he seemed to be standing right there beside her as she read the letter. It was almost unbelievable that Gordon McCarroll had become her real friend, and that though the sea now rolled between them, she felt nearer to him than she had ever done. When they were in school together and she had seen him every day, she had felt as if a great gulf were between them. It had never before seemed as if he belonged at all to the world in which she lived, and now he was acting as if she were just one of his world, and it was wonderful. She wished so much that her mother could have known that he was to be so friendly. How pleased she would have been!

She read the letter over several times, and then went to humming a little tune while she made her bed and tidied up her room. And she remembered how her mother used to say: "It's nice to have my little bird singing around the house as if she was happy!" and how she always used to answer, "But I am, mother dear! I have you, haven't I? And isn't that enough to make a girl happy?" And then her mother would slip up softly behind her and put loving arms about her, and a kiss on the back of her neck.

And now that mother was gone!

The tears came quickly into her eyes as she thought of it. And then as she brushed them away she hugged her letter to her heart and touched her lips softly to the written words.

"Silly!" she told herself as she realized what she was doing, reminding herself over again that that kiss he had given her had been a mere touch of friendliness in parting, because she had no one else to bid her farewell.

But the joy of the letter stayed with her all that day, as something so new and cheering. To think she had a friend in America who cared to write to her. Oh, he was probably only writing once or twice because he felt sorry for her, all alone in a strange land. But even that was nice. For she knew that he was going to be the kind of man to whom she could always appeal if she were in any sort of trouble, and that was a great comfort. Perhaps, she told herself firmly, some day she would know his wife if he got married, and maybe his mother, a little. That would be nice. He must have a nice mother. Perhaps something like Lady Campbell. Why, she might get to know them well enough to be bidden to the wedding, in case she ever went back to America.

But those thoughts brought a quiet little sadness into her eyes. It somehow seemed to put her so far from having anything to do with Gordon, to have to think about his wedding. But there! She must not think such things. And she must not make too much of his present kindliness. It probably wouldn't last. And why should she need other friends now she had all these nice cousins, her own folk?

So she took the book he had sent and gave herself a little while of reading. It was a book so filled with delight that again the boy who had kissed her good-by at parting, who had sent her flowers and a radio message, seemed to stand beside her, pointing out phrases in the written page, and calling her attention to certain paragraphs, till she felt right at home with him again.

So Rose sat down and wrote of her coming to Kilcreggan, and of all the dear relatives she had found here. She talked to him as if he were a dear brother far away in whom she might confide, and was very happy as she wrote, quoting a snatch from the book he had sent, telling him how she was going to enjoy it; describing the "kirk," and even quoting a sentence from a sermon she had heard there.

There was a softness and a gentleness about her face when she came among the family a little later that made them remark to one another how lovely she was.

And when Kirsty told David and Donald about the letter that had come for Rose that afternoon, David remarked cannily:

"She'll maybe be havin' a sweetheart, Kirsty, my dear, an' the letter'll be frae him."

"Oh, no," said their grandmother quickly, "I think not, Davie. I hed a lang talk wi' her yestreen, an' she didna say onything aboot him."

Davie chuckled.

"Mayhap she'll not ken it hersel' yet, but I'm thinkin' a gowan as sweet as oor Rose'll no stay onplucked for lang."

"Well," said the grandmother cannily, "a'd wish tae

be oncommon sure of ony mon that took my Gilbert's bonnie lassie awa frae us."

But of course Rose knew nothing about such thoughts and words and went her lighthearted way through the days, looking after her grandmother, doing any small tasks they would allow her, reading her book Gordon had sent, writing little letters now and then, bits of letters she would incorporate in one, in case Gordon wrote again and she had to answer; thoughts that came to her as she was about her tasks, as if he were around here and there with her and they were thinking their thoughts together. Now and again she would chide herself for having him always in mind that way, when he was only a friend in passing. She knew she had no right to make so much of him in her heart.

She had written her Aunt Janet, telling of her pleasant journey, and of how she had found her grandmother quite ill, but she was better now, and able to sit up for a little while each day. She had given a brief description of the lovely village in which they were living, a little description of the sweet house, "like the picture of Anne Hathaway's cottage in looks," of the pleasant family life, not leaving out a glimpse of the family worship around the firelight. She told it as a matter of course, just as if Aunt Janet would enjoy the thought herself. And then she thanked her again for the brief hospitality she had enjoyed and said that she hoped she might see her again some day before she went back to her American home. That was all. And she had no reply from the irate Lord and Lady of Warloch Castle.

She had written also to Lady Campbell, and given her the latest news from her beloved friend "Rose," the Aunt Rose who was living in Australia. She told her that she was at Kilcreggan where the Galbraiths now lived, and sent her a message from the old grandmother that she would be so glad to see "her Rosie's friend" if she ever came that way.

They had been several times to the "kirk" as they called the big delightful stone house among the trees, and Rose was charmed with the whole atmosphere, and with the marvelous messages that were given. There had been much the same spirit in the little chapel where she and her mother had gone for years, but not the same deep teaching. Here there was scholarship mingled with spirituality, and new wonders of the scripture were disclosed at every turn. How she would miss this when she went away! How she wished her mother could have had the comfort of such teaching. And then a new thought came to her. If Aunt Janet could hear something of this, wouldn't it make some difference in her? And Uncle Robert, too. Would he accept this wonderful Word? She didn't feel so sure about her uncle. He seemed so cut and dried and self sufficient, like one of the Pharisees.

Was it thinkable that sometime she might have opportunity to tell Aunt Janet, at least, how blessed it was to trust a God who cared supremely for you, who cared so much that He had given His own Son to die? Of course she must know those facts, but she did not give the impression that she ever took them into her heart and counted them true and dear. Yet there must have been a time when Rose's own mother had no more personal knowledge of the truth than Aunt Janet had now, for her mother had learned all this precious gospel from the Galbraiths. That night she spent time upon her knees asking the Lord to save Aunt Janet, and to use her if possible to tell her some day about it. For her dear mother's sake she wanted to do that.

So the days went rapidly, almost happily by.

She did not forget her mother's death, but the hardness of it was softened by the atmosphere of loving trust into which she had come for a time to dwell, and she was soothed and comforted.

Then one day a car drew up at the front gate, and the Warloch chauffeur came up the walk and knocked on the door.

It was Donald who opened the door, and looked at the man with keen, canny eyes.

"Is Miss Margaret Galbraith staying here?" asked the chauffeur, with something like condescension in his tone.

Donald gave him a withering glance.

"Miss *Rose* Galbraith is here," he answered with dignity. "Is she the one you wish to see?" Donald could talk as clear-cut English as could be if he chose, and he was not wasting his beloved Scotch dialect on this product of aristocracy.

"Why, I was told to ask for Miss Margaret Galbraith," said the man with a worried glance back toward the car standing outside the white gate in the hedge.

"Who wants to see her?" asked Donald with his most lordly manner.

"Lord and Lady Warloch are in the car and would like her to come out and talk with them."

"Tae come oot an' coonvarse with them!" said Donald relapsing into his native dialect. "Ye may tell my Lord and Lady Warloch they are wulcome tae come intae the hoose an' coonvarse wi' her as lang as they desire, but Miss Galbraith wull no be comin' oot tae thae car."

The chauffeur blinked, looked down thoughtfully, and then turned on his heel and marched out to the car.

Donald standing in the door noticed there was some little altercation between my lord and my lady, and finally the lady got out of the car and came up the walk attended at a respectful distance by the chauffeur. Ah, well Donald knew who the lady was. And his eyes twinkled as he further sighted the lord getting out irately and following indignantly behind. He looked mad enough to set fire to the house. He marched impressively up the walk with a stern eye fixed on what he considered that upstart of a young man in the doorway of the cottage. The idea of any man who lived in a cottage daring to order a lady from a castle to come into the house if she wanted to see her own niece.

There was a shade too of amusement in the twinkling eyes of Donald as he watched the approach. It was something he had expected to happen for several days past ever since Rose had told him that she had written to her aunt telling where she was. He knew that sooner or later there would be some move made, that is, if they wanted to have anything further to do with her. And in any event, he knew from what had happened in years gone by, that Rose's sudden flight during their absence would not be left unnoticed. So here they were.

He was quite as much the gentleman by the time they reached the house as Lord Warloch himself, and he ushered them into the wide immaculate living room, where even though the day was mild, a trifle of fire blazed quietly on the hearth, and the air was fragrant with a great bowl of sweetbriar roses on the table. He saw to it that both Lord and Lady Warloch were comfortably seated, and then he said with the grace and courtesy of a real lord:

"I will call my cousin Rose. I think she will be able to come very soon. She is with our grandmother just now, but I think she will not be occupied long. I will tell her at once."

"Do you mean that she is nursing a sick person?" inquired Lord Warloch haughtily.

"Oh, no, not nursing. My mother would be doing that whenever necessary. She was reading to her, I think.

But she will want to come at once I am sure, at least as soon as she can do so without disturbing her grandmother," and Donald left them to themselves.

There sat the lord and lady and gazed about them in utmost amazement. They could but recognize good furniture when they saw it. And there were the walls lined with beautifully bound books, and even a fine old portrait or two. It was incomprehensible to them. They quite resented it, that a mere cottage, though of course it had proportions more than most, should contain such valuable things.

"She must have money," murmured his lordship, "more even than we had supposed. She must have brought all these things over with her. Why did she not bring them to us at the castle?"

"No!" said Lady Warloch sharply. "They look as if they had been here always. They are Scotch things, not American."

"Nonsense!" said Lord Warloch. "You always pride yourself upon your discernment. But you are not always right."

Then there was a sound of footsteps and they relapsed into angry silence. They meant to punish the girl who had run away from them in their absence. They were sitting silently staring about them when Donald returned.

"My cousin will be here in just a moment," he said and drew up a chair genially, near to Lord Warloch.

"You drove up from Edinburgh?" he asked.

Lord Warloch replied by a reproving nod.

"It must have been a pleasant drive. It is a bonnie day."

The Warlochs evidently did not consider this remark worthy of an answer, though Lady Warloch lifted one corner of her lip, the side away from Lord Warloch, in a faint gesture, which left Donald in doubt as to whether it was assent or merely contempt.

Donald smiled sunnily again and launched into remarks about the region of the Trossachs that would not call for reply, and went rambling on until he heard Rose's step.

She entered as lightly as a bird, quite composed, and not in the least awed by their presence, which not only surprised the callers, but somewhat confused them. The attitude they had assumed did not seem to fit the occasion, and made no impression whatever. And an impression was evidently what they wished to make. A severe impression, so that no connection of this obnoxious family should ever dare cross them again.

"Why, Aunt Janet!" she said pleasantly. "This was lovely of you to come and see me!"

She reached over and touched her aunt's cheek lightly with her lips, and then turned and went over to shake hands with Lord Warloch. But Lord Warloch did not take very kindly to shaking hands and performed his part of the ceremony quite in embarrassment.

"You've already met my cousin, Donald Galbraith, haven't you?" she said, smiling toward Donald. "Sorry I had to keep you waiting a minute or two. I was reading grandmother to sleep, and she was just dropping off. I was afraid to stop at once lest she would waken. It means so much to her to get her afternoon nap, you know. She is very weak yet. But she won't sleep long, and she will want to see you when she wakens."

Rose settled down beside her aunt.

"No, really, we can't stop!" said Aunt Janet with a half-frightened look toward her husband. "We only drove over to take you back with us. The dinner to which you were invited has been postponed until tomorrow. It would have been sooner only that we did not know where to locate you until you wrote me."

"Oh," said Rose, somewhat dismayed. "I didn't realize that you wouldn't know the address. I should have left it, of course. But there was so much to do and to get acquainted with when I first arrived that I didn't get around to writing you again as soon as I should have done. You know grandmother was quite weak and ill. She is much, much better now, I'm glad to say, and she seemed so pleased to have me here. I was sure you would understand about my leaving in such a hurry. She was quite fearful lest she wasn't going to live to see me, and that seemed to mean a very great deal to her, as of course it did to me. But really, Aunt Janet, I couldn't possibly go with you today. I'm sorry that you've had all this trouble of coming after me for nothing, but I couldn't leave now, and I'm sure you can make your friends understand."

Then before there could be any protest from the guests Mrs. Galbraith came sweetly into the room, as quiet as a shadow, as gentle and refined as any lady of the land.

Rose jumped up quickly.

"Oh, and here's Aunt Jessie, Aunt Janet. I've been hoping you two could meet sometime!"

And then Lady Warloch looked at the other woman, who was every inch a lady as much as herself. Her hands were not as lily-white perhaps, for they had seen happy service for her beloved family, but they were well-cared for, and her face was far sweeter and more lovely with true spirit-loveliness than the grim dour visage of the many-times disappointed, selfish Lady Warloch, for all her castle and her ancestral aristocracy.

Standing thus, within her quaint, sweet home, by grandmother's door from which she had just emerged, with the deep shadows of the room about her, and the pale flicker of the fire lighting her eyes, she was almost beautiful, with a beauty that one could not help but remark, at least to one's own soul. And when she smiled, as she did now, holding out a friendly hand to the other woman who had done so much to bring sorrow into that home, she was certainly beautiful. Not pretty, but really beautiful.

In a daze Lady Warloch put out her hand to greet the other woman and was scarcely aware she had done so. She certainly had not intended to do it. But she found herself enfolded as it were in a great friendliness that surprisingly warmed her chilly heart and filled her with wide wonder. Were common people like this? was her fleeting thought. And then, Was this the charm that had captured her young sister Margaret and made her willing to surrender wealth and castles and a lordly estate? Dazed she sat down and listened to this gracious lady, watched her ease of manner, her lovely smile, and was almost charmed herself by the sweet Scotch accent that tinged her words. She discoursed of the day, and the way they had come, and the beauty of the season, and then spoke of the years when they had lived in the outskirts of Edinburgh themselves.

Then in came John Galbraith and his tall son Davie. They opened the door without ceremony and stood among them, looking about with clear gaze. Perhaps for the first time in many years Lord Warloch had the feeling of having been weighed in the balance and found wanting, though he only lifted his chin a trifle more haughtily in consequence, and stared at the tall Scots and saw that they were men of keen, wise bearing, men accustomed to holding their own in the world.

Then Rose stepped up.

"Uncle Robert, this is my Uncle John. And this is my Cousin David. Now they're all here but Kirsty. She stayed with grandmother."

And suddenly Kirsty was among them. A shy sweet girl, a younger duplicate of her mother, with the same fair skin, dark curls and wide dark blue eyes, and glowing color. A beautiful girl.

"Oh, here she is! This is my cousin Kirsty, Aunt Janet, Uncle Robert!" and Kirsty with a grace all her own gave a little courtesy, gravely smiling. And then she spoke.

"I came out to tell you that grandmother is awake and is very anxious to see Lord and Lady Warloch. Will you walk right in here? She is all ready for you."

They all arose in surprise. Lady Warloch with an anxious glance at her husband.

"But really, Margaret," she began, "we cannot take time to stop longer."

But it was a peculiar thing, how that procession formed toward the old Scotch lady's room, and fairly forced the two reluctant guests into it.

Lord Warloch was the last one to enter the grandmother's room, except John Galbraith, who had pleasantly herded him along, with genial talk about the prosperity of the day, and the financial state of the country. Somehow he had to keep constantly reminding himself that this host of his was far beneath him in rank and class, for in spite of him he seemed almost to be liking him. He hadn't had a man—or woman either—talk to him as if they liked him in many, many years. Could it be that there had been some mistake all these years, and these Galbraiths were really worthy people after all, even if they were not as great as the MacCallummores?

"But really," said Lord Warloch at the very threshold of that wide old charming room belonging to the grandmother, "we should be going on at once. It is a long drive home, and we must get home before dark if possible."

But John Galbraith only smiled and waved his guest

inside, calling out, "Mother, we've come, and here is Lord Warloch come to greet you!"

And in spite of his worst self Lord Warloch came about to face the great old four-poster bed that spoke of centuries of ancestry, and looked into the sweet delicate face of the little old lady in her white linen mutch and kerchief. He was startled into behaving for the moment almost like anybody. Instead of his lofty haughty bearing, he approached that bed with the ordinary interest of a person who was seeing something entirely new and astonishing. His eyes were on Grandmother Galbraith as if she had been a rare old museum piece.

And Grandmother Galbraith's eyes were on Lord Warloch's face as he approached. When he stood at the very foot of the bed looking at her with keen glance, she suddenly turned her gaze for an instant on Lady Warloch, who stood beside him, and a smile blazed forth on her fine old features.

"A'm rare pleased that ye've come," she said quietly, the Scotch accent only softening her speech and giving it a fine touch of what seemed unusual culture. "For many years a've been wearyin' tae look upon yir faces. A' cudna believe that luvin' people wud choose for that sweet lassie, Margaret, yir ain sister, riches an' a castle instead o' the luve of a lad she luved like her life! But I see noo, yir not luvin' fouk. But my laddie, Gilbert, wes indeed a lad o' pairts, an' prood ye micht hae been o' him gin ye'd but let yirsels ken hoo fine he was. An' he luved an' cherished his Margaret till he went hame tae Heaven, but ye never gied yirsels a chaunce tae ken him. A've always hopit ye'd coom tae see yir fault all in guid time. But time has gane intae years, an' the twa ye wranged are baith in Heaven where ye canna ask their pairdon the noo! Ye didna do it while there was time, an' noo ye hae the greater shame that the years hae not taught ye better."

The old voice, strong and clear now, paused as if to give opportunity for denial of her words, but the two stared stonily awestruck, as stiff as two straight-backed chairs.

"And noo," she went on sadly, "though it's ower late tae speir forgiveness of the two maist concerned, there's still time tae repent an' tae speir forgiveness o' God. For lord and lady though ye be, ye will baith stand some day before the throne of God, tae give accoont o' the deeds done in the body. An' the Lord your judge will na ask ye, did ye have great riches on the airth, or did ye live in a castle, or run in the royal social ways? He wull ask ye, 'Hoo did ye treat the Lord's ain bairns?' Sae I'm warnin' ye baith tae get doon on yir knees afore it is too late tae make peace wi' yir God for the wy ye treated the responsibeelities He gave. Ye are not sae yoong as once ye were. Ye've no sae lang ta live ony mair, an' yir ca' may coom ony day, sae waste no time. That's a' I have tae say. Good day to ye, Lord an' Lady Warloch."

She lifted one frail hand and waved them away, then dropped back on her pillow, closed her eyes and turned her face quite away from them.

It was her son John Galbraith who touched the image Lord Warloch had become, and whispered:

"She's awa tae sleep again, we'd better gang awa," and led them forth from the room, closing the door softly behind him.

"She's na sae althegither there at a' times," he explained sadly. "Times she wearies for her ither lassie Rose who married and went to Australia. It was for that reason we wanted the other Rose to come and help to comfort her. And she has indeed done much to help."

But Lord Warloch marched along with a grim bow of

his head, as if he were at a funeral and one of the pall bearers had spoken to him. He stalked straight through the big room looking at nothing, and over to the open door, a half-frightened look in his eyes, darting a quick backward glance now and then as if something terrifying were following him.

"Won't ye sit doon an' have a coop o' tea wi' us?" came Jessie Galbraith's sweet voice. "It's a' ready the noo. Kirsty, bring the tray. Sit ye doon, Lady Warloch!"

But Lady Warloch cast a frightened glance toward the lean stalking form of her husband as he stepped from the door and started down the path to the gate.

"Oh, no thank you," she said in an undertone, as if she feared Lord Warloch might hear her. "We must go. We really must go. It's a long drive back to Edinburgh." She fairly scuttled from the door and down the walk, leaving no room about her for the gentle voice of Jessie Galbraith who was trying to tell her how glad she was that they had come.

Tealess the Warlochs climbed into their car and sped away without so much as taking time for the gesture of a farewell bow. Into the sunset they went, while David stood in the doorway looking after them and said aloud:

"Well, I like that! They even forgot what they came for, they were so kriestled! They never said another worrud aboot takin' Rose alang wi' 'em. Grandmither's worruds must hae gane deep!"

Lady Warloch sat with bowed head by her husband's side with wet tears streaming down her face, and never an attempt to wipe them away. But the hard cold eyes of her husband did not even notice them. He was staring down at his feet like one accused.

They might have gone perhaps a mile out of the little town when Lady Warloch spoke.

"You know it was all your fault!" she said, and her tone was full of accusation.

Lord Warloch turned his head and looked at her, and she saw his eyes looked frightened.

"What was all my fault?" he asked fiercely. There was threat in his voice and glance, but Lady Warloch was not noticing.

"It was all your fault that my father and mother turned so against my sister. It was you who told them that was the way to manage her. And then after she went away it was you who said she deserved her own punishment, and they must never forgive her nor take her back, or they would lose prestige in the county. You said that she would be sorry by and by and would come back and ask to be forgiven and taken back; that then they could have that common marriage annulled and marry her to Lord MacCallummore in the end. You said it would bring them great wealth. You knew my father was in distressful circumstances so that he would listen to such an argument."

"What if I did?" asked the dour voice. "Your people might have had minds of their own, if they hadn't known I was right. They didn't have to do what I suggested."

"But you said the Galbraiths were a low-down family, and you threatened not to marry me if we were connected with such common people. You threatened to come down on my father for the money he owed you if he let my sister marry common people. You were wrong! They are not common people!"

"I am *never* wrong!" said Lord Warloch with grim set lips below his frightened eyes.

"Yes, you were wrong," went on the steady relentless voice of the woman who had not dared for years to speak her own mind. "You have seen today that you were wrong. Those are wonderful people, and my sweet little sister found it out, and you separated us from each other, and kept us separate all these years! And it isn't true that you are never wrong. You have been wrong all the way through. I could see that you believed it when the old lady told you. And it won't be long now before we have to meet God, just as she said, and then what shall we do? You won't dare tell God that you are always right!"

Lady Warloch was almost beside herself with hysteria. She had never so given way to her feelings before in her life. She had been brought up to reverence wealth and castles, and her husband, but now suddenly they had failed her, and she was a-jitter.

"Be still!" thundered the hard old voice. "I am your husband, and I am in place of God to you, and I say be still! I am never wrong!"

Then he closed his tight old lips and they rode in utter silence all the way to Edinburgh.

15

GRANDMOTHER Galbraith was very weak for several days after this visit of the Warlochs, and the family walked softly, not sure but the angel of death might be hovering near.

"It was a great strain for her to speak that way," said Donald gravely. "She ought not to have done it. It wasna what you'd call courteous."

"Na, I wudna say that, Donnie," said his father. "Ye canna tell what the Heavenly Feyther tellt her tae say. It was a' true, an' she hes had mony a year to con it o'er in her hert. Wha shall say the Lord Himsel' didna gie her the verra worruds? It mayhap have been the Lord's way o' sendin' Lord Warloch His message. Grandmither is on the borderland of anither worruld. A worrud frae her would na come sae ill as frae you or me. Didna ye see the lord's ashen face as she spake? An' he no took his eyes frae the face of her. We are no tae judge. But it went sair with my mither tae alloo sic worruds tae pass her gentle lips. She was e'er sae sweet spoken."

Around the fire that night at worship they felt the lingering shadow of death again, and prayed, one by one, that the beloved grandmother might be spared yet awhile in their midst.

Slowly she seemed to rally again and come back almost to normal. One day she came out among them of her own accord, with her old plaid about her shoulders, and sat down awhile and smiled at them all.

But she never mentioned the recent visit of the Warlochs, and they never mentioned it to her. Perhaps they hoped that she did not remember it. Certainly it was locked behind her sealed pleasant lips. Though they did notice that her eyes sought all around the room until Rose came in and sat down with a bit of sewing she was doing, and then her sweet smile bloomed out.

"The Lord be thankit that ye're here yet, lassie. A' was sair tribbled in a dream last nicht that ye had gane awa back tae thae castle."

"Oh, no, grandmother," said Rose happily. "I like it here best, the way my own mother did. I love you all. Some day I may have to go back to America, but not until you're quite well, grandmother!"

The old lady smiled tenderly.

"My lassie! My ain wee lassie!" she murmured, and then they could see that it was the other Rose she was thinking of, the Rose who was so far away in Australia, and whose letters seemed to her so far apart. "My wee lassie Rose," she said softly, "that used tae sit in her wee chair by my side an' smile at me!"

But one day there came a letter from that other Rose saying that she was coming home at last to stay. Her husband had a promotion and he was to represent his company in England. She wanted to know if there was room in the cottage for them all to come home and stay awhile, at least until they could look around and find a house for themselves.

And there was great rejoicing that day. Somehow the

weakness of the old lady seemed suddenly to become strength, and she was awake betimes and about the house, doing this and that and the other thing until the boys had to bring her bodily from the kitchen and tell her that she must not do any more, she must lie down and rest.

But how they did gather around the fire that night and talk it over, and plan how they would stretch the dear wide house and make it big enough to gather in all the "bairns."

"I don't need a whole room to myself," said Rose thoughtfully. "Can't I go into that tiny room at the top of the stairs? Or did you need that for one of the children? What I really ought to do, of course, is to go back to the castle for a few days and then take ship back to America and get at my teaching. But I would love to stay a few days just to see Aunt Rose, I've heard so much about her."

"You dear lassie!" said Jessie, looking lovingly at her. "Ye're na tae think of sic a thing. This hoose is plenty big for a' the family, an' we'd be sair disappointed tae hae ye gane when the ither Rose comes alang. Ye're sae muckle alike we're wearyin' tae see ye thegither. An' grandmither, here, wud miss ye sair."

And they all chimed in to assure her that she could not go.

"You'll come and sleep with me, of course," said Kirsty happily. "I've always wanted a sister and now I've got you. My room is wide and there is plenty of space!"

"But of coorse, gin yir hankerin' for a braw castle," broke in grandmother with a twinkle, "we'll na hold ye tae a cottage!"

"Oh, grandmother! If you only knew how glad I was to get away from that 'braw castle.' It was just my mother's portrait and her darling piano that kept me there as long as I stayed, but it would fill me with horror to go back. Oh, I'll be only too glad to stay here and have all the fun of getting ready for Aunt Rose."

So the very next morning, although it was yet many days before the Australians could be expected, the two girls began fixing up their room together.

"There's na need for you to disturb yourself yet, dear," said Jessie. "Better stay in the big room till juist before they coom."

"Oh, but we want to," cried Kirsty. "It's going to be fun. Mither, I've cleared out one of my two cupboards and Rose has her things hung there already, and we're going to have grand times together."

So they moved in together, for they had grown heart to heart already, and were happy in the change. And then they went at fixing up the guest room that had been Rose's, getting it ready for Aunt Rose and Uncle Harry. They brought down a quaint little mahogany crib for the new baby of whose arrival they had just heard, a third little Rose who would one day soon fit the little rocking chair that grandmother had been saving so carefully.

And while they were putting up the fresh curtains at the windows and arranging where the crib should stand, grandmother came walking in and looked around a bit, her eyes growing dreamy and sweet. Then suddenly on the alert she said to Rose, "Come ye! Come wi' me!"

She led Rose into her own room whose door always stood open wide except when she was asleep, and pointing to the little rocker she said:

"Tak the wee chair in tae the room for the wee bairnie. A've been savin' it ower lang. It's time it was used, the noo. Praise God, her name's Rose, too!"

So Rose carried the precious little chair into the room, and they all were gay and happy as they put the finishing touches to that room.

It was a very happy household with grandmother feeling daily more like herself, and getting about slyly, managing to do things that she wasn't allowed, just to feel herself a part of the general joy over the homecoming of her daughter and her family. It seemed wonderful to Rose to be in the midst of real happiness.

And then came another letter from Gordon McCarroll. Her heart gave a leap and sent the lovely color to her cheeks as the postman handed it to her at the door. It seemed to her that no handwriting had ever been so fine and clear and wonderful as the hand that Gordon wrote.

She slid it quickly inside her blouse and took the rest of the mail in to the family. Then slipping out the back door she made her way to the little rustic seat the boys had made between two trees back in the shady part of the yard, and there she settled down to read her letter. He had written again! He seemed to like to write to her. That is, he hadn't forgotten her.

It thrilled her inexpressibly, and there was a lovely look on her face as she read on. Jessie, from the pantry window where she was sifting flour for setting bread, caught a glimpse of her and smiled. "Dear child!" she said to herself. "How happy she looks! Oh, I hope it's not some silly sweetheart who is writing to her, making her uneasy to go back to America! She seems like our very own child! If Don and Davie did not each have a girl already I could think of no better wife for either one than this sweet Rose. But of course they're own cousins and it wouldn't be good. But I do dread something unpleasant that may be coming for this little girl, with no mother any more to guide her!"

But if she could have looked over Rose's shoulder and read parts of that letter she would not have been so worried.

I'm so glad, *wrote Gordon McCarroll,* that you have got away at last from that grim old castle. I had a feeling from the first that that wasn't the place for you. Queer, isn't it, when I don't know the place nor any of your people. But when you feel you know somebody pretty well and their reactions, you can't help forming some idea of what they are going through. And I've been thinking a lot about you since the night on the boat when we said good-by, and also since your letters have come. And somehow it seems as if I had known you very well always.

Why, I can look back to those days in school and see you standing beside the third seat from the front looking with such a clear untroubled gaze toward old Miss Criswell as she asked you questions in algebra. You were never caught napping, and I got used to listening when you got up to recite, because you always had something interesting and new, or else it was put in an original way. I mean this. I always admired the way you took your education, as though it was something you really wanted and not just something that was being stuffed down you. I'm not just trying to throw bouquets at you across the water. I'm only proving to you that you and I are old friends and have known each other always. That is, a long time. And we have a right to take it for granted that we understand each other's language, and enjoy each other's company. Is that all right with you? Because that's the way I feel about it.

So, after a long day's work in a hot city I'm enjoying coming back to the comparative coolness of my room and having a chat with you.

I liked your description of your Uncle John's cottage. I'd like to see it in person some day.

And your introduction of the whole family was rare. I'd like to meet them all. I think I'd know them if I passed them on Fifth Avenue some day.

And how great to have a grandmother like that! I like Uncle John and Aunt Jessie too. I'd like to be one of the group that kneels around the fireplace mornings and evenings to worship. That was never a part of my experience since grandfather died, but I wish it had been. I'd like to begin and end the day that way.

And I like the church you are attending. I'd like to hear that great, simple man. Not everyone can form a single sentence that can travel across the ocean and stir a fellow's heart the way the one you quoted stirred mine. You've given me food for thought for many days. I wish you would go to that church among the trees many times again, and tell me all about it every time. I mean it. I want to hear more.

She caught her breath and tears of joy sprang to her eyes. It seemed so wonderful to her that anybody from school should be interested in Christian things. The group she had known thought that high school was the time to cast away such outworn things as the Bible and church and prayer. Oh, some of them still went to Sunday School, but they didn't take it seriously. Therefore it rejoiced her that this boy, who had seemed so fine and far above the ordinary, should react toward this wonderful gospel she had been hearing with the same enthusiasm she felt herself.

A bird in the tree over her head fluttered out to the

end of a twig on the branch, turned his head this way and that, eyed her trustfully, and said "Tweet, tweet, tweet!" Then it hopped about and flew away unfrightened, and Rose, with a light in her eyes went on with her letter.

> There is just a possibility that I may get a long enough vacation this summer, probably along in September, to run across the water. If I do, will you let me call and see you?
>
> I hope you don't think I'm crazy with all this daydreaming. But I certainly would like to see you again and have a good long talk. We must have a lot of things in common that we never have talked over.
>
> Address your letter to the office unless I let you know otherwise.
>
> As ever, your friend,
> Gordon

Rose sat for some minutes over that letter. The very idea of Gordon's coming to call on her over here, fairly took her breath away. It seemed as if she must be reading a fairy story and trying to fit herself into the title role. It didn't seem real. What would some of the girls at school think if they knew she was corresponding with Gordon McCarroll? Corresponding! Yes, that's what it could be called now. He had spoken of her future letters as if he expected them to go right on indefinitely. She was really corresponding with the nicest boy in high school.

Of course high school was almost two years past now, and they were both grown up, but this friendship was so comparatively new and of such rapid growth, that it seemed more like a vision or dream than reality. But

Gordon, coming over here to call on her! She could scarcely make herself believe it.

Then suddenly she remembered that they were making jelly in the house and she was supposed to be helping, and she fluttered her letter quickly into its envelope and hurried in.

"Oh, I'm so ashamed!" she said as she came into the kitchen and washed her hands quickly in the basin. "I got a letter from an old schoolmate in America, and I got so interested that I completely forgot what else I was doing. Please forgive me. Shall I stem these currants?" and she seated herself among the rest around the big yellow bowl, with a pan of unstemmed currants in her lap and began to make her fingers fly nimbly.

"A letter? That's nice. From an old schoolmate? That would be interesting, of course!" said Aunt Jessie sweetly. "Ye needna have hoorried. We have a' the time there is! Was it a school friend you're verra fond of, lassie?"

Rose's cheeks flamed rosily.

"Oh," she said, embarrassed, "why, yes, he's a good friend. We're just friends. It happened he was on the ship seeing someone else off as I was leaving. He's been very nice and friendly."

"So, that's the way the land lies," grinned Kirsty. "I thought you seemed unco interested the time the last letter came. Or was that frae anither schoolmate?"

Rose gave an answering grin.

"Oh, no. It was the same one. He's been very kind. He knew my mother was gone, and he thought I was lonely. He's just being kind, that's all."

"Oh, yes?" said grandmother suddenly appearing in the doorway. "But yon's the wy they begeen. We maun look oot or our bairn will be speerited awa."

Rose laughed gaily, her cheeks still rosy.

"Oh, nothing like that at all, grandmother. He's just one of the boys that used to go to high school with me. And I'm out of school now nearly two years. I haven't seen him since we graduated until the day I sailed. So you see."

"That soonds verra weel," said the grandmother with a twinkle in her eyes, "but it's weel tae tak warnin'. Juist what sort is this lad wha presoomes tae write tae my gran'cheeld? Is he a lord an' hes he a castle?"

"No, grandmother, he's not a lord, though his people are nice Christian people and I think they have a nice home though I've never been in it. We did not know the family. I only knew the boy in school. We had classes together. We never knew each other well outside of that. But he's a Christian. He likes to hear about family worship, and the church we go to here. He was considered the brightest boy in high school. He has some kind of a position in business now, though I don't know what it is. We've only written a few friendly letters. It doesn't mean a thing, grandmother."

"Weel, he'd better mean a thing or he'll be havin' tae answer tae me! I'd like tae look him over!"

"Well," laughed Rose, "he said in this letter that maybe sometime he would get over here and if he did he would come and call on me, so maybe you'll get a chance to see him yet, who knows? Though probably by that time he'll have forgotten all about me. Please don't get worried. Now, Kirsty, are there any more currants to stem?"

"No, they're all in the kettle now but those. You can help me get the jelly glasses from the cellar, though, if you will. They must be washed and ready."

So the pleasant bustle of the kitchen work went on and Rose grew happy with the thought of the letter in her pocket. Wouldn't it be wonderful if Gordon would come over some time and stop to see her. That was something to dream about like that parting kiss, and the flowers he had sent her on the ship. Something to rest her when she was tired and discouraged. Something that would probably never come true and didn't seem real at all, but it was lovely anyway. She smiled over it and went and put away her letter safely in the little box in her suitcase that locked, whose key she wore about her neck on a fine little chain.

And then, the very next morning the young Lord MacCallummore drew up at the gate in a shining car and demanded of the grocery boy, who was just going into the gate with an order, that he ask Miss Margaret Galbraith to come out to the car and talk to him; he flung a couple of shillings at him as he passed. The grocer's boy threw the money back into the car, gave him a contemptuous grin and swung into the gate without a word till he was half way up the walk. Then he turned and called back in broad Scotch, "Wha d'ya think ye air, onygait?" And when he came out he swung into his truck and rattled noisily away with a wicked young leer backward. And that despite the fact that he was in Kirsty Galbraith's Sunday School class.

So young Lord MacCallummore sat for several minutes in his sporty chariot and waited for a lady who did not come.

16

THERE were pleasant sounds from the thatched cottage as the work of the day went forward. Low well-bred voices from what must be the region of the kitchen, the ring of a spoon in a glass, the clatter of a pan that slipped to the floor, the chime of loving voices laughing. All too evidently there was no one in that house preparing to come out and converse with the young lord in his royal chariot, and Lord MacCallummore grew more and more angry as the minutes went by. Were they daring to ignore his request? Or hadn't the hoodlum of a boy done his bidding?

He glanced down at the money lying at his feet, finally picked it up and restored it to his pocket, and then stared at the house for another while. At last he remembered his car horn and blew it angrily, but nothing happened. If any had heard no one looked out of the windows, for the prim white muslin curtains were not disturbed. Well, was he going to sit all day and wait in front of a mere cottage? Did the girl think she was worth so much that she could treat him like the dust under her pretty feet? She must have a very great fortune indeed to be so haughty. And perhaps all the more was she worth the winning. Lord Warloch had said that after investigation, without actually putting any more questions to the girl about it, he felt that her fortune must be ample.

So after waiting again, for he carried a sour grim pride in his lank ugly frame, he flung himself from his car and stalked up the front walk to the cottage door, giving it such a thump with his bony fist as sent a thundering noise through the house.

Grandmother looked up from the spiced currants she was concocting and gave a startled look toward her daughter-in-law.

"Wha wud that puir body be?" she asked. "Is it the old lord come back tae resent ma wurruds? Ye'd best tak yir grand'ther's old gun wi' ye when ye gang tae answer that knock."

But Kirsty only laughed and hustled away to the front door.

She appeared before the young lord in her plain little working garb, with a "bit ribband" tying back her brown curls, and her eyes full of laughter at her grandmother.

The visitor looked at her in astonishment. What? another good looking young woman! Was she servant, or lassie?

"Is Miss Margaret Galbraith staying here?" he asked, and noted the sudden tilt of the girl's chin in a haughty gesture.

"No," said Kirsty loftily. "There is a Rose Galbraith, and a Kirsty Galbraith but no others."

"Well, I want the girl that came over here from Lord Warloch's castle, whatever her name might be, and I want her quick. I've waited long enough outside. I sent a lad for her, but she did not come, and I want her to come outside and talk to me. I am Lord MacCallummore."

Kirsty's eyes were flashing angrily, but her voice was steady as she said with a sweep back from the door:

"Will you step inside and sit down till I call my cousin and see if she is willing to talk with you?"

"Willing?" said the visitor. "Willing? She'd better be willing. Tell her it's very important. No, I will not come in. I wish her to come outside."

Kirsty left him standing outside the door, with the door standing wide so that he could see the lovely room, and could hear the scorn with which his message was delivered to Rose.

"Rose! There's a puir creatur' ootside the door whinin' tae see ye an' talk wi' ye, verra important business, he says. But he scorns oor hoose, an' wull no come in. Div ye wish tae see him? His name is Lord Me-cal-no-more! Maun I tell him ye'll no come, or div ye wish tae do his bidding?"

Rose grinned at her cousin, and then answered in a clear voice that my lord could easily hear:

"No, Kirsty, I do not care to see him, nor to talk with him, but you don't need to give him the message. I'll go to the door and tell him myself, and get the matter over quickly." Rose put off her kitchen apron, and went all flushed with her happy work into the big room. But there was no grin on her face as she approached the door, and saw the gloating look in the gray fishy eyes of the young lord.

"You were calling for me?" she asked coldly.

"Yes," said the imperious lord. "Come out to my car. I wish to talk with you alone."

Rose flashed a look at the car standing outside the gate and another of disdain at the man.

"I'm sorry," she said coolly, "I wouldn't care to go out and sit in your car, and I have no desire to talk with you alone. If you want to see me you must come in to the house where I am living."

"But it is a private matter," he said as he drew nearer the door and gave a keen, searching look about.

"Really?" said Rose. "That wouldn't make any difference. My relatives are to be trusted."

"I shouldn't care to trust anybody with my private affairs," said Lord MacCallummore scornfully. "Get your hat and we will take a ride. Your aunt would like you to come back to the castle. I told her I would bring you. Come at once. I am in haste. If there is baggage to be brought we can send for it afterward."

"It is quite impossible for me to go with you anywhere, and I do not wish to go back to the castle at present. I am needed here, and here I am staying. You may tell my aunt if you please that if I ever find it right to come back to the castle I will let her know by letter. But in any case I do not wish to go with you. I have cousins here who can take me if it becomes necessary."

She looked like a young queen as she stood there in her little cotton print dress, with battle in her eyes. Young Lord MacCallummore had a glint of almost admiration in his eyes. She really could be made to look like a lady. Perhaps it was worth while to try for this.

With this thought in mind he swung into the house and dropped into a chair.

"Well, really, now, you don't understand me," he drawled. "In point of fact I came down here as a favor to your uncle, to get a few facts for some business he had in hand. He was not well enough to come himself. And your aunt particularly asked me to stop and get you. Since your uncle is not well she says she needs you."

Rose stiffened again and looked at him with hard unbelieving eyes. She could not forget his tone of voice and the words he had spoken that night when she came downstairs for her bag and overheard him plotting with her uncle to perpetrate a marriage, with herself as the bride.

"It is quite impossible for me to go," she said again coldly. "I will write and explain fully to my aunt."

"Well, I'm sorry you do not see your way clear to going this morning," said my lord in the nearest to genial he had in the way of a tone of voice. "You see, there are a few questions your uncle needs to know at once, and we can find them out only from you. He said that in case you were unable to come at once he would like you to answer those questions. It is a matter of reports and so on. Government reports, you understand, which he has to file at once. It will be necessary for you to fill in the answers to this questionnaire which he has sent by me, and I will at once convey it to him of course. I can wait while you fill this out."

He handed her a typewritten sheet containing the questions. She took it with a startled suspicious look at him. Perhaps if she had not overheard that conversation at Warloch Castle she would have thought this merely some queer modern demand by a foreign country requiring an alien to file a report. But instantly she was on the alert. Looking up quickly she saw the sly gleam of satisfaction in Lord MacCallummore's eyes.

There was no heading to the paper except the word "Questionnaire." Then the questions followed.

1. What is the worth of your entire estate?
2. Where is it now held?
3. How much is in stocks or bonds? (State what kind and names)
4. In what form is the rest invested?

5. Is all your inheritance under your own power, or is all or part of it held in trust? If so state names and addresses of trustees.
6. Have you a guardian? (If so give name and address)
7. When do you come of age?
8. Will all your property at that time be transferred to your own keeping?

Rose read the paper carefully, slowly through to the end. Then she suddenly held it out to the man.

"I'm not going to make out any such paper as that!" she said crisply. "The answers to those questions are none of my uncle's business, and they certainly are not things for your government to pry into or for you to know. I am an American citizen, and I do not care to discuss my financial standing with you or anybody else over here. If there is any more of this nonsense I shall consult someone who has power to have this stopped. I have a very good friend whose husband is connected with the English Government and I shall appeal to him. I am sure it will not be pleasant for anyone who attempts any further questioning of this sort."

Rose's chin was high and her air was assured, though to tell the truth she was mightily frightened. Her habitual method of keeping in the background made it hard for her to maintain this position, for all the time something kept saying what if she was wrong and there was something to all this? She had to keep remembering that night on the stairs and the cold hard words of both men as they speculated on her probable fortune.

She suddenly began to fold the paper rapidly, and crush it in her hand.

"You can go back and tell my uncle that I have

nothing to say about this matter, and I do not wish to discuss it at any future time, either."

She stood back as if she were waiting for him to go, and he rose slowly, eyeing her strangely a baffled look in his eyes. Then he stretched out his hand.

"I'll take that paper, if you please," he said autocratically.

"No," said Rose quickly. "I shall keep this to show to my uncle, and to my friend who is connected with the government. I shall have the matter investigated."

It was a sudden thought and she was not prepared for the almost fright that came into his light eyes as he took another step toward her.

"I warn you that that paper is government property," he said severely. "You'd better be careful what you do with that."

"There is nothing on it to show that," said Rose assuredly, "but I shall take good care of it, and if any fault is found with me I shall be sure to exonerate you by telling the government just where I got this paper and just what you tried to make me do."

Her voice was almost trembling now, but she was looking steadily at him.

"Give that paper to me!" he demanded in a louder tone, a very harsh rough tone.

"No," said Rose. "I'm going to keep it. And you'll have to excuse me now. I hear my grandmother is awake. I must go to her." Rose went swiftly into her grandmother's room and closed the door sharply. Lord MacCallummore could distinctly hear the old-fashioned wooden button as it turned. But he came on with a stride and took hold of the latch, shaking the door, an ugly look on his face.

"Yes?" said the sweet voice of Mrs. Galbraith appearing in the kitchen doorway, "and what wud ye be wantin' in thae room?"

The man turned with a start of surprise, then saw it was only another woman, and the cunning look came back in his eyes.

"I want that girl. That Galbraith girl. She has something that belongs to me. An important paper. I want it at once, or I shall call the police. I am Lord MacCallummore!"

"Oh!" said Jessie in her mild sweet voice. "Now, think o' that! Verra weel! Juist sit doon. I'll ca my husband. He's juist driven in. Excuse me." Jessie vanished into the kitchen again. Lord MacCallummore with a furtive look behind him darted out the front door, and was into his car and shooting off down the street and out of sight before ever John Galbraith could get into the house.

It was an interesting thing that the very next day Lady Campbell came riding up in her fine car to call on Rose. Grandmother was feeling better that afternoon and had come out to sit with the rest with her knitting in her hands. Jessie was there with her sewing, and Kirsty and Rose were hemming some new dish towels, made from old homespun linen sheets that were wearing thin in places. They were all laughing and talking and being cosy together, when Lady Campbell came knocking at the door. For she didn't send her liveried servant up to the door to demand the family's attendance, nor even to find out if that was the right place. She came herself.

"I was sure this was the place," she said gaily as Rose came to meet her. "Just from your description in your letter."

She kissed Rose like a dear old friend, and sat right down with them all, as if she were one of them, and such a nice time as they had together! Jessie Galbraith felt that she would always count Lady Campbell as a personal friend after this. She drew her chair up to grandmother's and watched her knit, and then asked her to show her how to make that particular stitch which was new to her. With her own hands Lady Campbell knit a round or two, just to be sure she would remember, and when she handed it back to the old lady, grandmother said, "I shull never let John wear that sock. I shull always keep it tae show how Lady Cawmill knit in it hersel'!"

When she got up to go she told them she was going back to London the next week to attend a big government affair, and she would like to take Rose and Kirsty with her to stay for a few days. She would like to take the girls around and show them a few sights in London. Perhaps they would catch a glimpse of Her Majesty the Queen, for she was to be in town.

The girls' eyes glowed like two pairs of stars and they caught their breath in delight. Nothing like that had ever come to Kirsty, and as for Rose she hadn't ever expected any such greatness in her life.

"Mother?" said Kirsty in wonder. And Rose's eyes turned toward her aunt with a question.

Jessie's smiling eyes looked from one to the other girl and then beamed at Lady Campbell.

"That is a beautiful invaetation, Lady Cawmill, and I ken the twa lassies are verra gratefu' tae ye. But I'm thinkin' mayhap they've not the gairments tae wear, an' ye wud be ashamed o' them baith. My niece may have fittin' raiment, as she came prepared for a holiday, but my Kirsty's not sae well supplied, an' mayhap I wudna have time tae remedy the lack."

The girls gave a quick look at one another, Kirsty's a withdrawing glance, and Rose's full of eagerness.

"Oh, Kirsty can have anything of mine she needs," said Rose. "I haven't much that's grand, but mother got me some pretty things before she went, and she would like me to share them. Kirsty and I are about the same size."

"Dear children!" said Lady Campbell. "That is lovely! But I don't think there will be any lack. And if there is it will be my dear pleasure to supply it. You know I have no daughters of my own and I have always wanted some. I shall be so glad if you will share your girls with me for a few days, Mrs. Galbraith. Just let them come with what they have, and if there are extra occasions I can lend them anything they need. I have a whole wardrobe in my house of garments my nieces have left when they came up to London to stay over to some affair. So you needn't worry. I'm sure we can fix them up if necessary. Don't let clothes worry you for a minute! And now, that's lovely, and I shall stop by for you early next week."

They arranged the time and she drove away leaving a much excited group in the cottage, the mother and grandmother no less pleased than were the girls.

And so it came about that early the next week when Lord MacCallummore returned insolently, he found Rose had gone up to London to Lady Campbell's. And it happened that he knew who Lady Campbell's husband was and what position he occupied in the government. He turned without a word, to hurry back to his car, when up came Donald and David, those two stalwart young men, and met him face to face! Like a barrier they stood in his way.

"Is there aught I cud do for ye?" asked Donald with the courtesy a better lord than MacCallummore might have shown.

And David squared his broad shoulders and scowled at the lord.

Lord MacCallummore's light blue eyes showed fright like a runaway horse and he said with a drawn attempt at a smile:

"No thank you, I'm just going!" and strode down the walk and made quick his departure.

17

WHEN the girls got back from London they had many wonderful things to tell.

"Oh, grandmither, it was sae wonderful!" cried Kirsty. "The palaces, the gardens, the towers. And grandmither, the parties! It was grand! But best of a' we saw the Queen. Ah, but she's bonnie! And grandmither, she smiled at me! Of coorse she didna ken me at a', but she lookit richt straight at me, and bowed and waved her dainty hand!"

The girls scarcely gave anyone else a chance to speak for days as they chattered on about their adventures.

Rose wrote to Gordon, a great fat letter, and there were a couple of paragraphs that Gordon read over and over thoughtfully:

> And just think who we saw and heard in London! Our own wonderful preacher from the "kirk" here in Kilcreggan! It seems he spends most of the winter in London, where there is a conference place very much like the one here.

I think I shall never forget his talk last week. It was on "the power that worketh *in us*."

He explained how God has an eternal purpose for His son, and we (Christians) are all wrapped up in it. To fulfill it He must fill us with Himself, and so conform every one of us to the image of His Son. His Holy Spirit is the power working in us.

He said we live too much in the realm we call "soul," the realm of "feelings" and outside influences, the realm where all the fret and worry are, the moods, the forebodings; and we get to thinking that that realm is the only real solid one, and that we must stand or fall according to what happens there. But this realm is not the deepest thing in a child of God. There is something stronger, more lasting than all that: the *power* within all the members of the Body of Christ. That is more than sufficient to meet and overcome everything in us or outside of us, which is contrary to the Lord Jesus Christ.

His conclusion was that if we really believed all this we should not be occupied with ourselves, nor our moods. We should not even worry about our own imperfections, because God is surely going to fulfill His purpose by His power that worketh in us. All we need do is yield for Him to do it. And His purpose for us is that we should be conformed to the image of His Son.

This seemed to put Christian living in an entirely different light to me and I am very thankful for that sermon. I do hope sometime you can hear him. I know you would see how helpful he is.

The rest of her letter dealt with the thrills of her trip to London, the celebration they attended, where they saw the King and Queen. She added a few shy thoughts of her own, how it would be when she some day saw the King of Kings in His Glory. And then, just at the end she wrote:

It seems very wonderful to me that I am writing all my thoughts from the inside of my heart to you. I hope you won't think me bold to do this. Just lay it down to the fact that I am greatly lonely at times, and that you are the one whom God sent to say a few pleasant words to me when I was leaving my own world behind and going to a strange land. And while I have found some very dear relatives and a few friends since, still I feel that you are linked to my old life in which my dear mother was with me. Even though you did not know her, she was the great thing in my young days, and you were a familiar sight every day in school all those years.

I really feel that you are very kind to continue this pleasant friendship, now, after those first few moments of my need are over, and it is a great pleasure to have some one outside of myself to talk to. I only hope I do not bore you too much.

Sincerely,
Rose

When Gordon McCarroll received that letter he was just starting for a week-end house party at the shore. One of his old friends from school years had found out where he was in New York, and had called him up on the telephone, begging him to come, as she had an extra girl, and her brother whom she had expected was unavoidably detained by business. Would he be good enough to take her brother's place at a last-minute call? Especially as it was only because she hadn't known his address sooner that he had not been invited before.

Gordon hadn't wanted to go. The friend was not a great favorite, and he was tired to death, for the week had been sultry and his work had been strenuous. But because the girl was so insistent he had finally said yes, and then discovered after he hung up that he had barely time to fling a few things into his suitcase and take a taxi to the train.

As he went out the door he discovered quite a pile of letters in the mail box. He snatched them out and stuffed them into his pocket, too hurried to do more than glance at them. The one on the top was from his mother, he saw, as he tucked them away safely. He was pleased to reflect that he would have it to read on the train.

He was too anxiously busy watching traffic on the way to the station, wondering if he were going to make it in time, to look at his mail. He was getting the taxi fare ready, so that he would lose no time when he reached the station. And even at that he had to sprint to get to his train gate and down the stairs in time. He swung aboard at the last minute.

The trains mountainward and seaward were full on Saturday afternoon always, and he had to walk through three cars before he sighted a vacant seat. He had asked for a chair as he passed the pullman conductor, but that official shook his head decidedly. "No sir! Not a chair! All taken!" So Gordon made for the vacancy, scarcely glancing at the woman who sat by the window, her head bent, as she pushed a small overnight bag a little farther over.

"Is this seat taken?" he asked courteously, touching his hat. He glanced at the full rack overhead, noting there was no room for his suitcase.

The lady looked up and then he heard his own name.

"Gordon McCarroll! How perfectly gorgeous! Where did you turn up from, and can it be that you and I are going to the same place? How perfectly spiffy!"

And there was Sydney Repplier!

Gordon was very much afraid his dismay showed in his face, but he tried to muster his courtesy, and turn a light of welcome into his eyes.

"Why, Sydney! This is most unexpected! I thought you were already on the way to the Pacific. Wasn't that what mother wrote me last?"

"Oh, but I didn't go!" said Sydney moving over toward the window hospitably to make room for him. "Fran Tallant called me up and stopped me just in time. So I turned in my ticket and stayed over. Say, isn't this perfectly spiffy, darling. You of all people! I thought you were so thoroughly engrossed in business that nobody could get anywhere near you. But luck does turn, doesn't it? Do you know, there isn't another soul I'd have been as pleased to find sitting down with me as you. It quite makes up for not being able to get a chair. It will be a consolation for having to travel with the angry mob. Are you really going to Silver Beach? Great day!"

Gordon swung his suitcase down in the aisle close to the seat and sat down firmly endeavoring to adjust the disappointment in his face. He knew that courtesy demanded that he should say the idea was mutual or words to that effect, but in spite of him he couldn't lie.

"Well, that's kind of you," he said amusedly. "And do you mean that you are going to Fran Tallant's? Well, now, that's odd, isn't it? And it isn't anything that I expected to do, either. I had just come in from a hard week's work and Fran called me up and said her brother had failed her and wouldn't I come. She didn't know who else she could reach in time. I tried to beg off for I was worn to a frazzle, but she pleaded so hard I finally said yes, and then had to rush to get the train. If I'd missed it I would have had to send a telegram instead of going, for I understand this is the last train out there tonight."

"Yes, so they told me. But say, isn't it grand you didn't miss it? I never met Fran's brother, and it will be darling to have an old friend instead to sport around with."

She gave him an adoring look. She had evidently taken up a new line, and she no longer attempted to tell him all she knew. That line had failed with him, and she was wise enough to try another.

"Gordon, do you know, your mother was perfectly sweet to me. She took me up to New York and did her best to interest me in the musician of whom I had been told such great things. But he turned out to be rather a flat tire, and I couldn't see being under him all winter in a strange city, so I decided to have a really good time while I was east, and just leave myself free to go anywhere. And that's what I'm doing now. And to think my first date led me to an old friend! How wonderful!"

She edged nearer to him. He could smell the fragrance of the perfume she was using. Not bad! Sweet and subdued and refined. Her dress too was most attractive. And she was wearing the prettiest transparent gloves of delicate mesh that gave her hands a most alluring look. A couple of diamonds she was wearing sparkled deliciously through the white meshes, and her little wrist watch, delicately encircled with more small but perfect diamonds, made the hand a lovely thing to contemplate. Once the little hand flashed over to his in a beautiful gesture, not exactly shy, but very frank and free.

"Gordon, do you know you have the darlingest mother?" she said in a low earnest tone, with a warm pressure of that meshed bejeweled hand on his.

He smiled and looked down at the little hand, half annoyed, half surprised. This wasn't like the former Sydney, this confiding childlikeness. He wanted to get away from her hand, yet not too obviously. He didn't like to be stirred by a warm well-tended little hand like that. And yet was he a fool? He didn't really belong to anyone else, and he mustn't hurt this girl. Perhaps he had misjudged her. After all, hadn't his mother sort of wished her on him once? Maybe mother was keener than he was. For mother's sake he mustn't hurt her.

"Oh yes," he answered quickly, "she's a peach of a mother." And then, "Excuse me," he said suddenly, "I've just remembered something. Some important papers. I wonder if I've left them behind me in my hurry. If I have I shall have to get off at the next station and go back, for I can't risk losing them."

He went wildly feeling through his pockets, and suddenly came upon the little sheaf of letters in the outside pocket next the aisle, the letters he had entirely forgotten. His mother's letter! And now there wouldn't be any chance to read it, as he had hoped. His mother's letters were always a delight, but he didn't like to share them with strangers.

He took the bunch of letters out of his pocket and ran them through lightly, as if he were hunting for some special paper, and it was then he saw Rose's letter, hidden between a business letter and his mother's. The sight of it and the touch of it thrilled him, as no dainty diamond-studded hand could do.

"Oh!" he said, shuffling the letters together and covering them deftly with his hand as he stuffed them into his inner pocket where they seemed to warm his tired heart. "Now I remember where I put it."

"Have you found it?" asked Sydney eagerly. "You don't have to go back, do you? Because you couldn't anyway. This train is an express and doesn't stop till we get to Silver Beach. What was it that was so important? Couldn't it wait till Monday morning? It's horrid that you have to be tied so to business. You don't seem like a business man to me. You ought to be having a good time. You're too young to settle down to business. What was your old paper anyway that was so important?"

"Just something that I was afraid I had mislaid, something that I was entrusted with that I couldn't leave around for others to see." Gordon was half musing as he spoke. Speaking in parables with a double meaning for his own soul. For the thing that he had really been afraid of losing, he told his own heart as he talked, was the precious loyalty that belonged to a kiss he had once given almost casually, a kiss that he found later had been real. And that little hand laid on his, those large handsome eyes looking warmly into his eyes had been reaching out for his fleshly soul and trying to seize that loyalty of his for their own. But he was glad beyond anything, with a great relief, that he had drawn away from that detaining little hand, and could now feel the letter over his heart. Perhaps he was fantastic but it seemed to him that that letter had come just in time to bring him to himself, before he dallied with a situation that would have always brought him a memory of weakness. He didn't want to have such memories in his life. They would seem to discount the memory of that kiss on shipboard. It had lived already too long in his heart for him to dishonor it now, even by a passing sensation that belonged to a girl he did not love. If he had wondered but a moment since whether she could ever become one whom he could love, he had no doubt about it now. He felt that Rose had come with a look of her clear blue eyes to make him sure that he wanted no girl like this one beside him.

"By the way," he said, animatedly, suddenly rousing

himself to distract her attention from the paper he had professed to lose, "have you ever been down to this house at Silver Beach? Do you know what an altogether delightful place it is? You know it is built practically out on the water, at the end of a long wide pier. And when there is a storm at sea the beauty is wild, tempestuous. You feel as if you were on a ship and about to go down."

"Oh, horrid! I shouldn't like that. Do you mean we'll be in a place like that tonight? Now, you've spoiled the whole thing for me. I shan't sleep a wink tonight thinking of a possible storm."

"Oh, you wouldn't anyway, with all the jamboree they'll have going on. They always have a gay time, lots of fun and frolic for those who like it."

"But don't you like it?"

"Well, some of it, but most of it is too sophisticated. I can't say I'm fond of the modern world. And besides I'm tired as the dickens after the heat and the hard work of the week."

"You poor thing!" pitied Sydney. "Why can't we go out in the woods? Aren't there woods around there? It seems to me I've heard that."

"There are trees, yes, and a lovely garden built on the pier, and quiet places here and there. Sometimes moonlight on the sea. But you seldom see much of it at such affairs. There's too much else going on. I fancy you'll find that out as soon as you get there."

"Oh Gordon! You're spoiling it all! And I thought we were to have such a wonderful time among the pines or something like that. But darling, couldn't you and I wander off and have a quiet restful talk together? That's just what I'm longing for."

"Try and do it!" laughed Gordon. "You'll probably find that everybody else would wander off with us. Besides, if I should go where it's quiet I'd probably fall asleep,

I'm that weary. But don't you worry. You'll find something pleasant for every hour of the day and night. Do you
play tennis? They have a wonderful tennis court, and a
swimming pool. Isn't that odd, a swimming pool right out
above the ocean. Me, I'd much rather have the real ocean
than to have it piped through a line and put in a painted
pool. However, everything there is odd as it can be, and
of course delightful. I'm told there is a very fine collection
of Chinese pottery there that the uncle has just brought
home from China. He's quite a collector. Are you much
up on that sort of thing? You've studied so many odd
subjects, have you ever looked into that?"

"Oh, yes," said Sydney dropping easily into her former character of mentor. "I spent quite a good deal of
time studying Ming. Do you know the characteristics of
that? It's fascinating. I'm just wild about them. I have an
adorable Ming bowl that I wouldn't part with for a
fortune." She launched into an intricate description of
her Ming bowl that lasted while they whirled past several
stations. Gordon, who didn't know Ming from a pussy
cat, had his mind dreamily on the letters in his pocket,
trying to decide which to read first when he got a chance
to read either one, then trying to think of another good
subject to launch with his young instructor that would
occupy the rest of the time until they reached Silver
Beach. The less he knew about the subject the better it
would be for she would have all the more to explain to
him. And while she was eagerly talking about something
in which she was interested she didn't seem to sit quite
so close to him, nor appeal to him with her dainty hands
on his arm or his knee quite so often. He loathed being
touched. He wondered why she did it. Was it a new line
she was practising? She had seemed too matter-of-fact to
be a real flirt, he thought.

It was queer about minds. You could keep them going,

asking an almost intelligent question about a thing of which you were wholly ignorant, if you tried, and yet in another part or section of your mind you could keep up a wholly different line of thoughts, with visions of absent ones, and imagined conversations running along much nearer to your real self than the actual conversation.

But at this stage the train slid into a station with the obvious intention of stopping. Sydney looked out, and then cried ecstatically, "Here we are at last! Silver Beach! And oh, Gordon, I'm so *proud* to be arriving in your company!"

She slid her pretty gloved hand inside his arm, and nestled closer emphasizing every word with a little sort of squeeze of his arm. My! how he hated it.

Quietly but firmly he removed her hand from his arm and arose, saying in a matter-of-fact tone, "Yes, it seems we have arrived. Is this all your baggage up here?"

"Oh, yes," she said deprecatingly. "I had to bring everything I had with me for I didn't know just where I was going next, you know. Don't you bother. Call the porter, please."

But Gordon swung her things down, bags and boxes and magazines, and a big box of candy, in addition to the suitcase at her feet, and piled them up, a barricade between himself and her, as he stood out in the aisle while the train came to a stop.

He was relieved to find a big limousine at the station waiting for them, with a couple of girls and a young man he knew already in it, and amid the clamorous greetings he managed to place Miss Sydney Repplier in the back seat with one of the girls and the young man while he and the other girl took the middle seats. He could see that Miss Repplier made several attempts to change with the other girl, without success, and he felt a wicked glee that he had escaped. What was it about Sydney, anyway, that made him feel almost afraid of her, afraid of that delicately pretty firm white hand on his hand, on his arm, afraid of her big pleading eyes looking into his. Why did he feel as if she had some kind of drawing power like quicksand that might even yet overwhelm him and spoil the beauty of his future? She was a nice girl, a beautiful girl in a way. But not a girl he wanted.

Amid the bevy of servants when they arrived at their destination, he managed to escape from her purring possession and was rejoiced to have a few moments in his room by himself to read his letters before the other fellows came in. Somehow he didn't feel a part of this affair at all. He wanted to get out and away. And after he had read Rose's letter he felt even more so. There were thoughts in that letter that he wanted time and quiet to digest. Thoughts that seemed too wholly sacred for any touch with this world in which he had been caught for the evening and the morrow. Conformed to the image of His Son! How could this experience in which he had allowed himself to be involved help in any way toward conforming him to the Son of God?

He was glad when they came down to dinner to discover that he was not seated next to Sydney, though he could see there was annoyance on her face, and he heard her telling in a clear voice that all could hear, that she had come down in company with Gordon McCarroll. He smiled affably at the young woman on his right, and absorbed himself so fully in conversation that Sydney could not possibly think he had heard her. And he managed to convince Fran whose troubled gaze was wandering up and down the table to make sure she had seated people pleasantly, that he was entirely satisfied with the way she had arranged matters, even if Sydney wasn't. He set his jaw a bit firmly in an interval of talk, resolving to make some excuse and find a way to get back to the city tonight or very early in the morning if it could possibly be done.

When the dinner was over and they drifted out on the great porch with the silver sea all about and the fresh breeze blowing in from the path the moonlight was making across the water, he suddenly found Sydney Repplier beside him, looking up confidingly into his face, slipping her white arm inside his. She was beautifully gowned in something white and silvery, and again he had that distinct sensation of a lure, the little hand on his arm, glittering with more jewels, resting so lightly, just touching his wrist, almost as if she had a right.

And anger rose within him as he stood there, and he was glad of the semi-darkness that hid the annoyance in his eyes. He just could not, would not, be taken possession of by this girl! It was outrageous. Just because her mother and his mother went to school together. School was a great bond, but it couldn't bind the children. He had a bond with his school too, but it was different from this. His girl wasn't running around fishing for a man, as so many girls seemed to be doing today, trying out this line and that, determined to succeed, as if the whole of life consisted in getting married!

He looked down at Sydney.

"Lovely night!" he remarked irrelevantly.

"Yes, isn't it," purred Sydney. "And you promised to take me down in the woods and the garden, you know. I think this would be a lovely time to go. Is this the way down?"

He followed her perforce, and they walked slowly down the flower-bordered paths, and out toward the denser foliage on the land side of the man built island.

"You know, Gordon, I think you're perfectly wonderful!" said Sydney earnestly. "You have so much strength of character. I was watching you at the table.

You never touched the wine. Everybody around you was drinking, having their glasses filled again and again, and you never touched it."

Gordon laughed.

"Why, that doesn't take strength of character for me," he grinned. "I was brought up without it. I loathe the smell and the taste of it, and I despise what it does to human lives and human souls. Sometimes I can hardly sit at a table where drinking is going on when I see nice sweet girls drinking, and fine men who are letting themselves in for being ruined. A good many of them do it just because everybody else is doing it. But it doesn't take strength of character to say no thank you. I wouldn't have to eat onions if I didn't like them just because I was afraid somebody would laugh at me, or call me peculiar, would I? I don't call that strength of character. I call it common sense."

"Oh, but you are wonderful!" said Sydney. "Your mother must be so proud of you!"

With relief Gordon saw someone approaching, just emerging from the woods, and as he drew nearer he recognized the man as Palmer Atkinson, the man he suggested that his mother "wish on Sydney." Here was his chance! He had never been glad to see Palmer Atkinson before, but now he really was, and glad too, that he was alone.

He made the introduction rather elaborate, professed to have long desired that these two should meet, asking the Atkinson one to go with them to the woods, and when they were well started, he paused, hesitated, and then said:

"Palmer, I wonder if you'd mind taking Miss Repplier down to see the pool in the woods. I've got to make a phone call, and I'd like to do it now before my party gets away for the evening."

"Oh, Gordon!" pouted Sydney. "Your mind is on your business all the time. You might just as well have stayed in your office the way you are doing. Can't you let your phone call go for for awhile? I wanted you to show me all those lovely places you spoke about on the way up."

"Oh, that's all right, Sydney," said Gordon amusedly, "Palmer knows those places. I think he knows more of them than I do. He's often down here, and I've never been here but once before. You go on with Palmer and I'll get through this as soon as possible. Maybe I'll catch up with you before you've seen it all. Thanks, Palmer. I'm sure you'll show Miss Repplier a good time, and I'll see you later." Then he turned and hurried back up to the house.

As he mounted the steps to the porch he saw a car drive up. A young man got out. That looked like Fran Tallant's brother Edward.

"Say!" he said eagerly. "So you got back, Ed! That's great! How come?"

"Why, I found I didn't have to go to Boston after all," said the young man. "Fran was so upset at my going that I thought I'd come back. I'm mighty glad to see you here."

"But I've got to go," said Gordon with sudden resolve. "I'm just going in to make a phone call now. But I ought to go back tonight. Is there any station near here where I could get a train? Aren't there taxis nearby? Couldn't I drive to some station that isn't too far?"

"Why yes, Gordon, our man could drive you over to Pelham. It's only a matter of fifteen miles, and there's a train that passes there at eleven ten. I often have to do that. Sorry you have to go, old man, but we'll fix it for you all right if you find you absolutely must."

What Gordon did was to telephone his mother that

he was coming home on the one o'clock out to Shandon, and please leave the night latch off as he had forgotten to bring his key with him. Then he went back, hunted up Fran and made his excuses, wrote a little note of excuse to Sydney for not coming back, flung his things into his suitcase and was off before anybody realized he was going.

He had quite a wait at Pelham for the train was late, and the quiet darkness around the closed station as he marched up and down gave him plenty of time for thought. The letter from Rose was in his pocket and seemed a talisman. It had certainly helped him to discern between the worthless and the precious. His whole soul revolted at the program that he would have had to live through during the evening and on the morrow. He did not enjoy the kind of thing he had just left behind, and he did not care for many of the people who had been assembled for a good time. He was glad to be away. He was glad to have a chance to think.

Here in the darkness with the keen stars overhead, and the moon slipping softly down in the west, he seemed to be seeing Rose again as she was that night on the ship. Rose! Beside her vision all the faces of those gay smart girls in the crowd he had just left, paled and were only painted toys.

He thought of some of the phrases that were in her letter and suddenly his heart was at rest. He knew for a surety that it was Rose he wanted, and that somehow he had to see her soon or go heart hungry.

18

MEANTIME, Aunt Rose had at last arrived in Kilcreggan. With her family of course.

Donald and David seemed to have been in the secret, and knew exactly when that ship was going to dock. They had slipped away in the night so that grandmother shouldn't be excited. They met the boat train and brought them home.

Yet grandmother must have had some uncanny way of knowing, for when they came softly in at the door, even the boys muting their heavy shoes and suppressing their shouts of greetings, there was grandmother coming out of her bedroom door with her stiff starched mutch, and her clean kerchief, an air about her of having been up a long time, as if she had known exactly when the ship touched the dock.

And such a happy time! Rose standing back out of the way watching them all, with her eyes shining and her cheeks rosy, thought how wonderful it would have been if her mother could have been there. How great it was to have real relatives, a lot of them!

They stood the two Roses together and said how they

resembled each other. And afterward they escorted the new arrivals into the big guest room and stood around while the wondering baby's little cap was taken off. Her mother Rose even sat her down in the little rocking chair that grandmother had cherished all the years, and rocked her a little. Then the littlest Rose looked about on them all and laughed aloud, a little chuckling baby laugh, half between a laugh and a crow. Then she bent her little head down and laughed louder, looking about on them all admiringly, showing off in the sweetest way to the great delight of everyone.

It was a beautiful exciting day, full of lovely work and charming errands to be done. And oh how Rose loved that darling baby, and enjoyed picking it up and hugging it and kissing each tiny pink finger on the roseleaf hands, and laughing into the soft pink neck, the baby laughing too.

That day also there was a letter for Rose, from Edinburgh.

She was feeding the baby when it came, and she slipped it into the pocket of her apron when they handed it to her and she thought no more about it until late that night. Then she opened it.

She had known it was from Aunt Janet, for they had had three or four such letters before her mother died, relative to their coming back to Scotland. Though the crest and coat of arms was blazoned heavily in embossed gold and green on the envelope, these letters had never brought a thrill of anticipation, and even less now did she care about them. Some more fault-finding perhaps, that was all she expected. So she read it with growing amazement.

Dear Niece Margaret:

Ever since I came to see you a few weeks ago I have been troubled with some questions that I would like to ask you. If you were here we would sit down some day and talk about these things and perhaps it would ease my mind.

The questions are about dying.

Did your mother, my sister Margaret, know she was going to die before she became unconscious?

Did she ever say anything to you about it?

What did she say? I think it might help me greatly if I knew just what she said.

Was she afraid to die? I can't think of her being afraid of anything. But then death is different.

If she wasn't afraid, why wasn't she afraid?

Did she have anything, any belief, to keep her from being afraid?

If you will answer these questions for me I shall be grateful.

I don't think we shall take any more long journeys. Your uncle has been ailing ever since he came back. He seems much depressed and is very feeble.

I wish you would write soon.

Your affectionate aunt,
Janet Lachlan Warloch

Rose was very much stirred by this letter. The poor old lonely soul was getting frightened over the fear of death, and it was her responsibility to answer that, to say something that would give life and hope to her. She was her mother's sister, and her mother would have wanted her to know how to be safe and sure when she died. And there was no one but herself who could help.

She tried to think whose advice she could ask.

Not grandmother. She had had too much excitement anyway, and besides she had an innate feeling that it would be breaking a confidence, if she told any of them. They were loving gentle kindly Christian people who would know well how to point the way of life and assurance to a frightened soul afraid of death, but they were not Aunt Janet's family, and Aunt Janet might resent their knowing she had written. She would, of course. In fact they were all aliens to her. They were a part of the thing that had torn her mother away from them all these years. No, she could not ask any of them. It would not be right to let them know.

She considered how it would be if she were to go up and ask the wonderful preacher at the church, and then she put that aside. No, that would not do. The question was a personal family question, and no one else must be involved in it, that is, no one around here.

The thought came to her that if Gordon McCarroll were only here she could talk it over with him. He was the only one who could be entirely impersonal about it. She had never talked of such matters as fear of death or anything like that with him, but she somehow felt he would understand and would help her to know what to say. If he only lived around here and they were near neighbors, perhaps she would try it, because he always seemed to understand so well what she told him and to enter fully into her ideas. But he wasn't here, and that was out of the question. This letter must be answered at once. If anything should happen to Aunt Janet before she got it answered she would feel responsible. She felt as if her mother were standing there beside her urging her to write at once.

So she sat down at the little desk and wrote by the light of a flickering candle which she shaded from Kirsty's eyes by piling up a couple of pillows in front of her cousin.

Dear Aunt Janet:

I am glad to answer your questions as well as I can. Yes, my mother knew she was going to die two days before she left me. But I think she guessed it even before that, for she said many things to me about the possibility that she might not get well. For one thing she told me she wanted me to go on with the journey as we had planned it, and be sure to see you, her dear sister.

No, I don't think my mother was afraid to die. She told me that if it only were not that she would have to leave me alone, she would be glad. She knew Heaven was going to be wonderful, and she wanted to see the Lord, and to see my dear father, and her mother and father.

I think the reason she was not afraid to die was that she was trusting in the blood of Jesus to cover all her sinfulness. She believed fully that Jesus died on the cross and took all the world's sinfulness upon Himself, every sin, and paid the full penalty for them all. She knew that whosoever would believe that and accept the Lord Jesus Christ as their personal Saviour would go right to Heaven when they died. My mother was happy in that faith, I know, and the Lord was very real to her.

The last words she said to me were spoken a few minutes before she died. She had been asleep and she woke up with such a lovely light in her eyes, such a look of love and happiness, and she said, "Rose, dear, I'm going Home to be with the Lord Jesus! Your dear father will be there, too, and all my dear ones. I shall tell your father what a dear child you have been, though I think he knows it already. And Rose,"— she always called me Rose, though I was Rose Margaret—"Rose, I don't want you to grieve for me for I am going to be very happy in Heaven, and it won't be long waiting till you come, because I shall be with those I love and with my precious Lord."

Dear Aunt Janet, I hope I have answered your question in a way that will be helpful to you. I know that you can have the same assurance and joy about death that my mother had if you will take her Saviour for yours.

I am sorry my uncle has not been well. Please remember me to him, and maybe you will tell him, too, about this wonderful Saviour. For He is my Saviour too, and I'd like you both to know Him.

I shall be praying for you both.

Very lovingly, Your niece,
Rose Margaret Galbraith

The letter went on its way the next day, and Rose, though her days were full with dear delights, remembered often to pray for the poor forlorn hard old woman who seemed to have sold the beautiful birthright that might have been hers for a life of rules and regulations, a castle in Scotland, and a dominating crabbed old lord.

Rose could well remember her father, and the new Aunt Rose reminded her of him constantly. The way her eyes lighted up when anyone spoke to her, the way she crinkled her eyes when she smiled, the way she moved and spoke, the sound of her voice and the motion of her hand. It was all a dear memory which made her love her aunt most tenderly.

The little boys were a joy, full of life and fun, twinkling eyes, unruly hair always in a curly tumult, daring dimples in the curves of cheek and chin, rollicking laughter, untiring bodies always ready for a hike, or fishing or blackberrying, not afraid of snakes or any other creature that came in their way, willing to work like all the rest of the family, and liking it. Their father was a good man with many of their kindly witty traits more gravely set, deeply devoted to Aunt Rose, as Rose remembered her father had been to her mother. Oh, it was a dear family to belong to, and the baby was a precious treasure. The days were one sunny group of hours after another. How would she ever bring herself to leave them all and go back to America and teach music, and live by herself? Yet she knew that some day she was meaning to do just that, only the time did not seem to have come yet.

If she ever stopped long enough to think it out to a finish she knew that somewhere in the back of her mind was a responsibility for the grim old relatives in Warloch Castle. Somehow she ought to do something about them before she went back to America. And yet she shrank inexpressibly from ever going there again. She shrank from contact with Lord MacCallummore. Every time she recalled the talk about herself that she had overheard she shuddered involuntarily. Again and again at night she was kept awake puzzling over that talk. Could it be that her uncle was very hard up and was trying to get money out of Lord MacCallummore? Or was Lord MacCallummore the one who needed it? Yet she had always understood that the MacCallummores were wealthy, owning more than one castle. Perhaps it was all owned by the father and the young lord wouldn't come into it while his father lived. That must be it. He had said as much that night to Uncle Robert, yet she hadn't been able to work it all out.

And then her uncle. Why, if he was hard up did they keep so many servants and live in a castle, and own a fine limousine? Why didn't they go down in the village and live in a simple little apartment where Aunt Janet could do most of the work herself and just get in a woman to wash and clean? She couldn't understand the pride that refused to bow to circumstances, that starved along at half rations rather than own to poverty.

And yet when she thought it over she wasn't convinced that Uncle Robert was poor, either. Was he merely penurious? There were such people as misers in the world of course; that is, she had heard there were, but surely not among decent families. Surely it could not be anything like that. But unless it was, why, oh, why had Uncle Robert been so hard against the young lord, refusing to do anything for him unless he paid some debt he seemed to owe him? What did it all mean any way? And why did they involve her in the questions? Why were they anxious to know how much money she had? More and more as she thought about it she was convinced that her own thoughtless answer to her uncle's question as to whether her father had left her anything must be responsible for Lord MacCallummore's interest in her. She shuddered at the thought. And often at night when she knelt in the darkness to pray for Aunt Janet she began to pray for Uncle Robert also. Poor disagreeable old man! How stricken he had looked when he had walked away from grandmother that day! Had her words gone deep into his soul, too, as well as into Aunt Janet's conscience-haunted mind? And were they stirring something deeper than just pride? Making them both see themselves, as mortal souls who might some day soon stand before their Maker and have to answer for the deeds done in the body?

It was several weeks after her first letter that Rose received a second letter from Aunt Janet. The writing was straggling as if the hand that held the pen was trembling and uncertain.

Dear niece:

Your uncle has had a stroke and the doctor doesn't know if he will ever get well again. He is paralyzed on one side and has lost his speech. It happened one day while he was talking with young Lord MacCallummore. He had not been well since that day we came to see you, but he had got up to see Lord MacCallummore. They were talking about money, I think, and your uncle was much excited. Just as I was coming down the stairs I heard them get up and come to the hall door. I heard him say, "I will have nothing to do with the transaction unless you pay up at once!" and then Lord MacCallummore said something angrily in a low tone, I could not catch it, and your uncle reeled and put his hand to his head and fell heavily.

Thomas got him to the couch, and he has lain so ever since. Sometimes he opens his eyes and looks at me with such agony, I know he wants something. I have tried to think of everything. I think he is afraid he is going to die. One day when he looked that way I got your letter and read it aloud to him. He seemed to listen. His eyes were sort of wild.

The other day I found a little old fine print Bible that used to belong to your mother. I thought perhaps you would know of some place I could read in it to comfort him. If you do, let me know, soon.

It was nice of you to answer my other letter so quickly, and tell me all that. I think it helped me, too.

Good-by. I wish you were here. There might be some other things I would want to ask, but I guess you'd better not come now. It wouldn't be very good for you. Lord MacCallummore is here too much, and I know you don't like him. He is trying to find something he says your uncle told him about.

Yours as ever,
Aunt Janet

Rose sat down weakly on the step and read the letter over again. Strange foreboding filled her heart. Poor things! And they had no one to help! They didn't know the Lord, and they didn't know how to find Him! Their stiff formal church had not given them any intimate touch with the Lord Jesus. Oughtn't she to go? She didn't want to, of course, not with Lord MacCallummore there, and especially when her aunt had told her not to come, but maybe she ought to go anyway! Oh, if there was only someone to ask!

At last she got up slowly and went into the kitchen where she knew Aunt Jessie was at work. Aunt Rose was with grandmother, trying to coax her to take a nap, the boys were down in the meadow playing, the baby was asleep, and Kirsty had gone down to the store. No one would interrupt.

Aunt Jessie looked up with a smile.

"What's the matter, dear? You look troubled," she said. "Oh, you have a letter! It's not from your friend in America, is it?"

"Oh, no," said Rose with a fleeting smile, "I wish it was. No, it's from Warloch Castle, from Aunt Janet, and I don't know just what I ought to do. What do you think?"

So she read the letter, and then she told her about her aunt's first letter and her own answer.

Jessie Galbraith had wise sweet eyes and she watched

the face of the girl tenderly, and her own eyes were filled with sympathy.

When the reading was over she said:

"The puir lone buddy! She'll be hungerin' for the bread o' life, an' there's nae mon to gie it her."

"What do you think I ought to do, Aunt Jessie? Should I go to her? She says not, but I can't help thinking mother would feel I should."

Aunt Jessie looked troubled.

"Read the bit letter again," she said. So Rose read it again.

"I doot not ye are needed," said the aunt, "but a'll na gie my consent that ye should gang alane. Wait till the laddies coom hame, an' see what they say. Wait till yir Uncle John cooms. It winna be lang, noo. A'll no consent tae have ye gang in the neighborhood o' that ill-mannered yoong lord, comin' here tae inquire concernin' yir fortune. He bodes nae guid tae ye, my lassie. Na, ye'll not gang alane. Donnie wad gang wi' ye, or Davie, but baith o' them wud be an offense tae the Warlochs. They have an auld grudge frae yir mither's time, an' it wud be better tae have some guid body no connected wi' the family tribble. Let me think a wee whilie till feyther comes hame."

And then suddenly there came a knock at the door, and Rose hastened to answer it. She opened the door and there stood Gordon McCarroll!

19

GORDON McCarroll had arrived at his home in Shandon Heights at half past one o'clock the night he came from Silver Beach. With a warm hug and kiss from his mother and a sleepy growl of welcome from his father, he had gone straight to bed, after assuring his mother, of course, that there was nothing wrong in the world with him. He just wanted to come home, so he came.

He slept late the next morning, and so did they all. But after a good hot breakfast they all gathered in the cozy library, father in his big leather chair, mother in her own particular rocker, and Gordon stretched on the comfortable old leather lounge that had been his favorite all through the years. And then he began.

"Well you see, mother, it was this way—"

Even after his strenuous day, and his exciting evening, and the unexpected journey home, Gordon had not gone to sleep at once. Instead he had lain there in his bed, that was more comfortable than any bed he had found anywhere, and got to thinking. What had he come home for, and just what did he mean to do now?

It was these questions that he was about to bring out for his parents' perusal and advice.

Oh, he had thrashed them all out thoroughly in the night and he knew just where he stood now. There was no uncertainty in him any more. He knew that he loved Rose, and that he wanted no other girl in his life but her. His next task was to make his mother and father understand that, and be ready to rejoice in it with him. Could he do that?

Through that long sweet night vigil he had seen Rose almost face to face, he had thrilled with the touch of her lips on his, he had held her small white hand, empty of jewels, and seen the beauty in it as he had not seen it in that other jeweled hand. In his thoughts he had gathered her into his arms, and held her to his heart with wonder and amazing joy. Would he ever do it in reality, he wondered?

And so when the morning dawned he went down to his father and mother and lay on the couch and began to tell them.

His mother looked up with a hungry fear in her eyes, and let her loving heart take in the great beauty that love gives to a face when it has just newly come there to dwell. As she studied the beloved face of her boy, somehow she was reassured. He had not done something rash. Surely, surely, all his years of dependableness were not going to end in mistakes!

"Yes?" she said breathlessly.

But the father sat with a casual glance at his son, and a quick half fearful one toward the mother, and hid behind a quizzical smile of content. He would bank on his boy every time, but he wasn't just sure how the mother was going to take—well, anything new he might be going to propose. He had never been quite sure just how she was going to take anything.

"About this girl we spoke of several months ago!"

"Yes?" quick, almost appealing. Oh, if he would only hurry and relieve the anxiety.

"Well, I told you she wasn't anybody new. She's a girl I've known practically all my life."

"Yes?" Oh if he would only tell her name and end the anxiety. The mother's eyes sought the father's and found quick warning in their gentle smiling depths. No, she knew she mustn't ask for that name. It had to come of itself.

"Why, you don't need to be so darned scared, little moms," laughed Gordon. "She was just a simple sweet girl who sat across the aisle from me the last two years I was in high school, and before that she was somewhere else in the same room. She was bright as a button and very quiet and shy. She was always well-prepared with her lessons and always stood well, sometimes at the head of the class."

"When you weren't occupying that place," said his father in a serio-comic tone of mingled satisfaction and teasing.

Gordon grinned at his father.

"She was there more often than I, dad. But, you see, our contacts at that time were just the usual class room stuff. We saw each other, we said 'Hello' or asked a question about lessons, that's about all. She almost never came to any class festivity unless it was in regular school hours. She was never at the parties, and never seemed to have any 'special' friends."

"But why?" interrupted his mother sharply. "Is there something peculiar about her?"

"No, mother, she was only peculiarly sweet and well-behaved. I don't know why she never came to things we had, picnics and the like. I judged perhaps it was lack of time. She may have had to work. She dressed very simply, becomingly, but plainly. She did not seem to have her mind on amusements. She was in school to get her education and she was doing her best to get it. Beyond that I don't know much even yet."

"But Gordon, are you *sure* she is all right? You are sure there is no reason—"

"Mother, let the boy tell in his own way!" said the father.

"Yes, Gordon. Go on, please!" Her voice was fairly trembling with eagerness.

"Yes, mother, I'm quite sure. But you'll have to hear the whole story! We went on like that through the whole last term, and I never knew her any better. Sometimes I caught a glimpse of her as she was studying, and had a passing thought of how interested she seemed, but I wasn't paying much attention to girls then. Only as I look back now it seems as if I had known her intimately always, since I was a little kid."

"But why, why, Gordon, didn't she have anything to do with the rest? Was it their fault or hers?" asked his mother impatiently.

"I think it was hers," said Gordon. "She just went home, disappeared as soon as school was over, and nobody seemed to notice. I think it must have been on account of her mother being sick. She hurried away as if she had urgent business."

"Was it only girls who held aloof? Was she a girl who was popular with the boys?"

"No, mother, she never seemed to look at the boys particularly. She was just a part of school, a lovely part, that we took for granted and thought little about. We were a selfish lot, and there were plenty of girls who hung around and got your attention whenever they could. Besides, I wasn't hunting for girl friends at that stage, I tell you. There's only one thing I remember about her and that was at commencement. She was dressed in white and her hair was fixed somehow different. She has brown curly hair, and it was all loose and fluffy, and she looked beautiful. I remember being surprised by her looks. She seemed almost like an angel. I suppose it was the clothes, perhaps, that got me, seeing her in white when I had been used to seeing her in plain dark cottons. But she was lovely and she made a beautiful appearance when she gave her commencement orations. She was the only girl who spoke at commencement. Maybe you remember her?"

"Was she small and slight?" His mother caught her breath with eagerness.

"Yes, that's the one."

"Name Rose Galbraith?" asked the father looking up casually, with no hint in his face that he had gone and looked up that old high school commencement program from among his archives, that first night when Gordon had suggested another girl whom he had known in school. He had treasured the name in his heart during the months of suspense.

"Yes, dad. How did you remember that? She's the girl whose speech you spoke of as being the best. Do you remember saying that?"

"Why, I remember thinking she was the best of the bunch or something like that," said the father dryly. "Nice girl. Nice voice. Nice name, Gordon. Galbraith. There used to be a man named Galbraith, wrote some pretty fine articles in the magazines. Gilbert Galbraith, I think. I suppose he's no relation of hers, though."

"Yes," said Gordon beaming. "That was her father. He died when she was only a little girl, and she and her mother had a right hard time getting along, I gather. Of course I haven't discussed things like that with her much yet."

"Well, but Gordon, I don't understand," said his mother with a worried glance. "How did you get to know her if you didn't know her any better than that in school? It's a long time since you graduated. Was she in New York? Have you been meeting her there?"

Gordon laughed.

"Yes, she was in New York, and I met her there, once, but only a very few minutes. That was all!"

"A few minutes!" his mother was appalled.

"Yes, just a few minutes. She was on ship board just starting over to Scotland to visit some of her relatives. She was all alone. Her mother had just died. They had planned to go over together, but her mother died a week before they were to sail. She was pretty well broken up, I think, but of course I didn't know it. I had been sent down to give some papers to a man who was sailing on the same ship, and as I came down the deck toward the companionway I saw somebody standing by the rail watching the people and her back looked sort of familiar. I stopped an instant to identify her, and sure enough, it was Rose Galbraith. I just impulsively stepped up and said 'Why, if this isn't Rose Galbraith!' or something like that. And she turned around and recognized me, and her face lit up. She seemed so glad to see somebody she knew. She said she was just thinking how she was leaving her native land, and there wasn't even an acquaintance down in that throng to say good-by to, and everybody else seemed to have friends. She said she was glad I had spoken to her. She was looking very sweet and pretty. Had something blue on and a blue hat that matched her eyes. I never saw her look so nice and like other girls before, and she seemed so pleased to see me that I lingered a minute or two. I asked her who she was going with and her eyes filled up with quick tears, though she smiled through them and said she was going alone, that her mother and she had been going together, but instead she'd had to leave her mother in the Shandon Cemetery. Well, gosh, that kind of got me, mother. I felt awfully sorry for her, and I stood there a minute or two more talking, asked her where she was going and all that, you know, and then I went to shake hands with her, and her hand was so little and shy and sweet in mine, mother, that before I realized—well, that isn't so, I did realize, but I did what we usually do when someone we know well is going across the sea or off anywhere for a long time, I just stooped over and kissed her! There, mother! That's the story! I suppose you and dad won't understand what I mean, but I tell you truly I can't get away from the memory of her lips, the look in her eyes, her little hand in mine! And it wasn't any mush-mush stuff, either! It's real. I've been testing it out ever since. I did my best coming home and trying to get interested in that 'Miss Know-it-all' that you had here for me, but it didn't work. I even tried her out again, just last night, for she turned up on the train when I was on my way down to Silver Beach where Fran Tallant had coerced me into going to fill in for her brother Ed. I stuck it out till mid evening, and then I decided I was done and the time had come to do something decisive. So I called you up, took a taxi to a poky old way train, and came home. And here I am! Now, what have you got to say?"

"But, Gordon," said his father taking a sudden hand, "do I understand that that scene on the boat is the last? You haven't seen her or had any contacts with her since?"

"Not on your life!" said Gordon. "I've been in touch with her right along. I stopped at the flower shop as I went down and ordered a lot of flowers sent up to her cabin before I got off. Then two or three days later I sent her a radio message on ship board. And ever since we've been corresponding. I've got her last letter right here in my breast pocket and you can read it, both of you, if you like. It's a pippin! Of course it's not a love letter. We haven't got that far yet. At least I have but I don't know where she stands as to that. We've just been corresponding as friends, so far."

"Oh-oh!" said Father McCarroll. "So that's the way it is! Well, son, I should say you had shown pretty good judgment as to how to go about things. Almost as good work as we got away with, isn't it mother?" and he came over and sat down on the arm of her chair and put a loving arm around his wife. "How about it, little mother, are you going to wish your boy godspeed?"

"Of course!" said Gordon's mother, wiping away the tears, and lighting up her own mother smile.

"But Gordon," she said a moment later, with a little puzzled look on her brow that almost verged on anxiety, "what are you going to do next? Don't you think it is time you began to inquire a little more about her? You know you scarcely know her at all."

"Not on your life, mother. I know her all I need to know. Whatever else I find out I'll find out from her own lips. The next thing I'm going to do is go over to Scotland and find out if she feels the same way I do. That's the most important thing, and I'm not going to wait any longer."

"You mean you are going to give up your job, or have they fired you?" asked his father.

"No, neither," laughed Gordon. "But I get two weeks vacation anyway, and I am reasonably sure I can kid my superior into giving me another week or two to do some business for the firm. The man who was going broke his leg last week, and I heard last night that he isn't getting on as fast as they hoped he would. I happen to know they are mighty anxious to have somebody from the company over there on the spot. I'm going up to New York tomorrow morning and see what I can do with them, and if all goes well I'll sail on the first ship leaving New York tomorrow. Will you wish me well or not, mother? Father?"

"Sure!" said the father happily.

"Why, of course, Gordon," said the mother in a small tight voice, "but don't you think you are being a bit precipitate? You know marriage lasts a long time. If it's all right—"

"It's all right, mother! Read that letter and see if you don't think so? She's a Christian girl, mother, and a darned sight better Christian than I've ever been with all my wonderful upbringing. And if she's willing to tie up to me I'll have to go some to keep step."

So Mother McCarroll read Rose's letter, and Father McCarroll sat and beamed on his son happily.

And when his mother had read the letter she passed it over to her husband.

"Yes, that's a lovely letter," she said, and got out her handkerchief and wiped her eyes. She was deeply touched. "Yes, she must be a lovely girl!"

So then Gordon started in to tell her all about the other letters he had under lock and key in New York, and Father McCarroll amid it all, trying to read the letter and yet attend to what was being said, nearly lost his mind. He wanted to listen and smile, and he wanted to read, but he managed somehow to do both.

Gordon described the castle, and the thatched cottage, and the grandmother and the evening and morning worship, and all the sweet Scotch habits and customs he was beginning to love. The parents listened eagerly, thoughtfully, and reflected that much as they had wanted to teach their boy to be a warm sincere Christian they had failed to establish a family altar in their home. It had been a long time since they had even thought about such a custom, though it had been a habit in both the homes in which they themselves had been brought up.

"Yes," said Father McCarroll. "That's a good thing, family worship. That's the way I was brought up. And you too, mother," nodding toward his wife.

She bowed her head in assent.

"Well, go on, son! When you get over there what are you going to do next? Get a job and stay there and go courting her?"

"Oh, no," said Gordon with a grin. "I'll do that the first few minutes, and then we're going to get married, if she'll have me, and I really think she cares. Believe me, dad, we're not going to let that sea separate us any more."

"Oh!" said the father. "And I suppose your mother and I can stay at home and suck our thumbs. You aren't even thinking of inviting us to the wedding, are you?"

Gordon's face lit gorgeously.

"Sure thing, dad, would you come? Do you mean you'd leave business and everything and bring mother over to the wedding?"

"Why of course, if we were invited," said his parent with a grin.

"Well, you're invited. We'll cable an invitation the minute we get the day settled. Say, dad and mother, you're both peaches! Of course I knew you would be, but somehow it's better than I had even wished!"

And then suddenly the dinner bell rang and with their arms about one another as they used to walk when Gordon was a little boy, they all three went abreast into the dining room.

20

SO there was Gordon McCarroll standing at the door of the thatched cottage in Kilcreggan, and Rose, opening the door, all unaware!

"Gordon!" she cried, a great light coming into her eyes.

He put out his hands and took both of hers in his own, and then with a kind of glory in his face he bent and kissed her. Then suddenly his arms went around her and he drew her close, his lips on hers.

"Rose! My little love!" he whispered softly, as she suddenly nestled closer to him and put her rosy face down on his shoulder. "Rose, I love you! Don't you know it? Look up, dear. Let me see what your eyes say."

For answer she lifted smiling eyes, and he laid his lips again on hers. "Oh!" she said softly. "Is this real, or is it just a dream?"

"It is real, little Rose," he said softly and held her close.

Then they heard footsteps coming toward the kitchen door, and Gordon quickly released her, and stood looking at her, his face shining.

The door opened and there was Aunt Jessie with a wondering look on her sweet face. Rose, all shining-faced and happy, took Gordon by the hand shyly and led him over to her aunt.

"Aunt Jessie, this is my friend Gordon McCarroll, from home."

Aunt Jessie turned a sudden quick look on the young man, and then apparently satisfied, beamed upon him.

"Yir verra welcome," she said extending her hand in greeting. "A' doot it's a glad day for oor little lassie tae see a frien' frae hame. Tak his hat, Rosie, an' gie him a chair. Air ye juist frae the ship, or came ye by Liverpool?"

"Yes, I came by Liverpool," said Gordon. "I landed two days ago. Had to stop in London on business for the company that demanded haste, and then I came right on here by train. I am so very glad to find Rose here. I was afraid she might have gone to the castle in Edinburgh, but I decided to try here first."

A quick look passed between Rose and her aunt.

"But I almost did," said Rose with a motion of her hand to her heart. "I was just saying this minute that I thought I ought to go at once, and Aunt Jessie was saying she wouldn't let me go alone, that I would have to wait till my cousins came back. It wasn't safe."

"Safe?" said Gordon with quick alarm in his eyes. "Why wouldn't it be safe?"

"Mayhap a' shudna hae mentioned it," said Aunt Jessie penitently. "I thocht ye micht know a' aboot it."

"Not quite all," said Rose with flaming cheeks, "but it's all right, Aunt Jessie. I'll tell him about it at once. I'm sure he'll understand."

"Well, sit ye doon in the shade in the yaird whiles an' talk, an' a'll get a bit meal on the table. Then when the lads come ye can eat an' go if gang ye must."

Hand in hand they went out in the yard to the rustic bench under the big tree and sat down, and Gordon put his arm about her and drew her closer to him.

"Darling!" he said, looking deep into her eyes. "Do you really love me?"

It was several minutes before they could tear their thoughts away from their delight in each other. But suddenly Gordon straightened up and said:

"But now, what is all this about going to Edinburgh? Can I go too? Because I'm not going to let you out of my sight while I'm here, and when I have to go I want to take you back with me."

Then they had to talk about that for a few minutes. Rose almost lost her breath entirely at the thought. Go back with Gordon as his wife! It brought a glow to her cheeks that lasted a long time. It was too new a thought to be dismissed lightly.

But then suddenly Rose realized that the boys would be coming back in a few minutes and they would be called to lunch. She must tell Gordon about her letter from Aunt Janet.

In the end the story was told very rapidly. But Gordon gave instant attention when she began to tell about Lord MacCallummore and her uncle's talk that she had overheard. His eyes were upon her lovely face as she talked, and now and again his hand would reach up and just touch her cheek lightly with the tip of his finger, as one touches something very precious indeed. And then at last she brought out her aunt's two letters which she had been comparing when he arrived, and while he read them her hand was in his, and she was watching him, and trying to take it in that henceforth he would belong to her, and they would be together as long as they both should live. How wonderful God was to her.

When he had finished he looked up, handing back the letters.

"Why, of course you will go," he said gravely. "You would always feel condemned if you didn't. It is a chance to do what you call 'testify,' isn't it?" And his face lighted like one who had succeeded in speaking a foreign tongue so that it could be understood.

She flashed back a smile.

"You have been reading the book I sent you," she charged.

"Yes," he said, "and it was great! And now I'm trying to live it. You know a book is no good unless you can put it into practice—unless it's *worth* putting into practice. And I've learned that about the Bible too. You read a little way till you find some direction and then you go out and live it until you find out what it was the Lord was trying to call your attention to when you read it."

"Oh, Gordon, it's going to be so wonderful to have us interested in the same things!"

"Isn't it!" said Gordon pressing her hand softly. "My sweet! My little sweet girl! And to think I went to school with you all those years and never knew how dear you were till you went sailing away out of my life, and I only had a chance to kiss you good-by."

And then the old car came rattling up to the gate and Donald and David came pell mell up to the house, and out again as soon as their mother had told them, to give that newcomer a "once-over." They were keen-eyed lads, those two, and they saw at once what like their cousin's friend was, and were satisfied.

And when the introductions were over:

"Shall we go?" asked David, impatient to be gone.

"Mither said come an' eat. There's Kirsty. Let's go!" said Donald.

They went into the house and Gordon stood among

them as one of them, exactly as if he had known them a long time.

"Three braw laddies," said Jessie looking at them pridefully. "I mind yir name's Gordon. That'll be a guid Scotch name."

"Yes," grinned Gordon, "I've been banking on that a lot to pass with you all. And now, Aunt Jessie, I may as well tell you the whole thing. I came over here to marry your niece and take her home with me. Now, perhaps, you won't want me to call you that yet."

Aunt Jessie gave a quick look at Rose, and then at the rest of them and smiled.

"Wha' wud hae suspected that?" said Aunt Jessie comically. "Wi' Rose a-snatchin' for yir letters as if they wes meat and drink! Now what a braw laddie! Anither new laddie to ca' me Aunt Jessie! God be praised. A' like ye fine!"

And then out came grandmother, with a clean starched mutch and kerchief.

"Sae ye've coom at last!" said grandmother, walking over and taking his hand in hers, studying his smiling face there above her.

"Ye'll dae," she said with decision. "A' can trust ye with my wee Rose." And suddenly she reached up her two hands to each side of his face and pulled him down, and kissed him fairly on his lips. "A guid laddie," she said, with his hands in hers. "A'm sateesfied!" Then she smiled.

Gordon bent and kissed her brow reverently where the silver hair parted on her forehead. And standing up straight and solemn he said:

"I'm proud to have passed *that* examination. I think that has meant more to me than a degree from any university would mean."

They sat down at the table and the old lady with her

eyes on the guest said: "Gordon will return thanks!" She looked straight at him like a challenge. Gordon with heightened color bowed his head. It happened that he had never been asked to serve in that way before, but he spoke with tender reverence:

"Lord, we thank Thee for this coming together, and for this food, and for the fellowship we have with Thee. Bless and lead us today for Thy name's sake. Amen."

No one said anything as they raised their heads and Jessie began to serve the rich Scotch broth, and to pass the bread. But there was a feeling in the air that Gordon had passed even a far greater examination than before.

Kirsty was quiet and busy, watching the guest now and then, and Rose looked up.

"Kirsty, you're going along with us. Can you spare her, Aunt Jessie? She can be seeing the sights of Edinburgh while Gordon and I go in to see Aunt Janet."

And so Kirsty went with them, and very soon they were on their way, the boys and their sister in front and Rose and Gordon in the back seat.

"You can talk better together that way," said Donald wisely, "and belike there'll be plenty tae say. Ye'll not be feelin' that we're watchin' ye a' the time, either," he added with a grin and a wink.

"Yes," said Rose a little troubled. "We must plan what to say when we get there. I must tell Gordon all about the MacCallummores."

"But do you really think that *I* should go in?" asked Gordon anxiously. "Won't I seem to be intruding?"

"Belike you'll gang in wi' 'er or she wull nae gang hersel'," said Donald fiercely. "It's no safe for her inside thae walls. Ye'll gang, or else I'll gang mysel', an' that winna be guid!"

So they began to discuss the matter, and Gordon said

yes, if it was a matter of Rose's safety, of course he would go.

But they had a happy drive in spite of the errand that weighed so heavily on them, and late in the afternoon they arrived at the castle. There was grave silence as they followed the winding drive up to the massive structure above them.

"I shall never forget this sight," said Gordon proudly. "It may be a thing of menace, but it's a proud one, and I'm glad I saw it."

After they had made an agreement as to the time they would return, Rose and Gordon got out and mounted the steps to the door, and Donald drove his old car slowly down the winding road, while David and Kirsty kept a furtive watch out for when Thomas would open the door.

"How do you like him?" asked Kirsty at last when the castle was a far thing on the rim of the sky and the lights of the city were beginning to appear.

"Mither says he's a braw laddie, an' if mither says so it's so!" said Donald firmly, adding with a grin, "an' I think so mysel'."

And so they proudly discussed him, rejoicing in him and approving of him. There was no denying that the three Galbraiths were greatly pleased with their new relative.

"And tomorrow Aunt Rose and her family will be back from visiting their sister in Glasgow, and then he'll have met us all," said Kirsty happily. "And that makes me think. I promised to call up Lady Campbell and tell her Aunt Rose is here. Mother said I might invite her to come out to dinner or something. Do you think it's all right to do it while Gordon is here?"

"Sure thing," said David. "She's likely heard of Gordon. Anyhow he fits, so what's the difference?"

"What bothers me," said Kirsty, "is where will those two get any supper? In that miserly old castle they won't expect them to stay, will they?"

"Well, they'd better!" growled Donald. "But I told them where we'd be, and Gordon will telephone if he wants us to come sooner for them."

So they found their hotel and got supper and spent the evening happily.

Meantime up in the castle Rose and Gordon sat in state in the great room where Rose's mother's picture presided in the distance, over the lovely old piano.

The twilight had possession of the room. Only two tall candles broke the gloom.

"Come over here and see my mother's picture," whispered Rose.

So, when Aunt Janet came down the long dim stairway and looked about her for her guests, wondering who the man might be, the two were at the far end, standing before the picture, and she followed them silently into the room and watched them a moment before they were aware of her presence.

Then suddenly Rose's low voice of explanation stopped and she was aware of someone else in the room. She turned quickly and saw her aunt.

"Oh, Aunt Janet! There you are! Excuse me, please, for coming in here while I waited, but I did want to see mother's picture once more, and I wasn't sure we should be able to stay long enough to make it possible. Aunt Janet, I want to introduce Gordon McCarroll. I brought him with me because he is the man I am going to marry, and I didn't know that there would be any other chance for him to meet you."

"Marry!" the cold lips almost twisted like a writhe of pain as she spoke the word. "I didn't know you were going to marry anyone. You never spoke of it."

"No," said Rose. "But, you see, I was here a very short time. Besides, we hadn't fixed the time then."

"Time?" there was another sharp note of pain in the voice. "Oh, is the time set?"

"Yes, practically. The wedding will be in a little over a week, just as soon as Gordon's father and mother can get over here from the States. But I wanted you to see him before we were married, of course. I got your note this morning and I hurried to come right away. I thought if I had Gordon with me it would be all right to come."

Aunt Janet cast a quick furtive look behind her, and caught a glimpse of Thomas passing the wide doorway.

"Thomas! More candles!" she ordered.

The candles came almost at once, and the lovely girl in the rich old gold frame stood out startlingly. Gordon turned and looked at it fascinated.

"She is very beautiful!" he said, and looked back at Aunt Janet.

"Yes. She *was,*" said Aunt Janet grimly with a heavy sigh. And then she looked Gordon over sharply, softening as she saw the look of admiration in his face for the picture.

"She looks like you, Rose. As you sometimes looked when you sat at your desk in school." He spoke thoughtfully, reminiscently.

"Oh, do you think so?" said Rose eagerly. "My father used to say we were alike. But my coloring was more like his."

And then she remembered Aunt Janet, who did not recognize the Galbraith side of the family.

But Aunt Janet was watching Gordon.

"Well, I don't know that I can blame you," she said with a sigh. "Of course he is nearer your age."

"Nearer?" said Rose with a startled look.

"Yes, I can't blame you. But where are you going to

be married? It seems like your mother's story over again," and she sighed heavily.

"Where?" said Rose. "Oh, why at grandmother's, I think. We haven't all our plans made yet, but we're sailing immediately for home. Gordon could only get away for a short time."

"Sailing?" said the woman forlornly. "But your wedding should have been here. Only now I don't think it would be wise."

"No, of course not. It would be impossible with uncle so ill. How is he today? Any better?"

The woman shook her head dully.

"No, no better. He may not ever be better. He may linger for years just this way. A living death. That's why I wrote you. I thought you would know some place where I could read to him. The print is so fine in your mother's little old Bible I can't seem to find any appropriate place. I don't know that he would understand it if I did try to read it either. I read so slowly and my voice isn't strong. I never was a very good reader. Your mother read better than I did."

"Yes, she was a beautiful reader. She made a point of teaching me. Would you like me to read to Uncle Robert a few minutes before I go? Or do you think he would not like it? He might not like to know I was here."

"Oh no, I don't think he would dislike to have you read. He never spoke as if he disliked you. Of course I don't know surely that he would understand, but the doctor thinks he does. You might try it. That is, if you're not afraid. I don't think Lord MacCallummore will be back again tonight. He has been here all day."

"What is he here for, Aunt Janet? Is he staying with uncle? Does uncle like to have him around?"

"No," said the aunt, "he seems to make him very

restless. Sometimes he moans in a terrible way. It's the only sound he can make. And sometimes he looks at me in a desperate way, as if he were pleading. No, I don't think he likes to have him here. I think it worries him."

"Well, why do you let him stay, then? Why don't you send him away? Get the doctor to tell him that it isn't good for uncle to have company."

"Oh, the doctor would never do that! The Mac-Callummores are very influential people around here. The doctor would not dare to tell him not to come. And I'm quite sure it wouldn't do any good if I were to say anything. He keeps telling me that he is searching for some papers that your uncle told him about, and that he has promised him he will find them. Of course I don't know anything about his business affairs. It may be so."

"Aunt Janet, I think you ought to keep him out. I don't think he has any business to be looking among Uncle Robert's papers or searching in the castle for anything. I'll tell you why. Once a little while ago he came over to Kilcreggan with a paper he said uncle sent, for me to answer the questions, about how much property I had, and what form it was in and who was my guardian. Things like that. He said it was a government paper and he must have the answers that day or it would make uncle a great deal of trouble. But I refused to sign it. I told him it was none of his business what money I had, that I was an American citizen, and I was sure this government over here had nothing to do with my affairs. I took the paper to Lady Campbell's husband who is a government man, you know, and he said it was all nonsense, there was no such government paper. Nobody had a right to ask me those questions."

"But I don't understand," said the aunt with a troubled air. "I'm quite sure my husband would not have sent you any such paper."

"That's what I thought too. I'm sure he didn't," said Rose. "And then another thing, you remember the night I was playing the piano, and then we went upstairs early? Well, I left my little bag on the piano and when I got upstairs I missed it and came down for it, and as I went back I heard Lord MacCallummore saying some very queer things to Uncle Robert, about not being able to pay him something he owed him. It seemed to have something to do with me, for he mentioned my name. I couldn't hear all they said, but I've never trusted Lord MacCallummore since. And anyway, Aunt Janet, my mother didn't trust his father. Perhaps you never knew all about that affair, but mother told me. And if I were you I would do something to keep him out of the castle. I'd send for a policeman if there wasn't any other way. I'm sure he's up to something, searching through uncle's things. Perhaps if you would appeal to Lord Campbell he would be able to help you. He's very kind and pleasant. You could say I suggested it."

By this time Aunt Janet was wide-eyed and trembling.

"Oh, my dear! Oh, my dear! I couldn't do a thing like that. I don't know what your uncle would say if I did a thing like that."

"But if you were doing it to protect uncle's rights, he couldn't blame you, could he? Besides, if he can't move or speak what could he do about it? He wouldn't know it, would he? I certainly don't think you ought to let him hunt around for things here. There might be some very important thing, some valuable, that would be missing if you don't protect it somehow."

"Perhaps you're right," said Aunt Janet. "I'll have to think about it. Of course I could send for your uncle's brother, but I've never liked him. Well, I'll see. It's all very queer though, I don't understand it. But I was worried about your coming because I knew that Lord

MacCallummore was anxious to get well acquainted with you. I think perhaps he wanted to marry you. But now, of course—Well, you're really going to be married, are you?"

"Yes," said Rose with a glory of loveliness in her face.

"That's just the way your mother talked." And then after a pause, "What have you got for a wedding dress? We must talk fast because if you're going to read to your uncle you'd better do it pretty soon. It might get him to sleep, and perhaps would make him less unhappy. But tell me, have you got a wedding dress?"

"Why, no, not yet," smiled Rose. "I'll get something simple. It won't matter much. We won't have a large wedding, just the family. I hope you will come."

"Oh, no I wouldn't want to come. It would make me think of your mother's wedding that never came off. I'd cry, and I hate to cry. But I was wondering if you would like to wear your mother's wedding dress?"

"My mother's wedding dress?" said Rose amazed. "But she told me she just had her plain little traveling dress that she came away from home in."

"Yes, she did. But she had a wedding dress, all beautiful with handmade lace, wonderful Carrickmacross lace. It was made especially for her wedding dress, and she never wore it. Instead she ran away with your father, and had to be married in a very common little traveling dress. But the real wedding dress that was made for your mother is upstairs now in a big white box, and if you would like to have it I'll give it to you."

"Oh, Aunt Janet. Why yes, of course I'd like to have it. It would be wonderful. Mother told me about that dress and I always felt sorry I couldn't see it. I would treasure it so very much, or I would send it back to you again after my wedding. If I could wear it, that would be wonderful."

"No, I don't want it back again. It would ease my soul to get it out of the house. Nights, often, I could not sleep, thinking of my little sister and all the things she gave up. But I guess somehow you've made me feel she was happy anyway."

"Yes, she was very very happy as long as my dear father lived," said Rose.

"Well, then I will give you the dress."

She touched a bell near her, and Thomas appeared.

"Tell Maggie to go up to the tower and get the very large white box on the top of the big mahogany dresser. Tell her it's the wedding dress. She will know which one I mean."

Then she turned to Rose again.

"Now, would you like to play on your mother's piano a few minutes while I go up and see if your uncle is awake so you could read to him?"

"Oh, yes," said Rose, "if you think it won't disturb him."

"Well, it's a very long way off from him. He won't be able to hear it very well. Anyway, he said once he thought you played well. Perhaps he would like it. Try it."

21

AUNT Janet disappeared, and in amazement Rose sat down at the piano and began to play, softly at first, tenderly; nocturnes, and scraps of lovely music that sounded of rippling water and waving ferns and flying birds. Then more tenderly still she melted into the dear old hymn tunes her mother had loved.

Gordon stood there and listened, watching her entranced. To think his dear girl could play like that. And all through the years he had never known it.

Then he began to wish that his father and mother could be here and see the grand old castle walls, and the exquisite painting of the lovely girl-mother; see the sweet girl playing there in the dim candlelight. Oh, mother didn't need to worry lest he was marrying a common girl. Why, she was rare and wonderful. Even mother would see she had an irreproachable background. If he could only just tell it to them as he was seeing it now!

And then Aunt Janet came back, with Thomas in her wake, bearing the big white box.

"We'll put it here on the hall table," she said, "till you

have to go. I'd keep you here all night, of course, if it wasn't for Lord MacCallummore. I wouldn't know what to tell him, and after what you have told me, he might make us trouble. I wouldn't want him to upset your uncle. Now, come right up, both of you. He's awake and the nurse thinks it may help him, put him to sleep, perhaps. Oh, his eyes look so restless. They seem to burn into you like coals of fire."

She led them upstairs to the big bedroom where the uncle lay grim and silent as a statue. Rose entered, with Gordon just behind her, a small limp leather-covered Bible in her hand, with a folded paper inside on which she had written a series of verses and references.

Her aunt motioned to her to sit by a table where was a shaded lamp and so seated she began to read.

"Hear my cry, O God; attend unto my prayer. From the end of the earth will I cry unto thee, when my heart is overwhelmed: lead me to the rock that is higher than I."

The eyes of the sick man came open wide and he stared straight ahead as if searching for the voice. Gordon as he stood across from the bed could watch him, the grim locked face that never changed.

The girl's voice went steadily on, with a fresh clearness that had an arresting quality.

"Have mercy upon me, O God, according to thy lovingkindness: according unto the multitude of thy tender mercies blot out my transgressions. Wash me thoroughly from mine iniquity, and cleanse me from my sin. For I acknowledge my transgressions: and my sin is ever before me. Against thee, thee only have I sinned . . . Wash me, and I shall be whiter than snow . . . Create in me a clean heart, O God; and renew a right spirit within me."

The room was very still. Aunt Janet was standing over by the door out of sight from the bed, and her eyes were

wide and almost frightened. The nurse stood near the
bed, her eye on the patient, and just out in the hall by
the doorway where they could not be seen stood
Thomas and Maggie, silently with bowed heads, as if
they were attending a sacrament. And Gordon stood
there quietly watching it all, thrilling with the voice of
his dear girl uttering the wonderful, hope-filled truths.

"Hear, O Lord, when I cry with my voice: have
mercy also upon me, and answer me. When thou saidst,
Seek ye my face; my heart said unto thee, thy face, Lord,
will I seek. Hide not thy face far from me; put not thy
servant away in anger: thou hast been my help; leave me
not, neither forsake me, O God of my salvation."

The reader paused an instant and fluttered over the
leaves and then went on again, with the clear ringing
statements.

"For God so loved the world that he gave his only
begotten Son, that whosoever believeth in him should
not perish, but have everlasting life."

Another fluttering of the leaves and then,

"How can ye believe, which receive honor one of
another, and seek not the honor that comes from God
only?"

Then, turning to another place,

"But these are written, that ye might believe that Jesus
is the Christ, the Son of God; and that believing ye might
have life through his name."

Suddenly Aunt Janet stepped up to Rose and motioned her to go over where her uncle could see her face.
She had noticed that his eyes were turning in almost an
agony to find the voice. So Rose got up and went quietly
over to stand at the foot of the bed where she could look
into the sick man's eyes. She smiled as she came near,
holding the little book up that he might see what she was
reading from. Then she read on.

"Now then we are ambassadors for Christ, as though God did beseech you by us: we pray you in Christ's stead, Be ye reconciled to God. For he hath made him to be sin for us, who knew no sin; that we might be made the righteousness of God in him."

It seemed to Rose as she lifted her eyes in her reading and looked straight at her uncle, that his eyes were fixed on her with intelligence. She was convinced that he knew her, and that he understood what she was reading. There was a kind of startled, understanding look in his expression, though the actual lines of his face had not altered. But she read straight on through the verses she had selected.

"He was wounded for our transgressions, he was bruised for our iniquities: the chastisement of our peace was upon him; and with his stripes we are healed. All we like sheep have gone astray; we have turned every one to his own way; and the Lord hath laid on him the iniquity of us all. Blessed is he whose transgression is forgiven, whose sin is covered. . . . I acknowledged my sin unto thee, and mine iniquity have I not hid. I said, I will confess my transgressions unto the Lord, and thou forgavest the iniquity of my sin."

Then the voice grew sweeter, with a comforting strain as she went on:

"Let not your heart be troubled: ye believe in God, believe also in me. In my Father's house are many mansions, if it were not so, I would have told you. I go to prepare a place for you. And if I go and prepare a place for you, I will come again, and receive you unto myself, that where I am, there ye may be also. And whither I go ye know, and the way ye know. Thomas saith unto him, Lord, we know not whither thou goest; and how can we know the way? Jesus saith unto him, I am the way, the truth, and the life: no man cometh unto the Father, but by me."

Rose closed the book and looked around with a tender almost frightened little smile. She had not considered what to do next. It seemed an awkward pause, yet these were all the verses she had prepared to read. What ought she to do next? Speak to her uncle, or just say good night and walk out? She looked uncertainly toward Gordon, and quietly he walked toward her and stood beside her where the sick man could see him. Reverently he bowed his head, and said in clear earnest tones:

"Father in Heaven, we thank Thee for these wonderful words from Thine own Book. They have cheered our hearts, and we know that if we lay hold upon them they will give us life, for Thou hast put them in Thy Book for that purpose. So we leave them with this dear one, and ask Thee to watch over him tonight and give him rest and peace."

It was all very still for a minute. Rose could see that her aunt was weeping, and then quietly she stepped to the bedside and stooping placed a soft little kiss on the sick man's forehead. She whispered, "Good night, dear Uncle Robert," and quietly as they had come they went out.

Almost in silence they started to walk down the winding way, until they were half way down to the level below. Then they stopped and turned and looked back up to the castle.

"It's a grand old monument to the past," said Gordon solemnly. "Seems almost as if it were built soon after the world was made, doesn't it? And yet, somehow, there's something arrogant about it, like the silent old man who owns it."

"Yes," said Rose in a voice of awe, "it is like that. But oh, Gordon, I'm so glad you prayed! It just made the right ending. It seemed as if it wasn't finished when I got done reading."

"Was that all right?" he asked anxiously. "I didn't know but you'd think I was butting in and spoiling things. An utter stranger!"

"You're not an utter stranger!" she smiled up at him in the starlight. "You're my very own. And it made a perfect ending. I'm so glad you did it. It's going to be so wonderful to have you able to *pray!*"

Then his arm went about her and there in the quiet loneliness of that mountain drive their lips met.

As they walked on they fell to talking about the uncle and aunt they had just left in their stately castle.

"Oh, I hope he heard, and understood what it all meant," said Rose eagerly.

"He did. I'm sure he did. I was watching his eyes. They took it all in, and sometimes they looked kind of frightened, and sometimes relief came, almost a light, as if he thought God was speaking to him. And when you went around and stood where he could see you, I'm sure he knew you and was grimly glad you had come."

"Oh, and I never thought I'd ever be glad about him," she sighed. "I thought he was the most disagreeable old party I'd ever seen. But now it's queer, how much I want him to find rest in his Saviour."

"Yes," said Gordon thoughtfully. "That's the Spirit of God that is in us when we accept Christ, I guess. That must be 'the power that worketh in us' as you wrote me, 'to the end that we might be conformed to the image of His Son.'"

He smiled down at her through the starlight.

"Oh, I've been reading all those little booklets that you sent me from your wonderful preacher, and I know a lot more than I used to know. From now on we'll be learning together, won't we? Perhaps we can coax your wonderful preacher to come over to the States and visit us next winter. We'll see what we can do. There are churches I know that ought to hear a message like that. I am just eager to hear him."

Rose walked on in the shelter of Gordon's strong arm, thrilled with the thought of the companionship that was before her. She lifted her eyes to the stars and wondered if her mother knew her happiness, and was rejoicing too.

At the foot of the mountain they found the cousins, drawn to one side of the road, waiting.

"We figured this was what you'd do," grinned Donald, "so we left word with the hotel to tell you if you phoned that we would be here until we saw the lights go out, and then we would come back there and put up for the night. We kept watching the windows, and as no more lights appeared in other windows we decided you would not stay all night. Now how about it? Shall we drive back tonight, or stay at the hotel and start early in the morning?"

They decided for the latter, as Kirsty wanted to get something at a store, and the boys had an errand or two. That gave Gordon a chance to send his cables, one to his father and mother bidding them take the next boat, the other to the engraver at home with whom he had arranged for announcements of the wedding to be sent out from a list he had left with them.

So the two girls, both excited and happy, went to their room and talked half the night.

"How well we are all going to fit together!" sighed Kirsty with satisfaction. "Isn't he just grand? Oh, how I wish you were going to live in this country. It would be wonderful to have you all time!"

"Yes," said Rose with shining eyes, "but we'll be coming over sometimes I expect, and you'll be coming to visit us."

And then they launched into plans for the wedding.

They opened the big white box and peeped in at the lovely old wedding dress, waiting there all these years for the daughter of the girl for whom it had been made. Rose tried it on, and found that it fitted her quite well.

Then they talked about what Kirsty would wear.

"You'll have to be my maid of honor, you know," she smiled at her cousin.

"Oh!" said Kirsty with a seraphic smile. "I never thought I'd be that. I ought to get a new dress. I'll have to, of course. I'd better look around tomorrow morning."

"Oh, why bother, Kirsty dear? There'll be no strangers there but Gordon's father and mother, and they will understand you didn't have time to get ready a dress."

"Yes, that's all right for you to say, you with that marvelous dress of your mother's to wear. But I can't just put on any old thing along with it."

"Very well then, isn't there some really old dress about your house you could wear, to go with mine? Didn't Aunt Rose, or your mother or even grandmother have a dress they've saved? Couldn't you wear it?"

"Yes, mother has," said Kirsty. "It was only a plain dimity with little pink sort of birds all over. It has fine little satin cords of white. It's sweet. I never thought of that. It wasn't her wedding dress, but it was a sort of party dress, and she's always kept it ever since because she thought it was so pretty. I think she has only worn it a few times, and it's quaint, made in old style."

"That's just the thing," said Rose. "We don't want newfangled things at this wedding. They wouldn't fit. Now, let's go to sleep. We've got a full day before us tomorrow."

When they got home the next day they were full of

plans, getting ready for the wedding. Even Aunt Rose's little boys were excited.

One of the first things Gordon and Rose did that afternoon was to go over to find the wonderful preacher, and ask him if he would marry them. They were in a great hurry to do that because they didn't know just what they would do if it turned out to be one of the weeks when he was away preaching at conferences. They didn't know anybody else they wanted to ask. Though of course there were plenty of good ministers in that region, this one seemed to belong to them, because they had been talking over his sermons and his little books. They were greatly relieved when they found he was free on the day that they had arranged for the wedding, and was glad to come and perform the ceremony.

"So that's fixed!" said Gordon happily as they started back. "And now, I guess that's the last necessity, so we can begin to have a good time."

"Oh, but I thought it had all been a good time!" said Rose joyously. "Even the hard things like going to the castle turned out to be one of the best times of all. I really believe Aunt Janet liked it. She kissed me almost tenderly when we went away."

"Yes," said Gordon thoughtfully, "she got me to one side and asked for our new address. She said she wanted to send you a wedding present. And you know I wouldn't be surprised at all if we were to see that poor old Uncle Robert come walking into Heaven some day. I think he got a little glimpse last night of how to get there. I really do."

"Oh, that would be the best thing of all!" said Rose. "And poor Aunt Janet! Mother loved her, you know, and I guess she wasn't always crabbed."

Then they went back to the house, that was already

beginning to smell of spice and a lot of nice things that were being prepared for the wonderful fruit cake Aunt Jessie had in mind to make for the wedding.

"Only the wedding'll be far too soon for the guid o' the cake. By rights it shud bide awhile an' mellow. But we'll have tae do the best we can."

There were a few invitations to be written. The family had talked it over, and decided on just a very few near relatives who would be hurt if they were not invited.

"Though they may na come," said Aunt Jessie.

Then a very few close friends of the family. There was Donald's girl, and Davie's girl, and Kirsty's young man, not definitely hers, but he thought he was going to be; Kirsty wasn't sure yet.

"An' there's Lord an' Lady Cawmill," reminded grandmother proudly. "Ye'll nae forget them! They'll na come, o' coorse, but they maun be invited!"

Rose wrote a sweet little note to Lord and Lady Campbell and another to Aunt Janet and Uncle Robert.

"She'll maybe show it or read it to Uncle Robert," explained Rose to Kirsty who was watching her.

Meantime, at the castle, exciting times had been going on. Lady Warloch had sent word to the best packer in the city to come over at once prepared to pack a valuable picture and a fine piano and ship them to the United States. And he had arrived promptly.

She had also sent word to Lord MacCallummore that she thought it best he should give up any further search, at least for the present, for the papers he was so troubled to find. His presence in the house seemed to be sensed by the sick man, and it disturbed him greatly.

Lord MacCallummore came over at once and tried to make Lady Warloch see how wrong she was. He said he made no noise in his search. The very gentle tappings of the wall that he had been making could not possibly be heard through those thick castle walls, and she did not realize how important the matter was.

But Lady Warloch took him to a little room as far as possible removed from the main part of the castle and told him very firmly that it wasn't important at all. All that was important was to make Lord Warloch comfortable.

Lord MacCallummore was most insistent, finally owning that the matter was at least important to him, because the main thing he was hunting for was an agreement between himself and Lord Warloch, certain papers which should have been destroyed long ago, and which he knew Lord Warloch intended to destroy, papers which referred to certain monies he had borrowed some years ago from Lord Warloch.

But Lady Warloch had been carefully thinking over what Rose had told her of the conversation she had overheard between the two lords, and now, putting them together with what she knew of her husband's miserly habits, had come to the conclusion that it was more than a mere paper Lord MacCallummore was searching for. She knew that it was her husband's habit to put away money in some hidden place in the castle. Lord MacCallummore perhaps suspected this and was trying to find it, thinking that she knew nothing of the matter. Therefore she was very firm.

"I do not wish any further searching for anything to go on in the castle while Lord Warloch is so critically ill," she said firmly. "I am sorry to disappoint you, but you will have to abide by my decision. Thomas," she spoke to the servant who was passing the door, "see that Lord MacCallummore's car is ready for him, and attend him to the door. I will let you know, Lord MacCallum-more, if there is any further change in Lord Warloch's condition. I am expecting Lord

Warloch's brother in a few minutes. I wish you good morning!" and she arose and watched him from the door, angry and puzzled, but relieved that she had rebelled.

So Lord MacCallummore went forth greatly disturbed in mind and wondering what had stirred up the lady. Wondering why the brother who had long been alienated from the lord should have been allowed to come now. Concluding that if Sir Lester Warloch was to be there for any length of time perhaps it would be as well that he did not go for the present. Sir Lester and he had never gotten on well together, and Sir Lester was far too canny a man to be convenient to have around when one was searching for a miser's hoard, though he was sure no one but himself knew of its existence.

Lady Warloch went up to the sick room and found the nurse writing a letter. "Has Lord MacCallummore gone yet?" she asked Lady Warloch as she came in. Lady Warloch went and stood at the foot of the bed and watched her husband's face as she spoke clearly.

"Lord MacCallummore will not be coming here any more for awhile," she said. "I have sent him away. I did not think his continual presence was a good thing for my husband."

And then she was amazed at the look of relief that seemed to come over the poor strained face there on the pillow. She had been right, then when she thought he looked worried at the little sounds of tapping here and there that attended Lord MacCallummore's workings. But just to make sure she sent the nurse on some trifling errand and then, looking straight at her husband she said distinctly: "Robert, are you glad I have sent Lord MacCallummore away? If you are glad close your eyes."

The old eyes closed instantly. That was one thing she had discovered the man could do. His eyelids were not paralyzed.

"Now open them."

The eyelids opened.

"All right, Robert. I won't let him come again. Not till you want him. Is that right?"

The eyes slowly closed again, and then opened.

"Well, it's a relief to know that, and that you can let me know what you want. Robert, we have talked together! Isn't that wonderful?"

A vague flickering of something like an attempt at a smile hovered over the lips that were locked in silence, like pale sunshine almost seen and then withdrawn.

So she went on.

"Robert, once several years ago you gave me a letter which you said I was to keep safely and not to open unless something happened to you. Do you remember that?"

The eyes closed quickly, and then opened again with an almost anxious expression in them.

"Well, Robert, is there any reason why you would like to open it now while you are still alive?"

The eyes closed again, and then slowly opened and watched her.

"Very well," she said calmly. "I'll go and get it. Now you go to sleep. Don't fret!" And then she stooped and kissed him gently on his poor silent lips, a thing she had not done for many years.

She went and got the letter and read it. It was brief but it sent her to a certain place for a certain key, that would unlock a certain panel in the wall behind a piece of furniture that she could easily move. A certain spot to press, and another panel swung open. At last an unexpected vault was revealed, large and roomy, and almost filled with wealth. Paper and silver and even gold in quantities!

Janet Warloch laid hold of the wall by which she stood and closed her eyes to steady the feeling that she was going to reel, and fall. She looked again, a breath-taking look, and then she turned away. She closed the panels one by one, locked the last one, and pushed back the piece of furniture. She placed everything as it had been, and then she went and put the letter away among her own private things where no one could ever find it, or would dream what it was if they did.

She found Lord Warloch sound asleep in the most restful sleep he had had since the stroke. But later, when he was awake, he found her sitting near him with her knitting and a pleasant look upon her face. He lay there a long time looking at her before she noticed he was awake, but when the nurse went out for a few minutes she came near and said:

"It's all there, I'm sure. Nothing has been disturbed. Now don't worry any more," and she laid her hand on his paralyzed one, and pressed his softly.

Then she spoke again.

"Did you like the reading the other night when Rose Margaret was here?"

His eyes closed again and opened.

"That's nice," she said with a note in her voice that reminded of her girlhood days. "Would you like me to read some more verses sometimes?"

The answer came after a steady, questioning, almost wondering look.

"That will be nice. We'll read together every day." Was she imagining the interest in his eyes, she wondered. She was silent for a time, knitting, and then she said, "I've sent for Lester, Robert. I thought it was time we both gave up hard feelings. He may be here today. Do you want to see him when he comes?"

Slowly Lord Warloch closed his eyes and opened them again and the look in them was one of satisfaction. There was no longer distress in his face.

The nurse came back and Lady Warloch withdrew to get ready for her brother-in-law's coming, and to prepare to read those verses that Rose had left for her. She was not accustomed to finding places in the Bible, but Rose had left her own large print Testament, that had also the Psalms bound with it. She had marked all the places with clearly written bits of paper, so her aunt found it was not going to be a hard thing to do after all.

Just then Thomas came up to say that the movers had the things on the truck ready to leave, and wanted to know if she wished to see them before they left. So she went down to make sure that everything had gone. For she had sent some boxes of books and other things belonging to her young sister who had gone away from her life so many years ago, and it was with great satisfaction that she stood in the castle door and watched the truck moving down the mountain bearing away the things that had for many years troubled her conscience, the things that should long ago have been sent to their young owner, and now were going to her child.

She had been worrying a little at the thought of what her husband would say when he found she had given these things to Rose, especially the piano and picture. But now, since her little talk with him, she had a feeling that if the time ever came when he was up and able to go about and see that they were gone, he would not fret about them. She had a feeling that somehow something had happened to his soul that had freed him from that great obsession of greed. Was she right? Oh, how much she hoped it was so.

And then she saw a car coming up the drive that bore her one-time-alienated brother-in-law to reconciliation, and she went in to be ready to meet him.

It was two days later that Rose's little note of invitation came.

22

IT was a beautiful, quiet wedding, celebrated in the thatched cottage, because grandmother was not able to stand the drive to the church and the excitement of it all together, and Rose could not think of being married without grandmother there.

So the house was made sweet and homelike, as in fact it always was, with flowers here and there. Grandmother wore her best soft gray dress which she had worn on all festive occasions for years, with a fine sheer white kerchief folded about her neck, and a thin sheer mutch starched smoothly on her white hair that still crept into little silver ringlets about her face if she didn't watch carefully. Grandmother sat in her old highbacked chair by the fireplace, where burned a lovely quiet fire "so granny would be warm." She sat with her hands folded, making a sweet gentle picture of herself and giving a holy touch to the whole room, dignifying it and making it seem like a hallowed place.

As indeed it was. For early that morning, before they ate the hasty breakfast, the whole family had assembled and knelt around that fireplace while John Galbraith prayed for the children who were that day to be united in the holy bands of matrimony. He asked for daily traveling blessings as they went on their way, and he called to mind the past with its dear ones who had already gone Home, that the memory of their blessed lives might help the young lives that were beginning. It was such a prayer that the children as they came and went through the room during the morning preparations, felt that the place was sanctified, and walked softly as before the Lord. For surely the Lord was a guest especially that day, for hadn't Uncle John invited Him that morning in his prayer? Even the little ones felt it.

Quite early in the morning for one who had journeyed so far since daybreak, Aunt Janet arrived. She bore a little white box in her hand which she gave to Rose at once, going up to her room to do so, where Rose was all ready except her veil—the veil that was to have been her mother's.

"These were your mother's pearls that she had expected to wear on her wedding day," said Aunt Janet as she handed over the box almost diffidently. "Our father—your grandfather—had bought them for her. But she never saw them. I thought perhaps you would like to wear them."

Rose's eyes filled with tears as she knelt to have Aunt Janet clasp the lovely string of real pearls about her neck.

"Oh, it was dear of you to bring these. It doesn't seem as if I should take them from you."

"But I am glad to give them," said Aunt Janet with a look of relief. "All these years they have weighed upon me, because I had helped to keep them from my sister. Now I know if she were here she would be glad to have her child have them for her wedding day."

Rose kissed her again, and hugged her close, and

thanked her many times for all she had done. And they spoke for a minute of the little service in the castle.

"He liked it," said Aunt Janet. "He can make me understand by opening and closing his eyes. And I'm reading more to him every day. He sleeps better after I do it."

Then there came word that the minister had arrived, and it was time for Rose to put on her veil and be ready. So Aunt Janet put her stiff bony arms around Rose and kissed her tenderly.

"You are like your mother as I saw her last," she whispered, and then came a quick shining of tears in her eyes, and one trickled down through the hard lines of her sad old face. Tears looked so out of place on that repressed face.

"And I've sent over your mother's picture and her piano as a wedding present," she burst forth as she turned quickly toward the door, "and there'll be a few things, her books, and some trinkets she loved. They've already started."

"Oh, Aunt Janet! You dear!" said Rose flinging her arms again about her neck. "How wonderful! But you shouldn't have sent them away. You will miss them."

"No, no!" said Lady Warloch, dabbling quickly at her tears. "No! I *wanted* you to have them. It pleases me. It really does!" and then with another quick kiss she was gone downstairs. And Aunt Rose slipped in to arrange the veil.

Downstairs the few outside guests had arrived. Contrary to grandmother's expectations Lord and Lady Campbell had both come, and Lord Campbell was standing in a group with Uncle John Galbraith and Malcolm McCarroll, as if they had been lads together. Over by grandmother, Lady Campbell and Gordon's mother were having a nice little quiet talk, getting really well acquainted, and liking one another immensely. Mrs. McCarroll found that all her fears about this new daughter-in-law, and the possibilities of her impossible relatives were rapidly vanishing away. Once as she glanced over toward her husband she met a twinkle in his eye, that plainly said to her loving understanding look, "There mamma, didn't I tell you our Gordon knew his onions?"

And over by the door was standing the distinguished preacher talking with Gordon McCarroll. The whole atmosphere was most unusual and satisfying, and Gordon's mother as she glanced about was proud of her son, and glad of the connection he was about to make with this dear family.

A sudden hush, and then came the bride in the lovely old gown made for her mother who never wore it; and Kirsty in the frail old pink dress that went with it so well, carrying lovely flowers that Gordon McCarroll had ordered.

There were banked flowers at one end of the room, and it was in front of these that Rose and Gordon took their stand, with Kirsty and Donald attending, and the minister standing in front.

Gordon's mother as she looked at them felt her heart thrill. What a handsome couple they were gong to be! She was going to be proud of this sweet girl whom her son was taking to wife, and the lovelight in their eyes was all that could be desired. But best of all was that they were both children of God. It made her feel so safe and happy about their future, whatever came. For she had felt, as none could help feeling, that Presence in their midst. She wondered that she had never noticed it before in any wedding she had attended. Everyone in the room must have felt it, even the children, for they were very solemn and sweet as they watched, wide-eyed, the whole ceremony.

Then the service began, a most unusual order. For this minister had a way of making the service a dedication to the Lord of these two lives that were uniting in one. It was very solemn and reverent, and Aunt Janet watching, listening, shivered quietly to herself to think what might have been if Lord Warloch had carried out his plans and married this sweet girl to Lord MacCallummore! Then she realized for the first time how her own young sister had wrought well instead of ill, even though it had brought separation from those who planned for her according to this world's standards.

Very tenderly and with great joy and pride they all went up to greet the bride and groom when the service was over. And as they were coming eagerly, Rose at intervals between her loving words, kept saying to herself, "I am married to Gordon McCarroll. Just think! I am the wife of that wonderful boy that I admired so much for years in school. To think he just passed by me on that ship, and our eyes met, and our lips, and then he came over the seas after me! Hasn't it all been just wonderful of God to care for me that way. How pleased mother must be up in Heaven now!"

And then the refreshments were being passed, delicious goodies that Aunt Jessie had planned and executed; not the least the great fruit cake which was delectable, even though Aunt Jessie didn't think it had had time to mellow. And there was nothing for any of them to be ashamed about before the lords and ladies, had they been self-conscious enough to think about such a thing. Aunt Janet, getting a new view of what life could really be, was thinking that! For she too recognized the presence of God in that house, even as she had recognized it that night in the castle when Rose had read the Word, and Gordon prayed that tender prayer.

Perhaps the voices were a little hushed, the tongues less prone to sharpness because of that Presence.

And even the little boys, standing in the doorway after the bridal party had driven away to the city, turned and looked about the house, and the big empty room, and one of them said to his mother, "Mother, did God go with them?"

"Oh, yes," said the mother smiling over at Agnes McCarroll and her husband who were standing near by.

The little boys stood still, looking all around once more, and then young Jamie lifted wondering eyes and said gravely,

"But mother, He seems to be here yet!"

Amid the smiling faces of the family group the mother stooped and kissed the eager young face.

"Yes, dear, but you know God is everywhere, and nobody need be without Him, if they are willing to let Him in."

"Oh!" said the little boy very thoughtfully.

Lady Warloch, standing by, about to make her adieus and depart, looked startled, as if that were an entirely new thought.

The cousins drove the bride and groom all the way to Glasgow, and waited till the ship left the dock.

Gordon and Rose stood on deck together, hand in hand, smiling and waving good-by to the family which had become so dear to them both. Rose, looking down at them all, getting the last glimpse of the beloved faces, her very own folks, thought what a contrast this was to the time when she had sailed away from New York alone, with that forlorn feeling that there was nobody anywhere who cared. True, she had had that precious unexpected kiss upon her lips then, but she had scarcely felt at liberty to think of it as more than a gesture of courtesy. But now she had the giver of that kiss beside her, her very own man! Her husband who loved her, and whom she loved! And now there were dear ones left behind who would miss her and be sorry to have her gone. Oh, the world wasn't so big and so far away as it had seemed when she left New York, and God was over it all!

At last when the land seemed very far away, and the group at the wharf but a dim blur, they turned and looked at one another, and Gordon stooped and laid his lips upon hers again. A sudden realization came to them that this was the beginning of their new life together, the new life of which that other first precious kiss had been but the pledge.

"Oh, Gordon, if my mother could know about us!" said Rose, lifting dewy eyes to his tender glance.

"I think she does, dearest," he said earnestly.

Later when the moon was rising they were walking on deck, and they came to stand in much the same spot in which they had stood in that other ship almost a year ago when they were about to be separated.

They were looking out across the water, standing hand in hand, watching the miracle of the moon as it sailed in stately splendor up from the horizon.

"Look!" said Rose eagerly, pointing out across the rail, "see that bright pathway of silver! It seems almost as if an angel might come walking on that toward us, almost as if God might be out there walking on the sea, making it safe for our first journey together!"

His arm drew her closer as he said reverently:

"He is nearer than that, beloved! He is within us. You have helped me to find that out. Isn't it going to be wonderful to serve Him together during all the days?"

About the Author

Grace Livingston Hill is well known as one of the most prolific writers of romantic fiction. Her personal life was fraught with joys and sorrows not unlike those experienced by many of her fictional heroines.

Born in Wellsville, New York, Grace nearly died during the first hours of life. But her loving parents and friends turned to God in prayer. She survived miraculously, thus her thankful father named her Grace.

Grace was always close to her father, a Presbyterian minister, and her mother, a published writer. It was from them that she learned the art of storytelling. When Grace was twelve, a close aunt surprised her with a hardbound, illustrated copy of one of Grace's stories. This was the beginning of Grace's journey into being a published author.

In 1892 Grace married Fred Hill, a young minister, and they soon had two lovely young daughters. Then came 1901, a difficult year for Grace—the year when, within months of each other, both her father and husband died.

Suddenly Grace had to find a new place to live (her home was owned by the church where her husband had been pastor). It was a struggle for Grace to raise her young daughters alone, but through everything she kept writing. In 1902 she produced *The Angel of His Presence, The Story of a Whim,* and *An Unwilling Guest.* In 1903 her two books *According to the Pattern* and *Because of Stephen* were published.

It wasn't long before Grace was a well-known author, but she wanted to go beyond just entertaining her readers. She soon included the message of God's salvation through Jesus Christ in each of her books. For Grace, the most important thing she did was not write books but share the message of salvation, a message she felt God wanted her to share through the abilities he had given her.

In all, Grace Livingston Hill wrote more than one hundred books, all of which have sold thousands of copies and have touched the lives of readers around the world with their message of "enduring love" and the true way to lasting happiness: a relationship with God through his Son, Jesus Christ.

In an interview shortly before her death, Grace's devotion to her Lord still shone clear. She commented that whatever she had accomplished had been God's doing. She was only his servant, one who had tried to follow his teaching in all her thoughts and writing.